At lightning speed the flame raced through Fiona's body. She had to leave straightaway or there would be no turning back. "I have to go," she murmured.

Gently, Joanna turned Fiona around to face her. Joanna's eyes were blazing. "Kiss me good-bye," she demanded, her voice husky. "Then you can go."

Helpless, like last time, Fiona just gazed into her eyes, looked longingly at her mouth. Joanna's hand glided down her thigh, found the split in her dress and slid inside. Fiona moaned softly. Joanna's hand moved higher, stroking. Suddenly, the fire engulfed Fiona and she threw her arms around Joanna's shoulders, kissing her passionately. Both Joanna's hands were under the dress, stroking her hips. Joanna was trembling. Fiona felt herself sway.

"We'd better lie down," Joanna whispered.

A street lamp cast a pale light through the bedroom window; leafy patterns danced on the walls as trees moved in the breeze. With Joanna holding her, while they devoured each other with kisses, Fiona slowly sank down onto the bed, onto her back. Leaning over her, Joanna softly kissed her throat.

LOOKING FOR NAIAD?

Buy our books at
www.naiadpress.com

or call our toll-free number
1-800-533-1973

or by fax (24 hours a day)
1-850-539-9731

The Other Woman

by Ann O'Leary

THE NAIAD PRESS, INC.
1999

Printed in the United States of America on acid-free paper
First Edition

Editor: Christine Cassidy
Cover designer: Bonnie Liss (Phoenix Graphics)
Typesetter: Sandi Stancil

Library of Congress Cataloging-in-Publication Data

O'Leary, Ann, 1955 –
    The other woman / by Ann O'Leary.
        p.   cm.
    ISBN 1-56280-234-8   (alk. paper)
    I. Title.
PR9619.3.0386084   1999
823—dc21

98-31633
CIP

For Helen

About the Author

Ann O'Leary's career began in film production and, except for a brief youthful and misguided dalliance with life as a restaurateur, has been focused on advertising. After several years working as a TV producer in ad agencies, Ann and her talented sound engineer partner opened an audio production studio producing TV soundtracks. Having traveled the world extensively, Ann is happily settled with her partner in Melbourne, Australia, where she was born. Sharing their wild garden with mobs of rainbow lorikeets and brushtail possums, they live in an area affectionately known as "dyke city," nestled between mountains and bay beaches, a few miles from the city center. When not out enjoying the restaurants and cafés for which Melbourne is famous, Ann spends much of her time writing.

Books by Ann O'Leary

Letting Go
Julia's Song
The Other Woman

CHAPTER ONE

Joanna woke up suddenly. Disoriented, her heart thumping, she lay still for a moment, clutching at the loose threads of her dream and trying to get a grip on reality. With a gasp, she caught sight of a dark, huddled form on the chair in the corner of her bedroom. Leaning on one elbow, holding her breath, she stared, trying to focus.

As her eyes adjusted to the thin, dawn light, she released her breath. "Idiot," she muttered, annoyed with herself. The night before, exhausted, she had carelessly dumped her clothes on top of the plump chair cushions before falling into bed. It wasn't like her to be untidy. The bedside clock read five-thirty. It was still hot. She turned toward the light seeping through the half-drawn, butter-colored Roman blind.

Getting up, she went to the window and opened the blind fully, hoping a breeze might drift through and cool her naked body. But it was motionless outside. Her gaze fell on the elm trees lining the street. Slashed in half by the low, watery shafts of the sun, the treetops were washed in a pinkish-yellow glow, the trunks in shadow. Like outstretched arms, the branches seemed to be begging for a life-giving breeze, the leaves gasping.

She pulled on a long T-shirt and headed out to the kitchen. Taking a bottle of water from the fridge, she poured a glass, drank it thirstily, then poured another. A few drops of water spilled, glistening on the stainless steel counter. She wiped it dry with a fresh, white tea towel before sitting down on one of the high-backed stools at the counter. Her recurring dream had woken her again, where she was trapped in a small room, completely dark, from which she could never find a way out. As she searched desperately, feeling her way around the walls of the unidentifiable room, she began to panic, and it was always then that she awoke.

Joanna sighed, and held the icy glass against her neck. She'd had a similar dream often when she was a small child. You could understand it back then, she thought, but not now. It was a child's fearful dream, but twenty or so years later, it made no sense.

Six months ago she had received word that her father, whom she hadn't spoken to for ten years, had been taken into a nursing home. Hearing about his

2

illness had stirred up memories of her childhood that for twenty years had rarely entered her thoughts. It was as though a door to an unused room in her mind had been opened, and the comfortable layer of dust coating an irrelevant past had been disturbed. Daylight memories could be largely suppressed, but apparently refusing to be ignored, they had evolved into a dream which regularly invaded her sleep. All the time, images of the dream hovered — a menacing shadow — at the edge of her otherwise contented life. Maybe she would take a vacation sometime soon, she thought. Life had become a bit predictable and a change of scenery would get her back to her usual self.

The sun had risen; yellow beams bounced off the counter into her eyes. It was still early, but she decided to get ready for work and make an early start. It was Saturday, and house-hunters would already be up, poring over the real estate pages in the papers. Prospective home buyers would be phoning her by seven-thirty. She finished her water, then padded across the plush living room carpet, up the few steps to her split-level bedroom and into the adjoining bathroom to have a shower.

A half-hour later, she ran her fingers through her wet, short dark hair, leaving it, as always, to dry naturally. Wide awake, she focused her thoughts on the busy morning ahead. In the real estate business, Saturday was the busiest day of the week. Apart from her taking buyers through property inspections and fielding countless phone inquiries, Saturday was also auction day.

In her bedroom, she pulled on a pair of linen, slouchy pants — light gray with a fine beige pinstripe — and tucked in a black silk sleeveless V neck. She slipped on the matching pinstriped vest, leaving it un-buttoned, wondering if her two auctions that morning would go well. It was a hot day and maybe a few of her wavering buyers would stay away.

She put on her small gold ear studs and gold rings. When she got to the office, she thought, she would call all her interested buyers, offering encouragement, and, of course, phone her vendors to reassure them. She didn't like jittery vendors. When they lost their nerve they often rejected the best offer of the day, even when it was within reasonable market value. When a property was passed in at auction, Joanna faced weeks of private negotiations before a sale was eventually made and her commission paid. There was no extra money for the extra work. So good preparation, in the four to six weeks prior to the auction, was essential. But she loved auction day. It was a test of her skills, and a gamble. She could never be sure how buyers and vendors would react under pressure. Adrenaline began to course through her body, her muscles coiling up like springs, her senses sharpened. She could make a lot of money today, or none at all.

It was seven o'clock as she put on her watch. Time to switch on the mobile phone, she thought as she headed for the kitchen.

Pausing at the antique French roll-top desk in the living room, she grabbed her organizer and phone.

The sun, beating through the kitchen window, was heating up the room. She lowered the Roman blind. She spooned coffee into the coffee machine, and in moments, the delicious aroma filled the room. Her pulse quickened, her mouth watering as she antici-pated that first, heavenly mouthful. As she poured the coffee, the mobile phone rang.

"Joanna Kingston."

"Hi, my name's Nathan Smith. We saw your ad for a couple of houses we — my partner, Robert, and I — want to look at. Our friend Tim Jacobs recommended you. You sold him and his boyfriend an apartment a year ago?"

"Oh, yes. Tim." Joanna couldn't really recall Tim from the hundreds of clients she had dealt with over the past year. The fact he was gay didn't help. Most of her clients were queer. With her free hand, she stirred some sugar into her cup.

"He said you were an absolute *darling*," Nathan said with a chuckle.

Joanna smiled. She liked hearing of recommenda-tions. Most of her business came from referrals. Thanking him, she checked her organizer and made an appointment to meet them at the first property in an hour. She needed to drop in to the office first, so she had to hurry. She gulped down her coffee, dropped her phone and organizer into her briefcase and went downstairs to the garage, accessible from a door opening off the entrance hall.

Pressing the remote control on her key ring, the garage door opened as she started the car. Apart from droning cicadas, the street was quiet as she backed out of the garage. Curtains were still drawn across windows. Blackbirds pecked around on lawns. A boy, gliding by on a bicycle, hurled newspapers that landed with a slap on concrete driveways. Joanna put on her dark sunglasses, switched on the air conditioning, punched in a rock station on the radio and, with INXS blaring, headed off to Inner City Realty.

It was close to eight o'clock when Joanna arrived at the office, which was already buzzing with activity. Sales consultants dashed in and out, mobiles glued to their ears. Karen, the receptionist and office secretary, was talking on the phone, and other lines were ringing. She gave a little wave and smiled as Joanna passed her desk. Joanna had worked there for eight years and Karen had been there for most of that time. Since Joanna was rarely in the office, she relied on Karen to take care of inquiries that concerned her when she was out of reach or her mobile was busy.

As a senior sales consultant, Joanna had a private office. She dumped her briefcase beside her desk and glanced across the corridor into Cathie's office, directly opposite hers. Cathie was the rental department manager. Talking on the phone, leaning back in her chair, she wore a short red skirt that exposed her thigh almost to the hip. Her shapely legs were crossed, and one red stiletto, dangling from her foot, rocked back and forth as she gently swung her leg. Smoke curled from the cigarette she held between her manicured fingers. Joanna could overhear snatches of her conversation.

". . . and some black olives, too, honey," Cathie purred in her breathy, cultured voice. ". . . and don't forget to take the towels out of the washing machine . . ." She was obviously talking to her girlfriend.

Joanna sat at her desk and took out her files. She had signed up two new vendors yesterday. She checked through the sales agreements carefully before placing them into new folders and neatly labeling them. On her way out, she would hand them to Karen to be processed. Nick, one of the company's auctioneers, appeared in her doorway.

"G'day, Jo," he said brightly. Nick was in his sixties, had been in the business all his life, and there wasn't much he didn't know about selling real estate. Joanna was always glad when Nick was scheduled to auction her properties. He was the best, enthusiastic but honest. Buyers trusted him and so did she. He knew by pure instinct when people were holding back. He could draw out that extra five or ten grand that a purchaser had to spend — knew they should spend — as easily as taking a rattle from a baby. Joanna needed to be able to rely on the auctioneer. For that heart-stopping half-hour or so, all her weeks of preparation were in the auctioneer's hands. There was nothing Joanna could do except move among the crowd, whispering encouragement to the buyers she had nurtured, pat her client's hand and hold her breath. "What've we got today," Nick said, rifling through the pages on his clipboard. "Ah, yes. Monteroy Street at twelve and Palm Avenue at one." He looked up with a grin. "Are your vendors sweet?"

Joanna smiled. "Yeah, they'll be fine. I'll give them a call in a minute."

"Great. I've got the boys out now, putting up the street signs and auction flags at the properties."

"I hope the heat doesn't keep the crowds away."

Nick shook his head. "No worries about the heat. Rain. That's all we ever have to worry about, Jo.

Bloody rain." He wished her luck, said he'd see her later and continued on his way.

Getting out her list of the most promising buyers, she prepared to call them. One of the most important things she'd learned over the years was to know a real buyer from a dreamer. She had often tried to explain this to the junior sales reps. But they never got it. She watched them chase after time-wasters, like puppies chasing a ball. The junior reps had the wrong attitude. For a start, they lacked any appreciation for architecture, took no pleasure in seeing the beauty in a house or in assessing its potential and market value. And they didn't get involved enough with their vendors and buyers, trying to understand them, matching them up successfully. They might as well be selling doughnuts for all they cared.

Cathie hung up her phone and looked over at Joanna. "Hi, sweetie," she said.

Joanna gave her a smile. "Hi. Busy morning?"

"Fucking unbelievable!" Cathie breathed, brushing her tawny blond curls off her shoulders. "I was hoping this heat would keep everyone at home today."

Joanna chuckled. "I want them out there in droves. I'm not on a salary like you are, remember."

Cathie's phone rang and she turned away to answer it. Joanna glanced from her own tidy desk, empty except for the open file in front of her, to Cathie's desk. As usual, it was a clutter of files, strewn papers, cigarettes, overflowing ashtray, makeup purse — open, its contents spilling out — and, today, a posy of violets in a small vase. Despite what appeared to Joanna to be alarming chaos, Cathie was very good

8

at her job and always knew exactly where to find everything.

Joanna smiled to herself. She and Cathie had been friends ever since Cathie began working there, six years ago. The day Cathie arrived, Joanna had stopped by the office briefly, to pick up some brochures. Karen was talking to a woman at reception and, overhearing them as she hurried past, Joanna realized the woman was Cathie Adams, the new manager of the rental department, due to start that day. Joanna was aware of a new, strong, sweet perfume hanging in the air. Cathie's name was already fixed onto her open door. A glance into her office revealed a cigarette burning in the ashtray — precariously close to a stack of papers, and a lipstick and compact open, ready for use.

Joanna had just sat down at her desk when she heard the four junior sales reps in the open-plan office next door talking about Cathie — making lewd comments. Angry, Joanna got up and headed out into the corridor, intending to tell them to shut the fuck up, when she was nearly bowled over by Cathie. Also heading for the open-plan office, Cathie stormed past Joanna like a tornado, forcing Joanna to flatten herself against the wall. Her face fixed in an expression of black fury, it seemed that Cathie had overheard the men's comments too. Fascinated, Joanna followed her.

"Listen, you stupid, fucking pricks!" Cathie shouted. The young men's eyes widened in shock. They seemed to shrink into little schoolboys behind their desks. Cathie's eyes were blazing, her fists clenched. "If I hear one more obscene, sexist remark from any one of you, I'll sue all your fucking arses

9

off!" Joanna gazed in delight at their reddening faces. "Have you bloody got that?" The schoolboys nodded dumbly, looking like they might burst into tears. With that, Cathie swept out of the room, heading for her office.

Impressed, Joanna went and introduced herself, asking Cathie out to lunch. In sharp contrast to her severe outburst, Cathie accepted warmly, with a disarmingly gentle charm. Joanna quickly sensed that Cathie was a dyke, which was a nice bonus. They left the office together, laughing, and after a lunch that went on longer than it should have, especially on Cathie's first day, and after a couple of drinks too many, they had become firm friends.

"Jo?" Cathie called out across the corridor. "You're going to Marie's and Louise's place for dinner tonight, aren't you?"

"Yeah. Should be good."

"That new doctor's going." Cathie lit a cigarette. Her glossy candy-pink lips matched her nails exactly.

Joanna was only half paying attention. She was selecting the brochures she needed for the morning's inspections and still had to make her calls. "What doctor?"

Cathie gave a loud, dramatic sigh. "God, Joanna! I've mentioned her before. Fiona! She works at the clinic with Sue and Marie." Sue, Cathie's girlfriend, was a physiotherapist; Marie was a doctor. "Fiona's an old friend of Marie's. I've only met her a few times, briefly, when I've popped in there to pick up Sue."

"Uh-huh." Joanna dialed the number for one of her vendors.

"She's gorgeous."

"Uh-huh." The number was engaged. Joanna looked up the other vendor's number.

"And single," Cathie added quietly. She drew on her cigarette, eyeing Joanna, swiveling her chair back and forth slightly. She had that matchmaker look in her eyes again.

Joanna gave a patient smile. "I've got to make these calls quickly or I'll be late for my first appointment." Fortunately, Cathie's phone rang again, and Joanna turned her full attention to her work.

A short time later, Joanna was ready to leave. Her vendors were optimistic. They had assured her that their houses were looking perfect with flowers everywhere, light classical music standing by on CD players, and her buyers still sounded keen. From her filing cabinet, she took out the two contracts of sale relating to her two auctions. Hopefully, they'd be signed before the day was over. She put them, along with the brochures she needed, into her briefcase. Grabbing the new sales agreements to hand to Karen, she paused for a moment, making sure there was nothing else she needed from her office for the next few days. Enjoying the freedom of being out on the road, she only came into the office when it was really necessary. Her days were spent driving around from one property to another, inspecting, giving valuations, negotiating, signing up new vendors and finalizing sales after, and occasionally before, auctions. When she needed a place to sit and make phone calls, write ads or meet with clients, she usually used her favorite hangout — Café Q.

"Good luck with your auctions, sweetie," Cathie said. "You'll still make it to cricket this afternoon, won't you?"

"Of course."

"Mind you," Cathie said, wrinkling her button nose, "it's a shit of a day to be playing fucking cricket."

"Don't worry, babe," Joanna said with a laugh. "We'll kill 'em." She said good-bye, then left to meet Nathan and Robert.

Joanna parked her car outside a townhouse in a row of modern terraces. Nathan and Robert pulled up behind her. She had just shown them an apartment on the other side of the city, which Nathan seemed to like but his boyfriend hated. From the hints Nathan had dropped about their budget, she suspected that they were viewing properties well above their price range. As she opened the house and invited them in, she felt, intuitively, that they were going to be difficult clients.

"The double garage is great, though, isn't it?" Nathan asked Robert hopefully.

Robert shrugged, looking sulky. "I don't like the carpet, and the light-fittings are hideous."

"But those things are easy to change." Nathan turned to Joanna, his expression apprehensive. "Aren't they, love?"

Joanna nodded. "It's best to focus on the layout and design. Don't worry about the decor. Just allow for those changes in your budget." Apart from the decor, the townhouse seemed to fulfill the requirements Nathan had outlined to her. His boyfriend was just being negative. "Why don't I make some notes about your likes and dislikes." Joanna got out her notebook. "Then, as we look at various places, we can build up a profile of what you both really want."

"I want an old place — Edwardian, or something that's got some character," Robert said in a whining tone.

Impatiently, Nathan ran his hands through his long, blond-streaked hair and sighed loudly. "You told me you wanted modern, honey!"

God! Joanna thought. Don't have a domestic. She had another inspection after this one, then her first auction at twelve, and she didn't have time to mess around.

"Why don't you both talk it over," Joanna said, smiling warmly. "I'll call you early next week and see if you want to view some period homes, okay?"

Robert shrugged and marched off toward the door. Nathan smiled and touched her arm. His manner was confidential. "Thanks, love. I'll talk to you later."

Joanna locked up the house and sped off to her next appointment.

CHAPTER TWO

The cricket match was due to start at three o'clock. With five minutes to spare, Joanna drove into the carpark beside the cricket ground that was in the center of a large, tree-filled park.

She strolled across the soft, green grass toward the group of players clustered together near the boundary fence. Lounging on rugs or sitting at picnic tables under the trees, there seemed to be around fifty spectators, mostly friends and partners of the players. As she got closer, Joanna could see Cathie and Sue among the two dozen players of both teams. Marie, their team captain, tall, lean and purposeful, was striding around organizing things. They were all wearing traditional white pants with white short-sleeved shirts. Joanna smiled. Marie was going to be annoyed with her for not wearing the correct clothes. Due to the heat, Joanna had decided to wear her white athletic shorts instead of the long pants, and a loose, white tank top. It amused Joanna that Marie took their amateur matches so seriously. Like most of the others, Joanna considered their games to be a bit of a laugh and good exercise. Although she liked her team to win, of course.

Cathie had introduced Joanna to Marie and her partner, Louise, two years ago. They'd been looking to buy a house, and during the course of house-hunting, which culminated in Joanna's finding them a great house they loved, they had become friends. Clients often became friends. Mixing business with socializing was what Joanna liked best about her work. Marie had formed their cricket team last year, and they played other dyke teams a couple of Saturdays a month during the summer.

"How'd the auctions go?" Cathie asked.

"Great. We had a good turnout. My buyers came through and the vendors held fast. Both properties went for more than the reserve price."

"You can take me out to lunch next week, then," Cathie said with a grin.

Marie had been talking with the other team's captain. Looking hot and bothered, she strode over to Joanna and the others, an unlit cigarette hanging from the corner of her mouth. She'd given up smoking months earlier but hadn't given up cigarettes. "They won the bloody toss and of course have elected to bat," she said peevishly.

Everyone grumbled. They would have to stand around in the heat, fielding while the other team relaxed in the shade, taking turns to bat. Marie shot a glance at Joanna's shorts. "What's with those shorts, Jo?"

Joanna smiled. "It's a hundred degrees."

Marie shook her long, black fringe out of her eyes and snatched the cigarette from her mouth. She pursed her lips. "Not very professional."

Joanna chuckled. "We're playing the Dykes on Bikes, not the bloody West Indies." The others laughed and Marie gave a reluctant grin.

"Yeah, Marie," Cathie said. "Give her break. You're just fucking jealous of Jo's gorgeous legs!"

Marie rolled her eyes and tossed her cigarette into a nearby rubbish bin. "Well, come on, let's get out there."

After an hour of standing and running around in the baking sun, Joanna was tired. Waking up early from an uneasy sleep, followed by a busy, stressful morning working in the heat, was taking its toll. It was a slow match, and she gazed off into the distance. The park extended down a hill to a narrow band of natural bush bordering a creek — an estuary of the Yarra River. The calls of bell birds rang out from the shadowy thickets of Melaleuca scrub. Joanna pictured her dark dream, and a sudden chill deep inside her made her skin prickle. Pushing the image from her mind, she looked up from the shadows toward the sky.

The city skyline stood tall above the trees. A helicopter, slowly crossing the sky, was fuzzy in the heat haze surrounding the steel towers. It hung, suspended like a tiny toy on a string, before landing on a helipad on top of one of the buildings. Joanna suddenly felt woozy. Rubbing her eyes, she turned her attention back to the game. The other team was batting well, and Joanna's team was losing. No wonder, she thought, glancing around at her teammates. Shoulders slumped, hands on hips, they all looked listless. Some were just staring at their shoes. Sue, on the far side of the field, had obviously decided, stuff it, and was having a nice lie-down on the grass.

"They're bloody saving up Killer Casey till last, when we're fucking worn out!" Cathie shouted irritably. She was positioned on the field not far from Joanna. Taking a tissue from her pocket, she delicately blotted her perspiring face. Her thick, long hair was piled up on her head, and she flicked impatiently at the wisps that strayed over her eyes. Just then, the ball was hit with a resounding *thwack* and it hurtled in their direction. Both Joanna and Cathie chased it, but it flew past Joanna, skimming the ground a few meters out of her reach. If the ball made it to the boundary fence, the other team would automatically receive four runs. Cathie was closer to it, and just before it reached the boundary, she threw herself on the ball. Scrambling to her feet, she tossed it with astounding accuracy to the wicket-keeper, just in time for the player to be caught out. Cheers rose from the crowd.

Joanna and Cathie did a high-five. "Good one, Cath!"

Cathie looked pumped up. "About fucking time we got one out!" Panting, she picked bits of dry grass from her shirt. Amazingly, her bright-pink lipstick was still immaculate. Joanna strolled back to her position.

It was close to four o'clock when Fiona drove into the carpark beside the cricket ground. Pleased to find a space in the shade, she parked her white BMW beside a long row of motorcycles. She was meeting Louise and had told her to expect her later in the afternoon. There was no point in rushing to catch the start of the game when she didn't know a thing about cricket anyway. Fiona had been tempted, considering the hot day, to remain at home, comfortably reclined on a deck chair under the pergola, reading. But she had promised Marie and Louise that she would come along. They had insisted it was a good opportunity for Fiona to meet some of their friends. And it was time, Fiona knew, to begin reestablishing herself in Melbourne after living in Sydney for the last three years.

She grabbed a bottle of Evian from the passenger seat and gasped at the heat as she got out of the air-conditioned car. At a sudden outburst of cheering, she turned and gazed across the park. Hopefully, Louise had one of those tables in the shade of the pine trees. As she locked her car, she cast an admiring glance over an early Sixties model Mustang convertible parked beside her. The top was on, no doubt to protect the immaculate interior from the sun. Sexy-looking cars, she thought, especially when they were in such excellent condition as this one.

The light breeze was pleasant, the lush green of the grass and trees inviting. She was glad she'd come. The last three months had been busy, moving her things down from Sydney, settling into her rented house and her new job. The breakup with Diane was beginning to recede into the past. Thankfully, Diane phoned less frequently now that Fiona was so far away, and when she did phone, she was less difficult. Happy to be home in Melbourne, Fiona was looking forward to the future.

Louise waved to her, smiling, from one of the tables under the trees. She didn't play but usually came along to watch.

Fiona kissed her cheek. "Have I missed anything exciting?" she asked with a grin as she sat down.

"No, it's been a pretty ordinary match so far. We just got one of them out, but we're still losing." Louise took a swig from her bottle of Coke.

Opening the Evian, Fiona drank some, scanning the field, trying to take an interest in the game. She smiled at the sight of Sue at one end of the field, sitting on the grass, and spotted Cathie across the other side. Her attention was continually drawn to a woman fielding close to Cathie. Unlike everyone else, she was wearing shorts — as short as panties. Her legs were superb — long and strong-looking. Her shoulders were square and broad, her hips narrow. Agile but graceful, she had a perfect athletic body. She walked with an easy nonchalance that was a pleasure to watch. With one hand, Fiona gathered her hair from her shoulders and held it up off her neck, allowing the breeze to cool her perspiring skin.

Suddenly alert, Louise shifted in her seat. A murmur rippled through the spectators. "Here comes Killer Casey," she murmured in a reverent tone. "She's the opposition's best hitter."

Fiona watched the woman lumber onto the pitch and take up the bat. She found it hard to believe that Casey, who looked like she weighed around one hundred and ninety pounds, could possibly be much of a threat. "Surely she can't run very fast."

"Can't run to save her life," Louise said. "But she doesn't have to. She whacks the balls with full force straight to the boundary." The crowd was hushed, the fielders tense as Marie slowly strolled to her position at the end of the pitch, preparing to bowl. "My sweetheart's a good bowler," Louise added, "but Casey's tough."

Marie began her run up, gained speed, then bowled. The ball bounced with a skidding spin in front of the bat, and Casey was forced to take an ungainly step sideways as she swung the bat. She hit the ball though, and it flew high into the air.

The crowd murmured again. "Great!" Louise said. "There's a chance she'll be caught out!" The fielders all moved around, watching the ball. Fiona found herself holding her breath as the ball headed, with the force of a missile, toward the woman in the shorts. Louise stood up, excited. "Joanna's going to catch it!"

She seemed to be perfectly positioned for the catch. The ball descended rapidly, then it seemed to glance off the side of her hands. It flicked up and struck her in the face. Fiona stood, shocked, as Joanna staggered and put her hands to her head.

"Shit!" Louise exclaimed. The crowd gasped. Fiona

20

knew that cricket balls were as hard as rocks. Someone else picked up the ball as other players gathered around Joanna. She wandered off the field, waving away Cathie who was attempting to accompany her. "I'd better go and see if she's all right," Louise said.

"I'll go," Fiona said. "I've got a first-aid kit in the car if it's needed." She turned to Louise. "She's a friend of yours?"

"Yeah. Joanna Kingston. She's coming to dinner tonight."

Fiona remembered the name. Marie had mentioned she had invited a Joanna Kingston to dinner, that she was very successful in real estate and the best person to help Fiona find an apartment to buy. Fiona watched Joanna sit down on the far side of the field, away from the spectators.

The breeze was a little cooler as Fiona walked across the park toward her. The sun, dropping lower in the sky, was losing some of its bite. Joanna was sitting with her elbows on her knees, head in her hands, and Fiona was worried that she might be badly hurt. As she got closer to her, Joanna suddenly looked up. She was stunning.

Fiona smiled and took off her sunglasses. She was relieved to see that the injury didn't look serious. "Hi. You're Joanna, right? I'm Fiona Maddison. That was quite a knock you took. I've come to see if you're okay."

Joanna's gaze moved over Fiona's face and flickered, subtly, over her body. She gave a dazzling smile. Two little dimples appeared at either side of her mouth. "Thanks. But I'll be fine if I don't die of shame for missing that easy catch." Her tone was relaxed, her voice attractively throaty.

There was a tiny split on her eyebrow which was bleeding slightly. "You're lucky it missed your eye. I'm a doctor. Do you mind if I have a look at it?"

Joanna grinned. "Fiona. You must be Marie's friend." She moved along the seat to make room for her. "Sure. You can have a look."

Fiona held Joanna's face with one hand, while with the other she carefully felt around her brow. If the impact had been hard enough, it was possible the bone was cracked. Joanna's skin was flawless, her olive complexion deeply tanned. It glistened with perspiration. Her short, dark hair was tousled, and around her forehead and the nape of her neck, it clung to her skin in little wet curls. Fiona was aware of her fresh, salty scent combined with an attractive spicy perfume. There was a hint of musk. She found herself focusing on a tiny rivulet of sweat trickling down from Joanna's throat into the shadow between her breasts. Joanna gazed at her, unabashed. Almond-shaped, her eyes were hazel-green with long dark lashes. Fiona cleared her throat. "Does this hurt?"

Joanna smiled. "No. It just stings a bit."

Fiona stood up and put her sunglasses back on. "It seems fine. You'll just get a black eye, that's all. I could clean up that little cut, if you like. I've got some stuff in my car."

"Thanks." They walked to the carpark nearby. The spectators began applauding and the players slowly walked off the field.

"I think your team lost," Fiona said.

"Bad day. And I didn't help." Joanna shrugged. "I believe I'll see you at dinner tonight."

Fiona smiled as she took the first-aid box from the trunk of her car. "Yeah. It seems we were destined to meet today, one way or the other." Cathie and Sue ran up to them as Fiona gently cleaned the cut with a cotton swab soaked in cleansing solution.

Cathie looked very worried. "Are you okay, sweetie?" Fiona finished off with a dab of antiseptic cream.

Joanna grinned. "Fiona thinks I'll live."

Fiona packed up the kit and closed the trunk. "Come and have a cold drink," Sue said. They headed back to join the others, but after a quick drink, Joanna excused herself, saying that she'd had a busy day and wanted to rest for a while before dinner.

Sipping her water, Fiona watched her strolling back to the carpark. She paused to chat briefly with a few women on the way. Then Fiona heard a bleep and the lights of the midnight-blue Mustang flashed as Joanna walked up to it. Fiona smiled. Joanna slid behind the wheel, the white top rolled down, and she put on dark sunglasses. The engine gave a healthy rumble, then Joanna quickly cruised away.

CHAPTER THREE

Joanna toweled her hair, then inspected her eye in the bathroom mirror. The cut was barely noticeable, but a blue-green tinge was developing across her eyelid. In a business where presentation was all-important, a black eye was hardly likely to impress new clients. Too bad, she thought. It couldn't be helped. She carefully touched the sensitive skin around her eye and remembered Fiona's hands — so gentle, yet confident. Joanna had thought she was hallucinating when she looked up and saw Fiona approaching her. The wind was blowing Fiona's hair across her face. She reached up and gathered it, a light honey-brown, and dropped it down her back. Longer than shoulder-length, with a slight curl on the ends, it bounced as she moved. She was taller than average, nearly as tall as Joanna, and her tight, faded jeans sat low on her curvy hips. Obviously for comfort in that heat, the top button had been undone, offering a glimpse of her firm, honey-tanned stomach.

Joanna went into the bedroom and took a suit from the wardrobe. It was lightweight, cobalt-colored with a slight metallic sheen. She put on the fitted pants and a white, sleeveless top. When Fiona had taken off her sunglasses and smiled, Joanna was mesmerized. She was beautiful. Joanna watched her, hoping for some sign of interest — a cute, suggestive smile perhaps, or a tiny flutter of eyelashes. But Fiona had been nothing more than friendly and kind. Joanna clipped on a fine gold chain, spritzed on her perfume, and slipped into the tailored jacket.

In the living room, she opened a black lacquered Chinese sideboard, casting an eye over the wine in the racks, and selected a bottle of Grange Hermitage to give Marie and Louise. Fiona wasn't the flirty type, Joanna decided. While she was clearly a warm person, she was also poised, self-assured. It was difficult to imagine her fluttering her eyelashes, acting cute. Anyway, how could she have expected Fiona to show the slightest interest in her? She had just fumbled a catch that a blind idiot could have managed and was sitting there, a sweaty, grimy mess with a cut eye.

Joanna grabbed her wallet and keys and headed downstairs. Feeling much brighter after a short nap and a long shower, Joanna was looking forward to dinner. At least Fiona was single, according to Cathie, and that was always a less complicated starting point. Maybe during dinner Fiona might show a spark of interest. Joanna hoped so. It had been a while since a woman had really turned her head.

Marie and Louise lived in the northern inner city, near Joanna. It was close to eight o'clock when she arrived at their house ten minutes later. Joanna particularly liked their house. It was of the Federation period. She loved the angled verandas and large boxed windows. The timber fretwork decorating the veranda was painted in traditional dark green, edged in deep red. It had been a good find, Joanna thought as she rang the doorbell, and would have increased in value already.

Cathie and Sue were already relaxing with drinks in the living room when Louise showed her inside. Louise went back to the kitchen while Marie fixed Joanna a drink. "How's the eye?" Marie asked as she poured Heineken into a long, frosty glass. "Having any dizzy spells?"

Joanna took the glass of beer. "Thanks. No, it's fine."

"Let me bloody see," Cathie said, coming up for a closer look. "Well, it matches your suit, anyway." Joanna laughed and sat down on the sofa.

Sue drew on her cigarette and grinned. "I bet it hurt a lot less after Fiona gave it the treatment," she said, her green eyes twinkling.

Joanna sipped her beer and smiled. "Well, she took my mind off it, anyway." Turning to Marie, she asked, "How long have you known her?"

Marie was at the sideboard, opening red wine to have with dinner. "Since medical school — around twelve years. Thanks for the Grange. I think I'll open it . . . no sense in saving it up." She glanced over her shoulder at Joanna. "You might remember my mentioning a friend's house in the country where Louise and I go occasionally? That's Fiona's place. Great property. While she was in Sydney for three years, she came down a few times a year and we all went there for weekends."

Joanna vaguely recalled Marie's mentioning the house once or twice, but Marie certainly hadn't said anything about the beautiful owner. "Why's she come back to Melbourne?"

"She only moved to Sydney to live with her girlfriend, Diane. They broke up six months ago, so she's come back." The doorbell rang. "That'll be her." Marie went to answer the door.

"She's gorgeous, like I said, isn't she, Jo?" Cathie said.

Joanna and Sue looked at each other and rolled their eyes. Keen to see her settled down, Cathie was always vigilantly on the lookout for Joanna's perfect partner. Clearly, Fiona was Cathie's latest candidate for the role. Cathie just couldn't accept that being "settled down" was most definitely not on Joanna's agenda. "Yes, Cath," Joanna said with a grin. "She's gorgeous, like you said."

At the sound of Fiona's sultry, smoky voice in the entrance hall, Joanna's pulse quickened. When Fiona came into the room, Joanna found herself instantly standing to greet her. Christ! Gorgeous was an understatement. Her willowy body was dressed in tight, black, tailored pants and a low-cut, fitted camisole, black and finely beaded. Her honey-brown hair, glimmering with sun-bleached streaks, tumbled around her shoulders. Her smile was breathtaking.

Joanna's usual laid-back confidence was shaken momentarily as Fiona, smiling, gazed at her with a disarming directness. "I see your eye's beginning to color up a bit."

Holding onto her composure, Joanna gave a casual shrug. "What can I do?" she said with a grin. "I'll just have to go around looking like a prize fighter for a couple of weeks."

Fiona chuckled. Her lips were moist with a warm, beige-pink lipstick. Her gaze, moving candidly over Joanna's face, felt like a caress, and Joanna was transfixed. "Oh, I don't think so," Fiona said quietly.

"Sloe gin and tonic, hon," Marie said, handing Fiona a ruby-colored drink clinking with ice cubes. Marie left them to help Louise in the kitchen.

Fiona moved away from Joanna to sit down, leaving Joanna to breathe the soft, seductive perfume left in her wake. Joanna picked up her drink from the coffee table and took a gulp. "So, how are you finding Melbourne, now that you're back permanently?"

Fiona leaned back on the sofa and crossed her long legs. "Great. I'm loving my job at the North Melbourne Clinic. I'm so lucky Marie managed to get the position for me. Another doctor was leaving, I was on my way here, and it was perfect timing."

"And Sue says you've had no shortage of patients," Cathie said with a grin. "She says every dyke in Melbourne is queuing up to meet the new cute doctor from Sydney."

Fiona smiled and shook her head dismissively. The others laughed. "Hardly," Fiona said. "But it's great that we cater mainly to the gay community. Most of my patients are lesbians." She paused to sip her drink. Joanna had no trouble imagining dykes all over town thinking up any number of fake ailments in order to spend ten minutes with Fiona. She almost wished another cricket ball would fly in out of nowhere and strike her in the other eye, just so she could have Fiona touch her again. "And unlike the practice where I worked in Sydney, we have a holistic approach to health at our clinic, which I like. It's wonderful having Sue's physiotherapy and massage skills, and we have an acupuncturist as well."

"And we're getting a reflexologist soon," Sue added. "We have quite a few AIDS patients there, and the alternative treatments are often really good for them."

Marie came and announced that dinner was ready, and they all moved into the adjoining dining room.

Louise placed a large golden fragrant pie in the center of the table, while Marie poured the wine. "I love coming here for dinner," Joanna said. "Louise always cooks my favorite food — comfort food."

Fiona looked amused. "Comfort food?"

"Yeah, you know. Pies, puddings . . . things like that." Joanna grinned. "Soba noodles, shiitake mushrooms, bean curd, crushed dried seaweed all have their place, but sometimes I just crave comfort food."

"To remind you of your childhood?" Fiona asked.

"God, no. I had a series of nannies and housekeepers, of every conceivable nationality. It was like the United Nations at our house, most of the time. They cooked the food they knew, and I only got food like this at my aunt's place."

"Sounds like an interesting childhood," Fiona said.

"Interesting" was one way of putting it, Joanna thought ruefully. Louise began to serve the pie. Under the flaky pastry was a filling of chicken, leeks and mushrooms in a white wine sauce. "And just for you,

29

Joanna," Louise said, "I've made a steamed chocolate pudding for dessert."

Joanna groaned in delight. "What a woman. If you weren't already married, I'd marry you myself."

Sue chuckled. "That'd be the day!" She turned to Fiona. "We've all given up hope of Joanna's ever getting serious. We've lost count of her girlfriends. God knows where she finds them all."

The others laughed while Joanna inwardly cringed. She knew Sue's comments were made in good humor, and ordinarily she would have laughed herself. But instinctively, she felt that Fiona would be most unimpressed by Sue's information. And Joanna wanted to make a good impression. It was untrue anyway. Feeling unsettled, often jumpy since old memories had begun gathering in the corners of her mind like crones whispering and gossiping, she hadn't, for months, been in the mood for dating.

Adopting a relaxed smile, she addressed Fiona, seated opposite her. "That's a complete exaggeration. Take no notice."

Fiona nodded and gave a perfunctory smile. Her expression was worse than unimpressed, it was uninterested! She sipped her Grange Hermitage. "Beautiful wine," she commented to no one in particular.

It bothered Joanna that she couldn't quite read Fiona. Usually, she had no difficulty picking up on how a woman felt about her. Sometimes Fiona's glances seemed sexual, other times indifferent. Ordinarily, Joanna would have decided that this one was too hard. She liked to see clear signs of a woman's attraction for her before she took things any further. Always careful to steer clear of serious entanglements, Joanna never did any chasing. She avoided responsibility and guilt by not being the one to start affairs that, almost always, she would bring to an end. But Fiona wasn't ordinary, and Joanna was becoming drawn in by Fiona's ambiguous demeanor. Combining a powerful, earthy sex appeal with a somewhat detached, elegant poise, Fiona was a fascinating challenge. Strangely, it was very important that Fiona liked her.

"Fucking *gorgeous* pie, Louise," Cathie said enthusiastically.

Joanna watched Fiona steal a scrutinizing look at Cathie. Flicking her curls off her shoulders, Cathie took a delicate sip of her wine without wetting her glossy lips. Marie placed dishes of baked butternut pumpkin, potatoes, and spinach tossed with toasted pine nuts, on the table.

"Yum!" Cathie exclaimed. "I just fucking *adore* spinach."

A smile twitched at the corners of Fiona's mouth. Drawing her gaze away from Cathie, she devoted her attention to her wineglass. Pivoting it slowly on its stem, apparently engrossed by the jeweled color of the wine glinting in the candlelight, she appeared to be suppressing the urge to laugh.

Joanna smiled to herself. Fiona hardly knew Cathie and was obviously still at the "Oh, my God! Did she really *say* that?" stage. Of course, no one else at the table took the slightest notice of Cathie's comments. But over the years, Joanna had often enjoyed watching the jaws of the uninitiated hit the floor as Cathie — her voice soft and sweet as summer rain — dropped profanities like bricks at wonderfully inappropriate moments.

"Jo," Marie said, "Fiona's looking to buy an apart-

ment, and I told her you were the girl to talk to."
Joanna felt a delicious tingle of anticipation. The idea
of calling Fiona to ask her out on a date was looking
increasingly daunting. Showing her properties was the
perfect excuse to spend some time with her.

Fiona smiled. "Just something small. I've got a
house in the country where I spend most weekends, so
I don't want a place in the city that requires any
maintenance."

"I'd be delighted to help you." Joanna kept her
voice low, not wanting to sound over-excited. "I know
of a developer who's converting an old Victorian man-
sion into studio apartments. They might interest you.
It's a beautiful building on large grounds in Carlton,
walking distance to the city. A good investment too."

Fiona seemed very interested. "They sound great!
At the moment I'm renting a tiny cottage in Carlton.
I love that area."

Joanna nodded. "Heaps of good Italian restaurants . . . great shops. Why don't I call you in a couple
of days. I could pick you up from the clinic, say on
Wednesday, and take you around — show you a few
different places."

"Wonderful. I'd appreciate that. Thanks." Joanna
was aware of an increase in her pulse rate as she
returned Fiona's warm smile.

When everyone had finished the main course,
Louise and Marie started to clear the table. Sue took
out a pack of cigarettes, offering them to Cathie, then
Fiona. To Joanna's surprise, Fiona accepted one. She
hadn't smoked earlier in the living room with the
others. It was another intriguing contradiction. She
just didn't look like the smoker type, somehow. But
with obvious enjoyment, she draped one arm over the

back of the chair, inhaling deeply. The smoke curled and spun, disappearing into her throat, then re-emerging in a silvery, drifting stream from between her full, moist lips. Joanna was entranced. How did Fiona manage to make something so ordinary look so erotic? She held the cigarette between the elegant fingers of a beautifully manicured hand, nails painted in the beige-pink color of her lips. She tilted her head back, slid her free hand beneath her long, lustrous hair, lifted then released it in a shimmering cascade behind her shoulders. The creamy-white of her simple pearl ear studs gleamed against her radiant, tanned skin.

Marie returned to the room with new wineglasses and a bottle of dessert wine. Joanna was only half listening to the conversation of the others as she watched Fiona. She wondered what it would be like to kiss that luscious mouth, hold her gorgeous body. What kind of lover would Fiona be? Would she melt in Joanna's arms, yielding, gasping, moaning? Or, fixing Joanna with her direct, smoky-gray eyes, murmuring in that sexy voice, would she be demanding, even dominating? What a delicious quandary! Joanna couldn't make up her mind. God! She closed her eyes, momentarily disoriented as an unexpected erotic heat pulsed through her. What was she doing? Joanna took a deep breath and brought her mind back to the present. Suddenly, horrifyingly, she realized Fiona was gazing at her. Joanna had been staring at her like an idiot. Fiona's eyebrows were slightly raised in a ques-tioning expression, as if waiting for Joanna to speak.

Hoping that Fiona wasn't a mind-reader, Joanna swallowed, madly trying to think of something to say. "Um . . . I thought doctors were all anti-smoking these days." She cleared her throat. "Supposed to be bad for your health . . . you know."

"God, Jo!" Cathie said. "Lots of things are bad for your fucking health."

"Yeah," Sue added. "Even fucking, some would say." They all laughed.

Marie poured the dessert wine. "She only smokes occasionally. Wish I could do that."

Fiona drew on her cigarette and smiled at Joanna. "Are you worried that my smoking is bad for *your* health?" Her tone was teasing.

Joanna grinned. "Yeah, I am actually. You look so sexy doing it that I'm worried I'll faint, fall off my chair and smash my head on the marble hearth." Everyone laughed again. "And I don't think I could take another blow to the head today."

Fiona held her gaze, her eyes sparkling. Under the laughter and under her breath, she murmured, "Well, you'd better hold onto your seat."

Joanna was losing herself in those misty, impossible-to-read eyes. She had to figure out this fascinating woman. She had to know her. And she had to be careful.

Louise arrived in the dining room, proudly bearing a perfect chocolate pudding on a silver platter. Glistening with chocolate sauce, its aroma was wonderful. Joanna was relieved by the distraction, and the general conversation turned to other matters.

CHAPTER FOUR

At four-thirty the following Wednesday afternoon, Joanna unlocked the door of a luxury townhouse and switched off the alarm system. She had an appointment to show the house to a prospective buyer. This was an easy house for inspections. The owners, two women, were overseas, and it was always immaculate. Not like some places where Joanna had to ensure she arrived well ahead of her client to tidy things up. Hiding bowls of pet food under sinks, emptying ashtrays, kicking clothes under furniture and even dragging bedspreads over unmade beds were often part of the job. It annoyed her that some people could be so careless, especially when they were trying to sell their homes.

She straightened the dining chairs and adjusted the position of an ornamental handmade Peruvian bowl, moving it slightly off-center on the dining table. It was a modern building, the rooms quite small, which Joanna disliked, but the French doors masked the deficiencies, she thought. Taking up most of the wall in the living room, leading onto a wide balcony overlooking park land, they were imposing and detracted from the low ceiling. She opened the doors to let in the fresh air.

Glancing at her watch, she hoped her client wouldn't be late. She was picking up Fiona from the clinic at five-fifteen, to show her some apartments, and could hardly wait to see her again. Joanna's thoughts had been preoccupied with her since dinner on Saturday night. The intensity of her attraction was unusual and worried her a little, but she felt in better spirits than she had in months. An exciting affair with a sexy woman like Fiona would put her life back in perfect balance. She only needed to find out if Fiona felt the same way. Hopefully, she would agree to have a drink with her later, maybe even dinner. Fiona had, at least, shown that she liked her, so Joanna felt reasonably confident that she would accept the invitation.

Her phone rang. It was Nathan. "You know that cute Edwardian house you showed us, love? The one with the adorable attic? We think it's perfect. Do you think you can do anything about the price?"

Joanna inwardly groaned. Nathan and Robert had insisted on looking through that house, but it was way over their price range. "Well, I know you'd prefer at least two bathrooms and you want a state-of-the-art kitchen, but the triple garage, heated pool and five bedrooms make it a rather expensive proposition."

Nathan whimpered. "But Robert just loves it. Could you talk to the vendor?"

Vendors often accepted good offers prior to auction, but no vendor in his or her right mind would consider fifty grand below the set reserve price before an auction. The word *no,* however, did not exist in the vocabulary of a good sales consultant. "Sure, I'll see what I can do." Joanna looked up as a woman walked in through the open door. Her client had arrived. Joanna quickly took in her pretty face, short, skimpy dress, nice legs, and gave her a friendly smile. Dyke? she wondered. The woman's eyes flickered over Joanna's body; she tossed her long, black hair and dropped a cute smile. Seemed she was. "Nathan, in the meantime, why don't you have another think about those other places I showed you. You might want to consider the option of renovating to suit your tastes." Nathan sounded satisfied for the time being, and Joanna, promising to call him in a few days, said good-bye. The woman had wandered over to the French doors and was gazing at the view. Smiling, Joanna extended her hand. "Tina. I'm Joanna Kingston. Nice to meet you."

"You too," Tina purred through red, glossy lips as she accepted Joanna's hand. "This is a nice place."

Joanna took her on a tour of the house as they discussed the price range and Tina's requirements. Tina said she would have a think about it and thanked Joanna for the inspection. Joanna showed her to the door, where Tina paused and handed her a business card. "Why don't you call me?" she said. "We could have a drink or something, talk about real estate . . ." She smiled. "Or something."

Slightly taken aback, Joanna glanced at the card. "Oh, yeah. Thanks." A woman who cuts right to the chase, she thought.

"Looks like you've been having a rough time." Tina was focusing on her bruised eye.

Joanna grinned. "Cricket."

Tina nodded, dropped a parting smile and left. Joanna locked the house and headed for the North Melbourne Medical Clinic.

It was close to seven when Fiona and Joanna arrived at Café Q. "I'm surprised Marie hasn't brought you here before," Joanna said as they headed for the bar. "I seem to spend half my life in this place."

Fiona was impressed with the four apartments Joanna had shown her. Attentive and unhurried, Joanna had explained the advantages and investment potential of each one. She clearly possessed an eye for design and knew her business well. Last Saturday, Fiona had found her to be charming, delightful company. Frequently, at dinner, she had gazed at Fiona in a manner that was candidly sexual, and this afternoon had been no different. With her relaxed manner and stunning good looks, Joanna was decidedly sexy.

"Hi, Jo," said the man behind the bar. Joanna intro- duced Fiona to Steve, who owned the café. She ordered a sloe gin and tonic for Fiona and a Barbados rum on ice for herself. Steve asked Joanna about business while he fixed the drinks, and as they chatted briefly, Fiona settled back on the barstool and looked around.

The bar, with high stools around it, was in the center of the large room. Blond wood tables and chairs, in a simple, angular, Italian style, filled the rest of the room. A wall of glass at the front was tilted back against the ceiling, opening the café fully to the street. Wooden fans suspended from the ceiling rotated slowly. The walls were partially exposed old red brick, the remaining jagged plaster sections sponged in an ochre wash. Up-market, art-directed grunge, Fiona thought. But it was nicely done and she liked the atmosphere. Large chalkboards displayed the menu; Barbra Streisand crooned softly from the speakers.

Just as Joanna handed her the drink, two women strolled in. Dressed in full leather, bike helmets under their arms, they greeted Joanna warmly. She slid off her bar stool and gave them both a hug. She introduced Fiona to Bev and Sandy. "These are two members of the monster team we played on Saturday," Joanna said, beaming.

"Casey felt a bit guilty about your eye," Bev said.

Joanna chuckled. "Why don't I believe that?"

Sandy looked her up and down. "When are you going to come to your senses, Jo, and get a bike to go with that gear of yours?"

"Get a bike? When I've got my vintage Mustang?" They chuckled.

Smiling to herself, Fiona scrutinized Joanna. In fitted black, fine leather pants and a silvery silk V neck, her leather jacket slung around her hips with the sleeves knotted at her waist, Joanna was a study in chic insouciance. Although it wasn't difficult to picture her astride a Harley, the image of her posed, nonchalantly, in a Calvin Klein ad came more powerfully to mind.

Bev and Sandy headed off to a table to join some friends. "Let's get a table before the place fills up," Joanna suggested. "Will I get you another one of those pretty red drinks?" Momentarily captivated by her smile, Fiona found herself focusing on Joanna's mouth. Her naturally deep-pink lips were full and beautifully shaped, her little dimples disarmingly cute in her strong face.

"Thanks," Fiona said brightly, hoping her gaze hadn't been obvious. She was determined to keep her attraction under control and not encourage Joanna's apparent interest. The comments made at dinner about Joanna's numerous and casual affairs only confirmed what Fiona's instincts had told her. She had seen it first at the cricket match, in those almond eyes that flickered over her body, and in the way Joanna walked and held herself. Her slight arrogance was offset by an unpretentious and gentle manner. A touch of arrogance in a woman who knew how to carry it off was a trait that Fiona had always found appealing. But she knew all about sexy charmers with drop-dead smiles who liked to keep on the move, and she was finished with that kind of woman. A friendship with Joanna would be ideal, and that was all.

They took their drinks to a table near the entrance. It was still light outside and the street was busy with people wandering along checking the restaurants and cafés, reading menus displayed in windows, choosing places for dinner. Quite a few people, mostly gay, it seemed, were coming into Café Q.

"Thanks for showing me around today," Fiona said. "The apartments you chose are just the sort of thing I'm after."

"My pleasure. I hope you're not in a big hurry to buy, though. New places become available all the time, and I'm sure I can find you something perfect within the next few months."

Fiona smiled. "I'll try not to be impatient, but I do tend to be rather impulsive."

Joanna held her gaze as she sipped her drink. She raised an eyebrow slightly. "Do you?" Her voice was soft and low, her tone provocative. A tiny, lustful ripple warned Fiona to watch herself.

"Hi, Joanna." An attractive woman had paused beside their table. Fiona was glad of the interruption. There was an intimacy in the way the woman looked at Joanna. "It's been a while." Fiona guessed they'd been lovers.

Joanna stood, smiling warmly, and kissed her cheek. "Great to see you, Linda. It *has* been a while. We'll have to catch up sometime."

Linda smiled pleasantly at Fiona as they were introduced, then continued on to the bar.

"You seem to know a lot of people."

"My work." Joanna swirled her glass; the ice tinkled. "Plus I spend a lot of time here. I eat here a lot, meet clients for drinks, you know. You get to know people." The waiter brought their second drinks. "How about dinner?" Joanna asked.

The café was filling up, becoming pleasantly bustling and noisy. It was growing dark outside; a gentle breeze wafted in; the lights were low. Fiona smiled. "Why not?" They quickly perused the blackboard menu and placed their order with the waiter, including a bottle of Chenin Blanc.

Joanna was stroking her glass, wiping away the condensation. Her hands were a nice shape, her nails short and manicured. She wore simple gold rings on most fingers, including her left thumb.

"You obviously love your job. How'd you get into real estate?"

"By accident, really, through someone I knew. I'd just dropped out of an arts degree. It bored me to tears, and I was desperate to become financially independent of my father. I wanted something that offered a challenge, something with some freedom. I started working with a friend, part-time, about fourteen years ago, and became really interested in it. I did some formal training while I learned on the job. I'm in a position now where I'm pretty independent." She sipped her rum and smiled. "I come and go as I please, do my own deals, handle my own marketing. If I perform well, the financial rewards are good. If I'm not careful enough, don't work hard enough, I lose money." She shrugged. "I like it that way."

"Was your family upset about your dropping out of university?"

Joanna chuckled. "My father had a fit. We never got on anyway, but that was almost the last straw." She finished her Barbados.

Fiona grinned. "What was the last straw?"

"When I mentioned I was a dyke, about ten years ago." She pushed the empty glass aside. "I haven't seen him since." Her expression was indifferent. Fiona had never been close to her parents, either, but there hadn't been any conflict, as was obvious in Joanna's case. "After I moved out, I used to drop by to see him once in a while. We had nothing in common and I never cared much for him, but I just thought I should keep in touch." She shrugged. "I was young and maybe still seeking some sign of approval from him. I was starting to do pretty well in real estate by then and had bought my first apartment. But during that last visit, he started raving on about how I was wasting my life, that I should have finished university, what a disappointment I was . . . you know the sort of thing. He often grumbled about all of that, and I usually ignored him. But that day, I felt like I'd had enough. I told him I was doing well, living the way I wanted, and furthermore, I was a dyke, and he could think about that whatever he liked." Joanna chuckled. "I never saw such a shocked look on anyone's face in my life. I thought he was going to have a heart attack! He said he was appalled, horrified . . . stuff like that. Anyway, it made me wake up. He was an old bastard, always had been, and I owed him nothing. That day, he gave me the excuse I'd probably been waiting for, to wipe him out of my life. Seems he's comfortable with that. He's never called."

Joanna spoke without any trace of bitterness, her tone relaxed and matter-of-fact. But clearly, her family background had been troubled. Fiona's curiosity was aroused.

The waiter brought their dinner: risotto with sun-dried tomatoes and mushrooms for Joanna, a warm chicken salad with croutons for Fiona. He poured their wine and placed the bottle in an ice bucket.

"Are you also involved in that other clinic with Marie, over in the western suburbs?" Joanna asked.

"Oh, yeah. The Crisis Center. We both only work there one night a week."

"Sounds like a rough, dismal place."

"It is. It was a shock to me when I first started there. Marie begged me to do it. She's a wonderful doctor, very generous with her time. Being a free clinic, the conditions are poor, the pay's terrible, but Marie's dedicated to doing what she can for the patients there. It was set up to compensate for the lack of hospitals and general health care in that underprivileged area. It's not good enough, but it's better than nothing. They have trouble keeping doctors, though. They're always leaving." With an attentive, thoughtful expression, Joanna was gazing at her. Absent-mindedly, she was slowly tracing her thumb along the line of her lower lip. A very kissable mouth, Fiona noted. Glancing away, taking a sip of her wine, Fiona focused her thoughts. "You never know what's going to happen. We get drug overdoses, people cut up from street fights, rape victims sometimes. The regulars are the street kids. They have all kinds of health problems, suffer lots of abuse. They're the ones, more than anyone else, who have kept me there." Taking the wine bottle from the ice bucket, Joanna topped up their glasses. Her metallic, silver top glimmered against her tanned olive skin. "We have the paramedics in and out of there all night, ferrying the worst cases to hospitals across town, and of course, the police, looking for drug users and criminals."

Fiona paused, thinking of the kids she saw regularly — some as young as twelve or thirteen. At first, regarding her with suspicion, they had been uncooperative and hostile. But when, after a while, they rewarded her with trusting smiles, revealing their warmth and remnants of childish innocence, her heart had gone out to them. A few came in on the nights she worked just to chat with her. There was a bathroom at the center, and when they allowed it, she helped clean them up, phoned around and found them hostels for the night and advised them about safe sex and drug use. She had often been enlightened by their stories, and by the dignity and humor they displayed. When she learned to look past her general assumptions about their lives, and concentrated on individuals, she often saw extraordinary tenacity and optimism. She had learned that things were not always what they seemed to be. It gave her great satisfaction to know that already, in a few cases, she had helped to make a difference. Only a few weeks ago, eliciting the involvement of a good social worker that she knew, she had helped to place a run-away twelve-year-old girl, desperate for a stable family, into a good foster home.

"I don't think I could handle it more than once a week, but on a certain level, I enjoy it now." Fiona smiled. "Marie helps to make it fun."

Joanna nodded, then gazed into the distance, slowly twisting a gold ear stud. A sconce light on the wall threw a soft glow across her face. Her determined jaw, high cheekbones, long lashes were defined, half in light, half in shadow. She was quite an enigma. Why, Fiona asked herself, did she find that quality so enticing? Words unsaid, eyes focused on distant, unknown places, the hint of secrets to be discovered always captivated her. Averting her eyes, she gulped down the rest of her wine. It was the danger. The very thing she tried to avoid attracted her the most.

Joanna turned to her with a smile. "So, tell me about your country house. It sounds great."

"It was my parents' house. They both died four years ago, so the house was left to my brother, Michael, and me. He lives in Singapore so he never uses it. Once, it was a homestead on a huge sheep property, but was subdivided years before my parents bought it. Now, the house is on twenty-five acres, backing onto a state forest. It's about an hour and a half north of Melbourne." She smiled. "You're interested in architecture. I'm sure you'd like the place. It's around one hundred and twenty years old; my parents restored it."

Joanna's eyes took on a dreamy expression. "Iron roof, verandas all around?" Fiona nodded. "My aunt's and uncle's house is like that. They're up that way. I spent all my school vacations there when I was young." Joanna stared down into her glass as she twirled it around on the table. "I loved it there," she murmured. She was silent for a few moments, apparently lost in her thoughts. Then she looked up brightly. "It must be hard to look after when you live in the city. And how did you manage when you lived in Sydney?"

"I've got an arrangement with a woman in the town nearby. She goes in regularly to clean, launder the sheets and towels and things. And the couple on the neighboring property run their horses on my place, which keeps the grass down. They're happy for me to ride, too, which I love. I've got a few saddles in the garage." Joanna nodded, listening intently. "Marie and Louise are coming up to stay the weekend after next. Why don't you come too?"

Joanna seemed delighted. "I'd love to. Thanks."

The waiter came and cleared the table. "How about dessert?" she asked. "They've got a wonderful sticky treacle pudding here, with custard."

Fiona chuckled. "Okay. Comfort food again?"

"Yeah, it's almost as good as Aunt Thelma's." The waiter took their order for dessert and coffee.

"Did your whole family go to your aunt's place for vacations?"

Joanna shook her head. "There was only my father and me, and he never went there. He was rarely home. He worked overseas, mostly in Indonesia. He was an engineer, designing dams, bridges and things. The latest nanny used to put me on the train in Melbourne and pick me up afterwards." She chuckled. "We went through a lot of nannies. I was a bad girl. They couldn't put up with me."

"What about your mother?"

Joanna's expression suddenly darkened. She glanced away, biting her lip. Fiona braced herself. Inadvertently, she had scratched the surface of Joanna's highly polished veneer and exposed a vulnerability. She felt herself weaken.

Joanna adopted an indifferent expression. "She left when I was five. I've never seen her since."

"Do you know why, what happened to her?"

Joanna shrugged. "When I was very young, Thelma told me she had to go, that she wanted to be with me but couldn't. She said my mother loved me and everything, but you *would* tell a child that. I never bought it, though. I can't remember a lot about her, but I've got a strong feeling that we were very close. Anyway, at the time, I just figured that she simply stopped loving me, and that was it." She smiled. "For ages, I was scared that Thelma would do that too."

Fiona felt her throat tighten. It annoyed her that she was so sentimental. Joanna was telling a story that happened over thirty years ago, and she didn't seem bothered about it. Fiona shouldn't feel bothered either, but her too-soft heart had often led her into trouble.

"When I was a bit older, I guessed that she had an affair with some guy and ran off with him. It figures — my father was rarely home and they had separate bedrooms. Maybe she had lots of affairs. I don't know." She looked directly at Fiona. Her beautiful eyes were bewitching, and Fiona felt her composure slipping. "It's odd that you mentioned her. I've been thinking a lot about all that lately. Having dreams since I heard my father had a stroke and was put into a nursing home." She gave another indifferent shrug. "God knows why. Since the age of eleven or twelve, I've never cared a damn about her."

Fiona watched Joanna stir sugar into her coffee. Her expression was unperturbed, but her laid-back manner had altered. She seemed tense. Fiona's gaze wandered over Joanna's strong, square shoulders, the clearly defined muscles of her arms. Staring down at her cup, Joanna's eyes were veiled. She seemed, at once, both powerful and fragile. An irresistible combination. Fiona's pulse quickened; desire stirred. God! She didn't want this. A muscle flexed in Joanna's cheek, and suddenly, Fiona's composure evaporated.

Glancing away, Fiona looked around the café, trying to divert her attention. Leaning back in her chair, she distractedly gathered her hair from her shoulders and dropped it down her back. The bar was crowded, the conversation and laughter fighting with the music. Glittering in Lurex, teetering on precariously high heels, a group of trannies sashayed up to the bar; men preened and flirted with one another; two women were locked in a passionate embrace. She had to ignore these feelings for Joanna, she told herself, or she would get into trouble. The volume of the music shifted up a notch — Madonna segued into Blue Boys.

"Nice place, don't you think?" Joanna said.

Fiona smiled, stirring her coffee. "Yeah, I like it."

Joanna asked her about the current scene in Sydney, saying she hadn't been there for a while, and as they finished their coffee, their conversation continued on a lighter note.

Around a half-hour later, they decided to leave, and Joanna insisted on driving Fiona back to her car, still parked at the clinic.

They didn't talk much during the short drive. Joanna seemed at ease with the silences, but Fiona felt the sexual tension between them building. The roof was on, capturing the earthy smell of Joanna's leather, mingling with her sexy, musky perfume. She was a fast, confident driver. As she changed gears, took corners in easy, fluid movements, her leather whispered.

Joanna turned into the carpark and drew up alongside Fiona's BMW. It was dark, except for one dull light in the far corner of the parking lot. The engine purred quietly as Joanna turned to her. Fiona's heart beat a little quicker as Joanna's gaze lingered on her mouth. Fiona gave a friendly smile. "Thanks for the lift," she said evenly. She opened the door and got out of the car.

Joanna got out too and stood beside her as she unlocked her car. "I'll call you about the weekend in the country," Joanna said.

Fiona wondered whether she had been wise to invite Joanna. An ordinary friendship with her might be difficult. "Yes. It'll be fun."

Then Joanna gently took her arm and kissed her cheek. A sudden electrifying spark made Fiona quiver. Joanna gave a little smile. Her mouth was tantalizingly close. Suddenly feeling helpless, Fiona was transfixed. Was Joanna going to kiss her mouth? Fiona's mind was screaming no, while her body ached for it. Why couldn't she just get into the car? Why was she just standing there? She closed her eyes for a moment and Joanna kissed her neck. Fiona felt the tiny flicker of her tongue and gasped softly.

"Goodnight," Joanna said quietly.

Fiona swallowed. "Goodnight, and thanks again." She left Joanna standing in the shadows beside her car.

CHAPTER FIVE

Panic-stricken, Joanna felt her way around the smooth, featureless walls of the small dark room. There must be a way out. Suddenly, the room was incandescent with a brilliant white light.

With a jolt, Joanna awoke, her heart thumping. A flash of lightning captured her bedroom in a ghostly freeze frame. Thunder rumbled in the distance, crawled closer, then exploded in a deafening crack outside her window. A cool change had arrived. She got out of bed and stood at the open window. A refreshing breeze cooled her body and wafted through the room.

Backlit by the streetlights, rain hung in heavy, silvery sheets. Bouncing off the pavements, it roared. She inhaled the acrid yet pleasant smell of rain on dusty concrete. The bedside clock read three a.m.

Going out to the kitchen, Joanna got a glass of cold water, then returned to bed. Piling the pillows up behind her, she sat sipping her water as the room grew cooler by degrees. When she had arrived home after dinner with Fiona, she was restless, thinking about her. It took a while to get to sleep. She kept picturing Fiona's face after she kissed her neck. Her eyes were closed, her luscious lips apart. Heady with the scent of Fiona's skin and her sexy perfume, it had taken all of Joanna's self-control not to grab her and kiss her mouth. She could swear Fiona had wanted to be kissed — the quiver in her body, her little gasp signaling desire. But unlike other women Joanna had wanted, Fiona's reserve made Joanna cautious. Fiona had recovered her composure quickly, her smile perfunctory as she drove away.

Obviously, Fiona felt some attraction for her, but perhaps not enough to want to do anything about it. At least, not yet. Joanna smiled. She had known women who would delight in being swept into her arms and ravished in a dark parking lot on a hot night. But Fiona probably wouldn't. With a shudder, she imagined Fiona's withering glare of disapproval if Joanna had tried anything like that. She sighed. She would have to wait until Fiona made some kind of move. God! Joanna couldn't believe herself. Wait for a woman to want her? That would be a first! Still, she had never before been so intrigued by a woman, wanted anyone so much. And she had a powerful sense that Fiona was going to be worth the wait.

Joanna finished her water and placed the glass on the bedside table. Three-thirty. She lay down on her stomach, facing the window, listening to the rain. Hopefully, the dream wouldn't wake her again. She wished she could put the past back in that little dark room in her head and close the door on it for another twenty-five years. But that wasn't going to happen. Her memories had taken on a life of their own, running amok, and, she had to admit, a long-dormant curiosity had been aroused.

Another flash of lightning lit up the room. Against the wall opposite her bed, reaching almost to the ceiling, stood an antique Japanese stepped cabinet. Having survived two centuries, and having held innumerable secrets in its deep, polished timber drawers, it was impervious to thunder, lightning and childish nightmares. In the flashes of eerie light, it looked real and solid and reassuring.

It seemed that the only way she would recover her peace of mind was to solve the mystery of why her mother left. She would have to find answers to questions that all her life she had refused to ask — been afraid to ask. Closing her eyes, Joanna gave herself up to the memory of that terrible night.

The night lamp illuminated her birthday cards, lined up on the black marble mantelpiece. In glitter and colored foil, the number 5 was featured brightly. Clusters of colorful balloons were suspended from the corners of her bedroom. Downstairs, her parents were arguing, shouting furiously. Joanna, curled up into a ball in her bed, was shaking with fright. Suddenly, her mother burst into her room, whispered a few soothing words, then gently lifted her from the bed, wrapped her in a blanket and held her tightly. Joanna threw her arms around her mother's neck and clutched her, relieved, knowing she was safe. Then, shouting as he thumped up the stairs, her father burst into the room and wrested Joanna from her mother's arms. Joanna kicked him and screamed, her mother cried and shouted at him, but they were powerless. Shoving her mother out of the room, he dumped Joanna roughly back on her bed and slammed the door as he left.

The shouting continued for a little while longer, and another door slammed. It sounded like the front door. Then, worse than the shouting, came a terrible silence. Trembling, Joanna crept out of her room onto the landing and peeped through the banisters to the entrance hall below. Her father was standing there, staring at the closed front door. Abruptly, he turned, marched into his study and shut the door. Too afraid to venture downstairs, Joanna waited. Knowing her mother had left the house, she watched the front door until, exhausted, she fell asleep.

It was barely light when she had awoken stiff and cold, curled up on the carpet, her arm threaded through the carved posts of the banister. Light bled from beneath the study door. Apart from the chatter of birds waking up in the trees, and the resonant tick of the grandfather clock in the hall, the house had been silent.

Joanna was shocked to find tears stinging her eyes. She wondered if any good could come from sifting through all that again. The thunder had rolled away, the rain had eased. Joanna turned over and drifted off to sleep.

* * * * *

The following Sunday afternoon was warm, the sun shining. Marie was coming over for lunch. Louise couldn't make it — she was a nurse and on duty that day. Fiona was preparing a cheese soufflé. Standing at the stove, she gradually added milk to the flour and butter in the saucepan, whisking the sauce base as it began to thicken and simmer. One of her favorite pieces of music, the third movement of Beethoven's *The Tempest,* was playing on the CD player. Having thought a lot about Joanna since their dinner on Wednesday, she wondered what Marie would be able to tell her. The last couple of days at the clinic had been busy and they'd had little chance to talk.

Stirring the grated cheese into the sauce, she brought it back to a simmer. Picturing Joanna's sexy smile, and her tousled hair, she realized that Joanna was the first woman to attract her since her breakup with Diane. In recent months, Fiona had tried to convince herself that she had only become involved with Diane because of her own emotional vulnerability at the time. They met three years ago at a medical conference in Melbourne. Then, Fiona was still coming to terms with the recent death of her elderly parents who had died within months of each other. Diane, with her charm and seductiveness, arrived at just the right moment, offering love and devotion. Fiona had fallen for her, although doubts niggled at the back of her mind. Diane's provocative smiles seemed to be distributed freely to any woman who looked at her twice — and many did. But Diane had genuinely wanted her and had big plans for their future together. They moved to Sydney, where Diane had a job as a psychologist. Fiona was happy enough to make a fresh start elsewhere and had easily found a position as a general practitioner in a private practice.

Fiona removed the sauce from the heat, and stirred in the egg yolks, seasoning and chopped chives. She folded in the beaten egg whites, poured the mixture into the soufflé dish and put it into the oven. Marie would arrive soon. She poured a glass of Evian and took it outside. French doors opened off the kitchen onto a wooden deck. She sat on a wicker chair under the pergola, entangled with lush, green grapevines. Clustered around the edge of the small deck were thick lavender bushes, their perfume hovering in the air along with the bees humming around them. Birds sang from the nectarine tree, flitting in and out of the gnarled branches heavy with fruit. Hydrangeas were bowed with the weight of enormous blooms in pink, mauve and blue.

After they had bought a house, Fiona gradually began to learn of Diane's many past relationships and infidelities. Diane, always clever at manipulating emotions, assured Fiona that those days were behind her. But Diane couldn't resist the attention other women showed her, and within two years had her first affair. Fiona was shattered. Diane begged forgiveness, offering a myriad of psychoanalytical excuses: her traumatic childhood, her resultant insecurities. Fiona had ended up feeling sorrier for Diane than for herself.

Too soft-hearted, Fiona chastised herself. And stupid. She sipped her water, listening to the music. A year later, Diane had another affair, and that time, Fiona had walked out. She sighed. She had ignored her initial instincts about Diane, and while she could partly blame the difficulties in her life at that time for

56

her lack of judgment, the truth was, she fell for women like Diane because they excited her. The wild ones. The complicated, enigmatic ones. Like Joanna.

The doorbell rang. Marie had arrived.

While Marie went to the fridge and got them both a drink, Fiona tossed a salad.

Marie handed Fiona a bottle of Heineken. "So, did Joanna show you any apartments you really liked?"

"I liked them all. You were right. She knows her stuff."

Marie took a sip of her beer. "You seemed pretty taken with her on Saturday night. And I don't think she took her eyes off you all night long." She shook her head incredulously. "Louise and I couldn't believe her. We've never seen her lock onto someone like she did with you."

Fiona sliced some crusty bread and put it into a basket. "Oh, come on. I've no doubt she's always like that." She recalled the way Diane had always flirted with anyone new. Amazingly, Fiona hadn't thought anything of it at first. She smiled to herself. She had even felt proud of Diane's irrepressible charm.

"No, she's not. At parties, or wherever, I've only ever seen other women come on to her." Marie took a cigarette from a pack on top of Fiona's sideboard and stuck it in her mouth. "Jo responds if she's interested, you know. But I've never seen her make the first move." She chuckled. "Cathie claims Jo doesn't *have* to do anything, that her natural sex appeal takes the work out of it for her."

"It's true then, what Sue said about her numerous lovers."

Marie pulled out a chair and sat at the table. Absent-mindedly, she drew on her unlit cigarette.

"Only up to a point. It's not so much that she has lots of them, more that they don't last long. You won't see her with anyone for months, then suddenly she'll turn up somewhere with a gorgeous girl no one's ever seen before. She meets them through her work, mostly. Then, after a short while, they disappear. Often, they're in relationships — playing around. Jo's always said that she likes to keep affairs light, no strings, you know."

Fiona leaned against the counter and crossed her arms. "You *do* surprise me."

Marie grinned. "Yeah, well, you're the expert on Joanna types."

Yes, Fiona thought ruefully. Clearly, like Diane, Joanna had a wandering spirit.

Marie gave Fiona a speculative look. "You're attracted to her, aren't you? I can tell."

Fiona shrugged. "I think she's attractive. Who wouldn't? But even if Joanna was interested in me, I've got no intention of starting an affair with anyone when I know it would be over in five minutes. I hope we'll become friends." She should have just had a friendship with Diane, instead of becoming her lover, she thought. Diane was intelligent, fun and basically good-hearted. It was only as relationship material that she was hopeless. And Fiona, unable to separate her heart from desire, was hopeless at no-strings affairs. A passionate glance or a sexy smile could virtually make her knees give way; she always became emotionally involved. She put the cutlery and napkins on the table. "The next woman in my life will be someone stable, loving and reliable who won't mess me around."

Marie laughed. "Do me a bloody favor! You've never gone for a woman like that in your life!"

Fiona took the soufflé from the oven. She couldn't blame Marie for being amused by that declaration. "News flash. I've changed." She placed the salad, bread and the soufflé on the table.

Marie took a swig from her bottle. "Yeah, right." She chuckled. "God, I remember when I first met you at med school. You were going around with that biker girl. What was her name?"

Fiona smiled, remembering her fondly. "Sage. But I think she made that up." She served the soufflé.

"She was bloody mad! I'll never forget that day when the dean was making an address in the Great Hall. Around eight hundred students, tutors and professors were there. Can't remember what he was going on about. But suddenly, the main door flew open and Sage burst in on her Harley, roared down the aisle and came to a screeching halt in front of the dean's podium."

Fiona chuckled. At that age, she had found Sage's irreverent, crazy behavior exciting and adorable. Sage was probably responsible for her continuing fascination for bad girls.

"I thought the poor old bastard would pass out," Marie continued, "while she sat there, revving the bike, in her tight leather pants and some kind of skimpy leather top."

"A bustier, actually. With studs."

"Shouting over the engine, telling him he was a sexist homophobe and a slave to the fascist establishment, among other things."

Fiona grinned. "He was."

"Then she turned around and yelled to you, 'Come on, babe.' You got up, sedately walked down the aisle, slid onto the back of the bike and with a screech, you both took off!" They laughed.

Fiona pictured Sage's long, dark hair, green eyes always sparkling with fun, and the way she strode around as though every place she set foot in, she owned. She was sweet though, and gentle. After the Great Hall incident, she had suddenly quit her law studies and taken off on her bike across the Nullabor Plain to West Australia. Fiona had thought she would die from her broken heart. "Yeah. I got into a bit of trouble over that," she murmured.

"So, what is it with you and women like Sage?"

Fiona laughed. "Give me a break! I was only twenty-one! She was my first serious girlfriend. I was besotted."

"She was only twenty-one, too. If you knew her today, at thirty-two, do you think she'd be much different?" Fiona shrugged. Marie's brown eyes twinkled. "She could be a psychologist." She gave a teasing smile. "Or a real estate consultant."

Fiona rolled her eyes and gathered up the dishes, taking them to the sink. Marie knew her too well. And she had confirmed what Fiona suspected about Joanna. But what Marie didn't know was that Fiona had never before experienced the instant, powerful attraction that she had felt for Joanna. She was the sexiest woman Fiona had ever met. If Joanna tried to take things any further, and if Fiona gave in to her own desire, she would fall for Joanna hard.

Looking thoughtful, the cigarette dangling from her lips, Marie reclined in her chair while Fiona put on the kettle to make coffee. "These girls are the antithesis of your serious, responsible nature. They don't give a rat's arse. I think it's their recklessness that turns you on."

"Oh, do you, now?" Fiona said, smiling. "I lived with Ms. Psychoanalysis for three years, so you can save that, thanks all the same." She filled the coffee plunger. Hoping her tone sounded light and casual, she added, "I've invited Joanna to join us in the country next weekend, by the way."

Marie raised her hands in a defeated gesture. "A very friendly thing to do. I'm sure that you and Jo will become lovely little friends." Clenching the cigarette between her teeth, she gave a cheeky grin.

Fiona chuckled. "I'm sure we will, too." She put the plunger and cups onto a tray. "Come on, let's take our coffee outside onto the deck."

Talking about other matters, they whiled away the rest of the afternoon.

CHAPTER SIX

It was a classic February day, hot and brilliantly sunny, as Joanna headed north up the highway the following Saturday afternoon. Wearing a strapless red bikini top with her worn, comfortable jeans, Joanna was enjoying the sun and the warm wind on her skin. An hour out of Melbourne, the city's radio signal was beginning to weaken and splutter. Turning off the radio, she put on a favorite Muddy Waters CD. She should do this more often, she thought. Out of the city, on the open road, the Mustang came into its own. Gliding smoothly, as if floating on air, the car was like an extension of her body. Maybe, with any luck, if things developed with Fiona, she would be making this trip more often in the future. Apart from a brief phone call to confirm arrangements for this weekend, she hadn't spoken to Fiona for ten days. During that time, she had considered phoning her again to invite her to dinner, but instead reminded herself to take things slowly. This weekend was a good start.

Relaxing in her seat, Joanna turned the music up loud. On either side of the road, farmland stretched out to the horizon. Golden hay bales were sprinkled liberally over the stumpy yellow grass. Dams glinted in the sun. The scenery reminded Joanna of her aunt Thelma and the farm she had loved so much. Thelma's and Ted's place was only a half-hour west of Fiona's. She should make the effort to go and see them soon, she thought. She spoke with Thelma on the phone a few times a year and usually saw them at Christmas, but it wasn't good enough. They deserved more than that from her. Thelma and Ted had been like parents to her. They were wonderful people, and apart from their only child, Adrian — a year younger than Joanna — whom she had spent so much time with as a child, they were the only people she had loved and trusted as she grew up. Joanna had allowed their relationship to drift over the years. It had been easier, somehow, to just let virtually everything and everyone connected with her past fall away, become engrossed with the life she had created for herself.

Sheep and cattle, their heads bent over hay and the edges of dams, seemed motionless as the car whipped past. Joanna remembered the farm set Adrian had been given one Christmas. He and Joanna connected up the plastic white fences, set them into the green base, and put the plastic buildings and animals in place. Ted had probably hoped to stimulate in Adrian an interest in farming, Joanna thought with a smile. Adrian, always as queer as fuck, had turned out to be more interested in fashion design. He lived in Sydney, but he and Joanna were still close and kept in touch.

Joanna turned off the highway onto a minor road. To get to Fiona's property, she had to pass through a small town, then through the forest. She tingled at the thought of seeing her again. Maybe this weekend, Fiona would make the move Joanna was waiting for. It was a worry, though, that she was becoming a bit obsessive about Fiona. Why didn't she call Tina? She had Tina's card in her wallet, and she wouldn't have to spend time wondering how Tina felt, what she wanted. No mysteries there. Joanna sighed. The thing was, Fiona was an absolute dream. No one else came close.

It was nearly six o'clock when Joanna arrived at Fiona's property. After closing the gate behind her, she drove slowly up the long, gravel driveway. The silver of an iron roof glittered in the distance as she wound her way through the trees. Bright pink galahs shot in front of the car, squealing as they alighted in a gum tree. Already occupying the tree, a flock of white cockatoos, crests raised in blazing yellow indignation, shrieked at the invasion. Red bottlebrush flowers, gold-tipped, drooped from weeping Callistemons. Joanna breathed in the smell of eucalyptus.

There was a movement through the trees ahead of her. Suddenly, on horseback, Fiona appeared, cantering toward her. Between the tufts of wild grass, dust rose from the horse's hooves. Joanna stopped the car and gazed at her. Fiona's hair tumbled around her shoulders. Wearing a tiny, emerald-green bikini top with short, cut-off jeans, the muscles of her arms, stomach and thighs were taut and strong as she guided the horse. Joanna's pulse quickened. The poised, sophisticated image of the Fiona she knew was transplanted by this earthy, wild-looking beauty. She could hardly believe her eyes.

Fiona pulled up the horse beside the car and dropped one of her gorgeous smiles. "Great to see you," she said, panting. Her tanned skin glistened with perspiration. Joanna's gaze lingered on her silky-smooth legs, hugging the horse's flanks. Her mind froze for a moment, picturing those legs wrapped around her waist, Fiona's head thrown back in wild, passionate abandonment. She felt herself tremble.

Joanna blinked and swallowed. "Great to see you too."

"I'll race you to the house," Fiona said with a grin. Expertly, she turned the horse around and galloped off into the trees.

A little farther along the driveway, the trees cleared and the house emerged. A classic, grand, stone homestead, it squatted majestically on the hill. The wide driveway curved in a circle in front of the house. A heat haze shimmered above the iron roof, the corrugations reflected in the streaky clouds suspended in the powder-blue sky. High-pitched, the roof extended out to form broad verandas all around. White-painted veranda posts supported the vivid purple flowers of sarsaparilla vines.

Joanna parked her car at the side of the driveway in the shade of a River Red gum, then grabbed her overnight bag and some wine she had brought to give

Fiona. Marie and Louise were reclined on blue and white striped canvas deck chairs on the stone-paved veranda. Fiona was dragging the saddle and bridle off the horse. She tossed them under the veranda as the horse wandered off.

"No trouble finding the place, then?" Fiona asked. Joanna shook her head, then took Fiona's arm and kissed her cheek. Her skin smelled deliciously salty, with overtones of her seductive perfume. Fiona gazed into her eyes for a moment. Her direct, clear expression was searching. Her gaze flickered over Joanna's mouth, then she smiled. "You must be dying for a drink. Come inside."

Joanna kissed Marie and Louise. "How was business this morning, Jo?" Marie asked, chewing on a cigarette. "Make a shitload of money?"

Joanna chuckled. "I wish. It was okay." Fiona was holding open the carved timber screen door. Joanna followed her inside.

A wide hallway ran down the center of the house, interrupted by three ornate carved arches. The burnished hardwood floor was a rich golden brown. The ceilings were high, and Joanna admired the pressed metal ceilings. It was rare to see them in such good condition. Refreshingly cool, the house exuded a mellow, peaceful atmosphere and the soothing smell of old timber, antique furniture and beeswax polish.

"It's amazing," Joanna breathed. It reminded her of Thelma's place but was much bigger and grander.

"My parents did a lot of work to it," Fiona said as she opened doors off the hallway. There were four huge bedrooms, two on either side of the hallway, each with French doors opening onto the side verandas. Large fireplaces were framed by elaborate polished pine mantels. Pretty Liberty printed fabric, in muted colors, curtained the windows in generous swags. Bedspreads in matching fabrics were draped over each of the large, antique wooden beds. Two renovated bathrooms, one on either side of the hall, were perfect Victorian reproductions, replete with tessellated tiled floors, and sparkling black and white tiles.

"God, they sure did," Joanna said.

Fiona led her into one of the bedrooms. "This is your room."

Joanna watched her as she opened the white painted French doors. She looked achingly sexy in those very short cut-off jeans. Joanna wondered what Fiona would do if she just went to her and took her in her arms. Joanna would bury her face in that lustrous hair, then turn her around and kiss her gorgeous mouth. Staring outside, her back to Joanna, Fiona gathered up her hair in one hand and dropped it, shimmering, down her back. God, Joanna thought, does she know how sexy that is? Tearing her gaze away from Fiona, Joanna looked through the doors at the straw-colored, rolling hills. Blue-gray gum trees stood in clumps, still and droopy in the heat. Her eyes were drawn to a shadow moving slowly over the yellow grass. A wedge-tail eagle hovered, black against the sky. Suddenly, it swooped, lightning-fast, then vanished.

Fiona turned to her with a smile. "Come on out to the kitchen."

A stained-glass door at the end of the hall opened into the next section of the house. A dining room with an antique walnut table and chairs to seat ten was on one side; a large living room was opposite. Behind the dining room was the kitchen. Blackwood counters and cupboards lined the walls. Appliances were sparkling white. In one corner, the original black, cast iron combustion stove nestled into the chimney cavity. With a large, scrubbed, old pine table in the center of the room, it was at once slick, modern and cozy.

"Thanks for the wine," Fiona said as she placed it in the fridge. "We'll probably get through that tonight."

A round vase on the table was crammed with sprigs of eucalyptus. Some leaves were dark and glossy, some pale with a felty nap. Flowers in red, pink and white glistened with sticky nectar. Entranced, Joanna watched a tiny, native bee hovering over the flowers, its high-pitched hum barely audible. An old clock on the wall ticked solemnly. Thelma had a table like this one, and her kitchen had a similar, homey feel. For a few moments, Joanna was captured by memories, and her mind drifted back twenty-five years.

Nine years old, she was sitting at Thelma's kitchen table, scraping cake batter out of a mixing bowl, licking it off the wooden spoon. There was the aroma of cakes baking. Thelma was at the stove stirring something; Adrian, sitting beside Joanna, was drawing on large sheets of butcher's paper. Thelma wiped her hands on her apron, then turned a page of a book that was resting against the sugar canister on the counter. She was reading a poem about a boy who one day rode off on his horse into the bush, got lost and never returned. His mother waited at the farm gate for him to come home, but the reader knew the boy was dead. For days the mother looked and longed for him, but the bush took him, wild bluebells grew over him, and his body was never found. Joanna loved that poem. Imagining her own mother looking for her, longing for her, she asked to hear it over and over, although she knew it by heart. The words had danced in her head and beat a rhythm in her body.

"What would you like?" Fiona asked. She was holding the fridge door open.

Disoriented, feeling suddenly exposed by Fiona's warm, smoky eyes that flickered almost imperceptibly over her breasts, Joanna nearly answered truthfully. She'd like to take Fiona into one of those pretty bedrooms, lock the door, and slowly kiss every inch of her salty, honey-colored body. Perhaps her thoughts showed on her face. Fiona averted her eyes, fiddling with her hair that was brushing against her breast. Joanna sensed that Fiona's feelings for her hadn't changed. The sexual tension between them was mounting, although they were both doing their best to politely ignore it. Joanna smiled. "A beer would be nice, thanks."

Fiona handed her a Heineken, took one for herself, and they went outside to join the others.

Sipping her beer, Joanna surveyed the view. It was still very warm, but the sun was dropping in the sky and the burning heat of the day had passed.

"I'll start to get dinner organized, shortly," Fiona murmured. She took a sip of her beer. Sunlight, glinting through leaves moving in the soft breeze, danced on her skin.

Louise stretched and sighed. "I'll get the seafood ready." She playfully tousled Marie's hair. "You going to do the barbecue, darling?"

Marie nodded. "Do you know anything about real barbecues, Jo? Ones where you burn wood?" She looked apprehensive. "I'm used to gas ones."

Joanna chuckled. "Of course. They're the best kind. We had wood barbecues at the farm all the time when I was little. I'll help you with it."

She only half-listened as the conversation continued around her. Rainbow lorikeets darted among the trees, pausing to sip at the nectar in the flowers. Far away, kookaburras laughed raucously. Bush-covered hills rose against the horizon. As a young child, she had spent a lot of time playing by herself in the bushland surrounding Thelma's farm. Nearly got lost a few times, too, like the boy in the poem. It was easy to become lost. Provoking curiosity, the bush was seductive. From a distance, it appeared to be dense, impenetrable, but from within, it was the spaces between the trees that dominated. Broad, open spaces, flooded in sunlight. Scrubby undergrowth scratched around your knees, the heady smell of peppermint rising from the leaves crushed underfoot. It seemed benign, like unkempt parkland, until you went too far in and tried to retrace your steps. In every direction, everything looked the same. No paths led in, and none out. Those bright, open spaces, where a child could fantasize about hiding away, building a little house and living in solitude forever, suddenly became traps. The trees were huge fence posts, the scrub, barbed wire. But there were no neat borders, no end to it. You lost perspective; it swallowed you up as though you were drowning in the hot, dry, minty air. And the silence. Apart from the occasional, startled shriek of a bird, the shivering of leaves, your own breath, there was a shocking silence.

"It's seven-thirty." Fiona stood and stretched languidly. The light was fading, the deep pink streaks across the sky looked like they'd been sketched with a fat crayon by a careless hand. Arms raised, head back, Fiona shook her hair. Joanna had to stop herself from reaching out to touch it, to take masses of it into her hands, draw it to her face, inhale its sweet fragrance. "We'd better make a start on dinner," Fiona added. She and Louise went inside.

Marie stood. "Come on, Jo. Let's start the barbecue."

It was a brick barbecue, built close to the house near a stand of trees. There wasn't much kindling stacked underneath to get it started, so Joanna sent Marie off to collect some twigs or whatever she could find. When Marie returned with an armful of twigs covered in green leaves that she'd torn from the trees, she looked bewildered when Joanna laughed, shaking her head. "Why don't you set the table," Joanna said. "I'll fix this." She scouted around, found some dry wood and soon had the fire burning well.

A wooden table and chairs were set up at one end of the veranda. Marie laid out white plates, napkins, cutlery and glasses, while Joanna cooked the prawns and marinated chicken Louise brought her. Smoke from the barbecue and delicious cooking aromas hung in the air. Marie handed Joanna another ice-cold Heineken, and they stood, comfortably silent together, watching the sun slowly sink behind the hills. Birds squabbled noisily over their roosts as they prepared for the night. Crickets and frogs struck up a chorus.

Around eight-thirty, they sat down to dinner. A candle burned in a glass holder in the center of the table. Marie poured the chilled French Beaujolais and Louise set down a platter of oysters with wedges of lime on a bed of crushed ice. Fiona brought out a big basket of French fries and a bowl of salad. The sky was crimson, and Fiona's skin glowed in the reflected light. Showered, perfumed, dressed in fitted black linen pants with a white satin camisole, her country wildness had vanished. Lips glossy with her warm pink lipstick, it was the poised city woman who sat down opposite Joanna.

During dinner, Fiona occasionally looked across at Joanna, holding her gaze, and Joanna's desire, by degrees, became more urgent. She would have to find a moment to be alone with her, she thought. She had to hold her. Joanna gulped her wine. She had to kiss her. It seemed that Fiona wasn't going to make a move, and Joanna couldn't stand the waiting game for much longer.

Louise drained her glass of wine. With a satisfied sigh, she ran her hands through her short fair hair. "Has Diane called you lately, Fiona?" she asked as Marie topped up her glass.

A shiver ran down Joanna's spine. Fiona was still in contact with her ex?

"Not for weeks, thank God." They had finished eating and, reclining in her chair, Fiona lit a cigarette. Marie took one too, clamping it tightly between her teeth as if determined to overcome her obvious desire to light it. "Since I moved back here, she's stopped the constant talk of reconciliation." Fiona exhaled slowly, looking thoughtful. At least Fiona had apparently lost interest in her, Joanna thought with relief. "But until she finds someone else to hold her hand full-time, she'll call me when she has a problem."

"To hold her hand until she starts screwing around again," Marie said in a disdainful tone.

Diane screwed around? How could you want a

committed relationship, be unbelievably lucky enough to have Fiona, then screw around? Diane was clearly an idiot. With one hand, Joanna played with her napkin, rolling it into a tight cylinder. "Must get on your nerves, her calling you."

Fiona smiled. "Not anymore. Not as long as she only calls occasionally." She gave a little shrug. "At arm's length, Diane's quite sweet, really."

Sweet, my arse! Joanna thought. She had no time for women who made false promises, who lied. She'd had flings with some of those women who prowled around on the loose behind their partners' backs. Risk-takers, they were mostly fun, and usually lacking emotional depth; they were no problem in that department. But Joanna had little respect for them, just the same.

Marie and Fiona cleared the table, and Marie returned with a bottle of Armagnac and glasses. "Fiona's just making some coffee," she said. She put her arm around Louise and kissed her cheek.

Joanna's heart leapt. At last, a chance to spend a private moment with Fiona. "I'll go and help her," she said, quickly heading for the door.

Fiona put the last of the plates into the dishwasher and switched it on. She sighed. She was deluding herself if she really thought that she and Joanna could simply be friends. For God's sake, every time Joanna turned that smile on her, looked her over with those bedroom eyes, Fiona tingled. She switched on the kettle and spooned coffee into the plunger.

Joanna was great company, but it had been a mistake to invite her to stay.

While she waited for the water to boil, she went outside to the back veranda. The paddocks were awash with moonlight, the stars like sequins on black velvet. The gentle breeze was balmy. Already, she cared too much for Joanna.

She sighed, picturing Joanna stepping out of her car, grabbing her things, flicking the door closed, then strolling over to the house. There was a boldness in her walk, in the easy roll of her hips and forward thrust of her shoulders. Her stride took the ground with confidence, her feet branding the earth with every step. She had run a hand through her hair, pulled off her dark wrap glasses and dropped one of those smiles. Joanna made even the most basic outfit look sexy. Her jeans, worn right through at the knees, hugged her tight hips, the bikini top just covered her small firm breasts. Watching her, waiting for her, Fiona had found herself breathlessly anticipating Joanna's kiss hello.

The hinge of the screen door squeaked, and Fiona jumped. Joanna stepped outside, in silhouette against the light from the kitchen. "There you are." Her voice was low.

Fiona's pulse quickened. "Just waiting for the kettle."

Joanna came and stood beside her. Fiona could smell her light perfume, feel the heat of her body. "It's a great property," Joanna said. "Peaceful." She gazed at the sky. "I can never believe how many stars you can see in the country."

Fiona began to feel uneasy. Being there alone

together under those stars, in that balmy air, she suddenly, desperately, wanted to hold Joanna, to kiss her. Her voice came out in a whisper as she said, "I'd better see to the coffee." She turned toward the door.

Joanna took her arm. "Just before you go, there's something I want to do." Fiona felt helpless as Joanna drew her into her arms, looked into her eyes for a moment, then kissed her with a passion that made Fiona's head swim. Lust raced through her body like wildfire. Her heart pounded as she returned the kiss with a hunger that shocked her. As Joanna's arms tightened around her, Fiona's hands explored the sleek, muscled satin of Joanna's back and shoulders. Joanna groaned. She leaned Fiona against the broad veranda post, parted Fiona's legs with one thigh and gently pressed her body against her. Fiona's mind was going blank. She'd never been kissed like this.

China rattled in the kitchen. Fiona came back to earth with a jolt and she pulled away quickly. Joanna gasped, put her fingers to her lips and stared at the ground. It seemed she had gotten carried away too. Agitated, Fiona ran her hands through her hair while she took a deep breath, trying to compose herself. Joanna looked up at her. In the moonlight, her eyes were dark with passion. Embarrassed, Fiona murmured, "I'm sorry."

"Don't be." Joanna's voice was breathy.

Fiona headed for the door. "I've got to . . ." She gestured, unnecessarily, toward the kitchen. "You know . . ." Joanna's intense gaze remained fixed on her. She said nothing. Quickly, Fiona retreated inside. Marie was placing the cups and coffee plunger on a tray. She looked up as Fiona came in. Fiona averted her eyes and cleared her throat. "Have you found the white milk jug?" Joanna was going to walk through that door any moment, and she wanted to look busy.

"Yeah, hon," Marie said, pointing to the jug filled with milk, on the tray.

"Oh, good."

The door opened, and Joanna came in. Catching, from the corner of her eye, the calm smile she gave Marie, Fiona grabbed a dishcloth and began wiping the already-clean counter.

"It's cooling down," Joanna said in an easy tone. "I think I'll put on a T-shirt." She left the room and Marie looked at Fiona with a grin.

"It's great to see a friendship blossoming between you two so quickly."

"I got carried away, that's all."

Marie chuckled. "I'm not surprised. The chemistry between you two is palpable. All through dinner, I was waiting to see actual sparks flying."

Fiona sighed as the tension left her body. "God, can she kiss! I'm glad we were interrupted. I can't honestly say how far things may have gone, otherwise."

"What happens now?"

Fiona took a packet of dinner mints from the fridge and put them into a compote. "Nothing!" She smiled. "Okay, she's sexy. But if I started anything with her, it'd be a disaster. You know me. I couldn't play along with the simple little fling that Joanna would have in mind."

Taking the tray, Marie began to head outside to the veranda. "Uh-huh," was all she said. Feeling composed once more, Fiona picked up the compote and followed her.

Joanna was lazing in her chair, chuckling about something with Louise, when they arrived with the coffee. To Fiona's relief, she seemed perfectly relaxed and unconcerned. Fiona poured the coffee, and as Joanna poured the Armagnac, she gave Fiona a small but warm smile.

Later, Joanna lay in bed staring at the ceiling. An hour or so after the coffee came out, Marie and Louise had left to go to bed. Joanna had hoped that she and Fiona could spend some more time alone, but Fiona had quickly gathered up the cups and glasses, taken them inside, then said goodnight. Joanna felt she had hidden it well, but the last hour of small talk after that kiss was torture. A fire, unlike any she'd known before, had ignited inside her. Unable to will her lust away, keeping the flame low was the best she could manage. Whether Fiona was prepared to face it or not, an affair had already begun. And Joanna knew affairs were never over until they were over. Fires always died eventually. Even a raging one like this would have to die, but only after all the erotic dynamics had been explored and satisfied.

She grabbed her watch from the bedside table. It was three a.m. After everyone else had gone to bed, Joanna had stayed out on the veranda for a while, listening to the night sounds, trying to calm herself in the tranquillity of the surroundings. Gazing at the black outline of the forest against the sky, then staring deeply into the starlit abyss above her, she sought, in the face of much grander wonders, to put her passion into perspective. But they had only served to sharpen her sensual images of Fiona's arms around her, stroking her back. God! That kiss was almost like sex. It wasn't just the way Fiona kissed her in return, it was the way she accepted Joanna's mouth. Fiona's body melted into hers as her mouth seemed to drink her in, almost taking Joanna inside her. The intensity, the intimacy of it had shaken Joanna. At first, she had felt a breathtaking, lustful heat between her thighs — where lust belonged — then it had swept powerfully through her body, delivering a sharp kick in her chest before exploding in her head.

Remembering it, Joanna moaned softly in the dark and trembled. Since pondering the complexities of the universe hadn't helped, she had downed a few more glasses of Armagnac before heading off to bed. She had quickly fallen asleep for a couple of hours.

With a sigh, she threw the sheet off her naked body. Her skin shone in the moonlight streaking through the French doors. Her legs were apart, her hand on her thigh, fingers slowly caressing her skin. Aching, she knew she was wet. God! she thought. You're going to lie here and play with yourself while you fantasize about her? Picturing Fiona lying in bed in the room next door was driving her crazy. You're not that desperate yet, she chastised herself, as she got up and pulled on a long T-shirt. Unaccustomed as she was to running after a woman, the idea of cautiously chasing Fiona was exciting. Imagining the reward when she caught her was tantalizing. There was no doubt that Fiona's feelings were as strong as her own. After the kiss, her poise had completely abandoned her. Obviously a very sexual woman, Fiona wouldn't be able to hold out for long. The question was, Joanna thought as she grabbed the glass of water from the bedside table, why Fiona was holding out at all.

She opened the French doors quietly and went outside. Sitting down on a teak chair, gazing across the paddocks, she sipped her water. Mutual attraction was usually a simple matter, and Joanna was used to women who just went for it. Dinner, a bar or dance club, maybe a show, then sex, no problem. Keeping dates casual and irregular was the way to avoid complications. Then after a while, dates would peter out altogether. The women Joanna dated went by the same rules, and she had rarely encountered any upset when the time came to move on. Maybe, she thought, Fiona was just being cautious since the breakup with her girlfriend. Didn't want to get caught up in another mess. Joanna could never understand why so many women went in for committed relationships. As far as she could see, playing house was a game that nearly always ended in tears. Once Fiona understood that Joanna had no such intentions, wouldn't give her any heartache, she'd be fine.

She heard the French doors in the next room open, and turned to see Fiona step outside. Joanna's heart raced at the sight of her. Wearing a short, terry-cloth bathrobe, she smiled as she scooped back her hair. Trying to distract herself from the thought that there was nothing underneath the robe, Joanna returned the smile.

"I heard you come out here," Fiona said quietly. "I couldn't sleep, either." She leaned casually against a veranda post and crossed her arms, seemingly keeping a safe distance.

Joanna pulled her gaze away from her and focused on the dark shape of a horse, snoozing under a tree.

Before tonight, she had fantasized about how Fiona would react if she just swept her into her arms, helped herself. Now Joanna was confident that if she simply went to her and held her, Fiona would respond passionately again. She would give one of those little groans as Joanna kissed her, that tiny growl that came from deep in her throat. It made Joanna quiver just thinking about it. But she held back. She wasn't sure yet what Fiona's game was. What if she stopped at the kiss again? Joanna didn't think she could cope with that. She took another sip of her water. "It's a lovely night."

"I thought maybe one of your bad dreams woke you. Are you still having those?"

Joanna was surprised Fiona remembered her passing reference to the dreams. She smiled. "No. Too much Armagnac, I think. I still get the dreams, though." With a grin, she added, "Perhaps you could give me some sleeping pills, doctor."

Fiona chuckled. "I don't think they'd help."

"No." Joanna watched the horse. It was moving around, its head down, having a snack. "I've decided to do some investigating. The questions in my mind keep mounting, getting on my nerves. It seems I need to get some answers."

"Wouldn't your Aunt Thelma know the story?"

"Yeah, but I'd rather not bother her with it. Besides, I know she had some contact with my mother during my childhood. It's unlikely, but she still might have, and I'd hate for my mother to know that I was suddenly interested."

"What *do* you know about her?"

"Her name's Isabella Martinez. She was born here but her parents were Spanish immigrants."

"That explains your Mediterranean good looks." Fiona was smiling. Joanna rippled with pleasure at the compliment. Unfortunately, it seemed that Fiona hadn't intended to be flirtatious, averting her eyes, sliding her hands into the pockets of her robe.

"Thanks." Joanna swallowed. "She was very young, barely twenty when she married my father. I've picked up that she was pregnant with me when they married." She shrugged. "Not much else."

"What can you remember about her leaving?"

Joanna wondered why Fiona was so interested. It wasn't exactly a riveting story. But she was glad that Fiona wanted to talk with her anyway, and up to a point, she didn't mind talking about it. "It's funny. I can remember her leaving so clearly, it's like a movie running in my head. My parents were both fighting one night. I hadn't heard them screaming like that before. Then she left. Went out the door. My father went into his study and stayed there for the rest of the night. I could hear him in there when I woke up early the next morning. I searched the house for her, and the garden. I couldn't believe my eyes. She'd been there every minute of every day, as far as I remembered. I went into her room. She had this beautiful, four-poster bed with curtains around it. Filmy, silky ones. White."

Joanna paused for a moment, picturing the full-length window that was open slightly. A breeze was moving the pretty curtains. The bedspread was aqua-colored satin; cushions were piled up along with the satin-covered pillows. Joanna used to dive into them after her mother had made the bed. Laughing, she would pick up Joanna and cuddle her, then straighten the bed. Joanna would dive-bomb again and they both laughed like mad as the game went on.

To Joanna's annoyance, her throat tightened. She swallowed. "I climbed into her bed and snuggled into the pillows because they smelled of her. Then I fell asleep. All day, my father stayed in his room. My aunt Beatrice, his and Thelma's sister, a horrible woman, came to look after me. He said my mother wouldn't be coming back, but for ages, maybe weeks, I didn't believe him. I waited every day, sneaked into her bed every night. Then one morning Beatrice caught me in there and bellowed at me to get out."

From the doorway, Joanna had watched, wide-eyed in disbelief, as Beatrice stripped the bed, contemptuously tossing the sheets onto the floor. Going to the wardrobe, she had dragged out her mother's clothes and tossed them onto the heap, as if building a funeral pyre.

"She packed up all her things and sent them away. Then I knew she was gone." Fiona quickly wiped at her eyes. Anxiously, Joanna hoped she wasn't upset by the story. Maybe it was a mosquito or something she was wiping at. Joanna smiled to lighten the mood. "I'll just go over to my father's place and have a look around in the attic. There used to be boxes of junk and papers up there. Beatrice wouldn't have thrown them out. I might find some letters or something that'll explain things."

"I hope so." Fiona's voice was barely more than a

whisper. She cleared her throat. "We'd better get some sleep." She started for her room.

Joanna's mind worked rapidly. When would she get another chance to be alone with her again? She had to seize the moment. "Will you have dinner with me this week?"

Fiona hesitated, gazing at her. Her expression was doubtful. "About earlier, you know." Looking agitated, Fiona toyed with a lock of hair. "You know how I feel about you." Joanna's heart beat faster, that low flame leapt to life. "But I don't want us to have a sexual relationship. I can't be as casual about those things as I think you like to be." With a sigh, she stared out into the night. The moonlight shone on her hair. She was exquisite. With a smile, she gave a little shrug. "I'd make things difficult for myself, even if not for you."

Make things difficult? God, Joanna thought, only if you keep this up. That "sweet" Diane had obviously really hurt her. Joanna ached to hold her, to reassure her. But she didn't want to push her. Smiling, she said, "You don't have to worry about anything with me. I only want us to have a good time together. No tricks, no lies, no problems." Fiona didn't seem reassured. Joanna chuckled. "You've had me here as your houseguest and you won't even let me take you to dinner? That's not very fair."

Fiona's expression slowly softened. She smiled. "Okay. That'd be nice."

Relief flooded Joanna's body like a shot of adrenaline. They agreed to meet the following Friday evening at an excellent Japanese restaurant that Joanna recommended. With the tension dissipated between them, they warmly said goodnight and returned to their rooms.

As Joanna lay down in bed and pulled up the sheet, she felt confident that things would work out for her. It was understandable that Fiona wanted to avoid emotional difficulties. And that, Joanna thought with a contented sigh, suited her perfectly.

CHAPTER SEVEN

The following Thursday afternoon, Joanna unlocked the door of an Edwardian cottage and invited Nathan and Robert inside. It was four-thirty and, thankfully, her last appointment for the day. The last few days had dragged by, and uncharacteristically, Joanna was feeling short-tempered.

Fixing what she hoped was a friendly smile on her face, she showed them around the house and garden. With other things nagging at her mind, Joanna wasn't in the mood for Robert's sulkiness. In the last two and a half weeks, she had shown them close to a dozen properties. Among the array of modern town-houses, period terrace homes and apartments of all kinds, Nathan had seen many that he seemed to like. But Robert hated everything. He was the client from hell. A classic time-waster. With genuine buyers, the process of helping them find the perfect balance of taste and price was a challenge she loved. But she knew that Robert didn't want to buy a house. She wondered when Nathan would figure that out. If it weren't for Nathan, who was a pleasure to deal with, and so keen to find something to please his boyfriend, she'd politely get rid of them.

"So, anything here that appeals?" Joanna asked brightly. Robert stuffed his hands into the pockets of his tiny, tight shorts and stared at the floor. Aggravatingly, with the toe of a Nike-clad foot, he tapped the wooden leg of a chair.

"It's a bit small," he mumbled. So's your budget, sweetheart, Joanna wanted to say. "I want a dressing room."

Nathan looked at her helplessly. "What do you think, love? Could we build one in?"

Christ! Where? Joanna thought. In the fucking roof? This was getting silly. She took a deep breath and smiled. "I could arrange with the vendor for you to bring in a builder and get a quote. Or I can arrange a builder, if you like."

Nathan turned to Robert. "We could try to build one for you, honey," he said in a gentle tone. Robert gave a disinterested shrug, the little pain in the arse. "But the garden's lovely," Nathan added hopefully. "Let's have another look at it."

They wandered out to the back garden, and with a weary sigh, Joanna slumped against the living room doorframe. She hoped they wouldn't linger. There was something she had to take care of this afternoon that made her sick with dread, and she wanted to get it over with. She focused on the door and architrave. They were thick and lumpy with white, gloss paint. It amazed her that people could be so insensitive to the beauty of the original carved woodwork. Paint had been slathered on for years, so that the sculptured shape was barely visible. It should be burned off, right back to the wood, she thought, then carefully repainted. She gently ran her fingers over it, and a flake of paint came away, fluttering to the floor.

She had phoned Aunt Beatrice that morning, to tell her she was coming to the house. Thelma told her years ago that Beatrice, who had never married, had moved in with Joanna's father. After he went into the nursing home, Beatrice had stayed on in the house alone. After not hearing from Joanna in a decade, Beatrice had been shocked at first, then, typically, she became hostile. It bothered Joanna that she'd had to summon up the courage to even call her. The thought of seeing Beatrice and the house again made her chest heavy and tight. It would be like stepping into another world, going back there, hunting around in that attic. A world from another life that Joanna had hoped not to see again.

But she had something to look forward to as well, she reminded herself. Dinner tomorrow night with Fiona. Since the weekend, the image of Fiona had shone constantly, like a beacon in the night. The weight in her chest lightened just at the thought of her.

She wondered how her clients were going and headed out to the kitchen. Through the glass door, she watched Nathan pointing out the merits of the well-established camellias and daphne shrubs. Robert was looking bored.

Fiona had even made a guest appearance in one of those dreams last night. The walls of the usual small dark room had been transparent in that dream. Outside the room, the light was dazzling. In silhouette, someone had been moving around, peering into the darkness. Joanna had stood still, trying not to be seen. Which was odd, because in the other dreams she was always trying to get out of there. You'd think you would call out, she thought. Take the chance to escape. When she awoke, she had a sense that the person was Fiona.

Nathan's voice came wafting in. "I don't know if even a small pool would fit, honey . . . maybe a jacuzzi . . ." He sounded doubtful, and no wonder. There was barely room for a bloody bird bath in that courtyard.

It was probably just that she had Fiona on the brain, Joanna thought. Her subconscious was muddling everything together in her dreams. With any luck, Fiona would begin to dominate her dreams in a much more positive way, and her nightmares would disappear.

At last, Nathan and Robert were coming back inside.

Robert sped past her, making for the front door. Nathan smiled weakly. "Thanks, Joanna." He looked disappointed that Robert was still unsatisfied. "I don't know what's wrong with him."

It was tempting to tell him that Robert was wasting their time, but obviously Nathan was hanging on to the fantasy of their buying their dream home and living happily ever after. Joanna didn't want to disillusion him. Robert would do that soon enough. Meanwhile, it wouldn't hurt her to go along with Nathan. She gave him a warm smile and shrugged casually. "He's just a bit stressed, that's all. House-hunting's hard work. All those decisions, you know . . . figuring out what you want." Nathan nodded, looking a bit brighter. "Try and relax on it. Put houses out of your mind for a few days. I'll call you some time next week."

"Yeah. Good idea." Nathan grinned. "Thanks, love."

She showed him out and locked up. Then, bracing herself for a confrontation with Beatrice, she headed across town to the tranquil, leafy suburb where she had grown up.

Joanna turned her car into the driveway of the substantial, two-story Federation house. It wasn't looking as pristine as she remembered. Her father used to be fastidious about the house and gardens. There always seemed to be tradesmen or gardeners around. Getting out of the car, she gazed at the upper-story windows and balconies. The two dormer windows of the attic jutted out of the gabled roof. As a child, she had spent much of her time playing in the attic. She had hidden in there whenever Beatrice was around, and when her father came home from business trips. It all needed a coat of paint. She wondered why Beatrice hadn't taken better care of the place. She had plenty of money and, no doubt, access to her father's money as well. Too tight-arsed, Joanna thought. Pumping herself up, she knocked at the door.

A thin dusty-looking old woman answered the door, and Joanna was taken aback. Beatrice's heavy hips and breasts had dissolved away. Her hair, drawn into an untidy chignon, was white. She wasn't as tall as Joanna remembered, either. She narrowed her cruel, ice-blue eyes. They hadn't changed. "I told you not to come," she hissed. She began to close the door. Quickly, Joanna put out a determined hand and pushed it wide open. Beatrice stumbled slightly as she stepped back out of Joanna's way.

"It's delightful to see you again, Aunt Beatrice," Joanna said sarcastically, with a forced smile.

She cast an eye around quickly as she headed for the stairs. The Persian rugs in the hallway needed cleaning, and the banisters were overdue for a polish. At least Beatrice had kept the beautiful old clock ticking. She paused for a moment, picturing her mother holding her up, letting her wind the clock, teaching her how to read the time.

"You've got no right to be here!" Beatrice barked, and Joanna tore up the stairs.

"Fucking old bitch," Joanna muttered to herself. Gloom descended upon her as she walked along the hallway. In her old bedroom, her bed and desk stood stripped, empty. Isabella's four-poster bed was still in her room, and her antique dressing table. Also stripped and bare, like skeletons. Joanna recalled standing behind her mother, chin resting on her shoulder, watching her in the mirror while she sat at the dressing table putting on her makeup or painting her nails. Suddenly, tears stung Joanna's eyes. Even the curtains around the bed were gone. The knots in her stomach tightened as she continued along to the attic-stairway at the end of the hall.

The bright, bare light bulb revealed years of dust

and cobwebs. It appeared that no one had been in the attic since Joanna last saw it. The old rocking chair with the broken seat was still in the corner, her baby cot, a box of old toys, and boxes of her father's engineering plans were stacked around. Two big armchairs, with horsehair stuffing poking out of holes in the threadbare velvet, sat on either side of one window. A scratched coffee table was placed between them. This was where Joanna had entertained her friends, and her first girlfriend, Sara.

After the age of twelve, Joanna didn't have a nanny. There was only the live-in housekeeper, Lucy, who had been with them for years. Lucy hadn't snooped like the nannies had, and she pretty much left her to her own devices. Joanna and Sara had been fifteen when they came up here, locked the door, played at sex, smoked cigarettes and dope. While Sara rolled a joint, Joanna would pop down to her father's cellar and grab them a nice bottle of red. She was careful to only take the good stuff because she knew he never went near that part of the cellar. That wine was an investment, he always said. Joanna wondered when he noticed it was missing. He had never said anything. But all that vintage French Bordeaux hadn't been entirely wasted, Joanna thought with a smile. She and Sara had tossed it back like Coca Cola, but it had probably helped to educate their young palates.

At one side of the room, there was a cupboard built into the space beside the chimney. It had always been padlocked. Her father had told her it contained business papers and to leave it alone. If there was anything of use to her, it would be in there. The lock was rusty. Looking around for something to force the lock, Joanna grabbed a brass fire poker. Slipping it into the loop of the padlock, she wrenched it hard. The lock came apart and she opened the door.

Her heart skipped a beat as her gaze fell on a large, framed picture of her mother. It was a copy of the photo that Thelma used to show Joanna when she was very young. Joanna had forgotten how beautiful she was. No more than about twenty-one, she was holding Joanna, six months old, or so. Her hair was long, dark brown and slightly curly, her brown eyes dewy, her mouth curved in a gentle smile. Joanna, thumb in her mouth, was asleep on her shoulder.

Staring at her mother's face, Joanna thought about the letter Isabella had once sent her. Joanna had gone to visit Thelma and Ted just after her eighteenth birthday. She recalled driving up to the farm in the car her father had given her for her birthday. A red MG. He hadn't chosen it, of course, just picked up the bill. Thelma had baked her a triple-layer chocolate cake. Adrian was there too. Before Joanna left that evening, Thelma handed her an unsealed envelope. Thelma's expression was anxious as she said, "This was posted to me, to pass on to you."

Inside was a letter from Isabella, saying that she wanted to see Joanna. Shocked, sickened, Joanna shoved the letter back at Thelma. "No!" she shouted. "Tell her to leave me alone!"

With tears in her eyes, Thelma sighed. "Give her a chance," she said. "She's your mother."

Stubbornly, Joanna shook her head. Life was working out very satisfactorily for her. About to begin an arts degree at university, she had total freedom, thanks to her father's absences, a generous allowance and a new girlfriend in tow. She had almost forgotten her troubled childhood. The letter was like a kick behind the knees. Shadows of the past loomed once again, and Joanna was furious. Thelma's tears upset her, though, and without further argument, she took the letter. A few days later, she wrote a brief, curt reply, telling Isabella she wasn't interested, that she had all but forgotten her and wanted nothing to do with her. She sent it to the address in Sydney that was written at the top of the letter. To Joanna's relief, Isabella respected her wishes and she had never heard from her again.

Now Joanna couldn't help regretting her decision. If only she'd taken the opportunity then to get the story. With Isabella making the approach, Joanna would have had the upper hand. If she was forced to approach Isabella after all those years, she would feel at a disadvantage. She'd look like a pathetic lost dog, sniffing around, scratching at the door. Anyway, in the meantime, Isabella might have grown hostile.

Joanna's heart was pounding as she looked through the cupboard. On the top shelf, her teddy bear with one shiny, beady eye watched her as she sifted through the boxes. There were more photos of Joanna with Isabella, and some with her father included. In one, her father had his arm around Isabella; Joanna was perched on Isabella's hip. All smiles, the photo could have been lifted right off the campaign leaflet of some boring, idiot politician spouting a load of crap about family values, Joanna thought.

To her disappointment, the remaining boxes contained nothing but useless, outdated business papers. Feeling strangely disoriented, she closed the cupboard. She had put herself through all this and achieved nothing. Suddenly, on impulse, she opened the cupboard again and grabbed the framed photo of Isabella, tucking it under her arm. Turning off the light, she left the attic and headed downstairs.

Beatrice was skulking in the shadows at the foot of the stairs. "What have you taken? You've got no right to your father's things!"

"It's a photo of my mother."

"Why would you want that! She made a fool of him!"

Trying to appear unmoved, Joanna gave a casual shrug. "That wouldn't be hard."

Beatrice raised her chin. Her papery lips formed a thin, bitter line. "She was rubbish. A slut!"

Like a sudden gust of icy wind, the words threw Joanna off-balance. Anger welled in her chest, although she wasn't sure why. Determined not to show her feelings, she swallowed hard, forcing the fury down. Keeping her voice low and even, she said, "I had no idea she had such redeeming qualities."

Beatrice was bristling. The cloying smell of her stale, overly sweet perfume hung in the air, like the truth that Joanna so desperately wanted to hear but knew Beatrice would never tell. Joanna felt sick. Quickly, she made for the door, brushing past Beatrice who seemed to rustle like dead leaves.

The door slammed behind her.

CHAPTER EIGHT

As Joanna toweled her hair in front of the bathroom mirror, she was pleased to see that the bruise
around her eye had finally disappeared. Feeling
excited, she smiled at her reflection as she combed her
fingers through her hair. At last, it was Friday night.
She spritzed on her perfume, then headed into her
bedroom to get dressed.

The evening was mild, and she had decided to
wear her favorite outfit. She put on a lightly starched,
pure-white shirt. The fine quality cotton felt good on
her skin. Leaving the shirt open at the neck, she

pulled on the suit pants, then slipped the jacket on. Two years ago, for the annual Dyke's Ball, she'd had the suit tailor-made. Providing the tailor with a picture to copy, the suit was a classic Thirties style. In a light-weight, quality wool fabric, it was charcoal gray with widely spaced light gray pinstripes. The pinstripes ran diagonally across the front of the long, double-breasted jacket; the lapels were wide. The cuffed pants were a perfect cut.

As she put on her gold ear studs, Joanna smiled, remembering the ball that year. Cathie had turned up in a floor-length shimmering blue beaded dress. Low-cut, it was so tight that she could only take tiny steps. It frothed at the bottom, and although it was spectacular, it gave an unmistakable mermaid impression. Cathie was obviously disappointed that the dress made dancing impossible. As the evening wore on, and Cathie consumed more Champagne cocktails, the restriction of the dress became too much for her. Late in the night, along with a dozen or so other women, Cathie peeled off her dress, and in her bra and panties, had treated everyone to some tabletop dancing.

Joanna wondered what Fiona would be wearing. All week, her mind had played with sexy, contrasting images of her. The sleek, refined city doctor swirled and merged with the wild, wind-blown country girl. Desire washed over her as she remembered their kiss. With a sigh, she hoped Fiona had reconsidered the situation and relaxed about the attraction they both felt.

She grabbed her keys and wallet and went downstairs to the car. The restaurant was only a couple of kilometers away, and she had booked the table for eight o'clock.

The head waiter showed her to a table beside the indoor garden in the center of the restaurant. Beautifully designed and carefully lit, the garden of bonsai and ferns was luxuriant. From a bamboo pipe, water trickled down terraced rocks into a small lily pond. Light, instrumental jazz played quietly. The lighting was low.

The waiter handed her a wine list. "When my guest arrives," Joanna said, "could you bring us some Averna, please. Warmed."

He nodded with a smile as he left her to peruse the list. At the tap of heels hitting the polished stone floor, Joanna looked up to see the waiter escorting Fiona to the table. Throughout the restaurant, heads turned. Her dress, made of black, double-silk organza, was softly wrapped around her body in diagonal layers, following the curve of her waist and hips, clinging to her thighs like a shimmering cocoon. Capped sleeves accentuated the line of her straight shoulders. Low-cut with a V neck, the dress came to just above the knee. As she strode elegantly in her black patent-leather stilettos, a deep split on one side of her dress revealed a tantalizing glimpse of her thigh.

Joanna smiled and stood to kiss her cheek. Looking radiant, her eyes sparkling, Fiona's gaze flickered over Joanna. "Gorgeous suit," she said in her smoky voice, a smile on her luscious mouth.

"Knock-out dress," Joanna said with a grin. They chuckled as they sat down. Joanna was relieved that Fiona seemed completely at ease; there was no awkwardness between them. The waiter brought their apéritifs and menus.

"Mmm, the Averna was a good idea," Fiona said, taking a sip. Her lipstick was a deep rose-pink, matching her nail polish.

Joanna glanced over the menu. "I like this place because they change the menu all the time."

"You know the place. Why don't you order for us?"

Joanna decided on a selection of dishes and placed the order. "I've got a couple of other properties to show you," Joanna said. "One's a converted Victorian cottage that's mostly open plan, with a loft bedroom."

Fiona looked interested. "Sounds nice. Maybe we could have a look at it next week."

Joanna said she would call to make a time, already mentally planning the dinner date to follow the inspection.

Their first three dishes arrived: tuna sashimi, tiny, lightly pan-fried parcels of succulent asparagus rolled up in paper-thin beef, and minced ocean trout in small pastry cases. The waiter poured the white Burgundy.

Fiona tasted the food and smiled appreciatively. "This is a great place." She took a sip of her wine. "Did you go to your father's house? Do the search you were planning?"

"Yeah, but I didn't find anything." Joanna shrugged. "I suppose I'll have to speak to my father. Can't stand the idea of it, though."

Fiona swept her hair off her shoulders. Diamond ear studs glittered. "You mentioned he'd had a stroke. Do you know if he's capable of talking to you?"

Joanna played with her chopsticks, turning them over in her hand. "Thelma told me he gets a bit confused but hasn't completely lost it. He might just refuse, though. I've never asked him about any of this stuff before."

The waiter brought the other dishes: sushi rolls topped with avocado, prawn dumplings cooked with vegetables in a clay pot, and steamed rice. Joanna was flattered by Fiona's interest, but not wanting her boring problems to dominate the evening, she changed the subject. "Your brother lives in Singapore, didn't you say? What does he do there?"

Joanna learned that Michael owned an export business dealing in Asian antiques, and she was pleased to discover that Fiona shared her interest in Asian antique furniture. They discussed the subject for a while, and chatted about vacations they had both spent in Singapore.

As dinner progressed, Joanna found herself increasingly captivated. She couldn't help imagining Fiona in her arms, kissing her again. More than once, Fiona's gaze lingered on Joanna's mouth. She seemed to remember the kiss too. Joanna wondered if Fiona would come home with her, wondered if she would allow another kiss, and wondered whether another kiss would, this time, take them all the way.

At the end of the meal when they were ready to leave, Joanna took her chance. With a warm smile, she said, "My house is only up the road a little way. Would you like to come back for coffee?" Fiona hesitated. Looking into the distance, she fidgeted with her heavy, gold bracelet. "You mentioned, once, that you'd like to see my house."

Fiona nodded and chuckled. "Yes, that's true. I'd like to see a real estate consultant's house." Thrilled, Joanna gave her simple directions in case she lost sight of Joanna's car, and they left.

* * * * *

Joanna was waiting for her, standing in the doorway, when Fiona pulled into the driveway. Leaning casually against the doorframe, hands in her pockets, she was smiling. Joanna had outdone herself in that suit. As she headed across the brick-paved courtyard toward the door, Fiona wondered if she had been wise to come for coffee. Determined to suppress her own desire, she had been relieved, during dinner, that Joanna seemed to have the same idea. A few times, she had felt caught by Joanna's gaze, sensing her sexual interest, but thankfully Joanna hadn't pushed it.

The entrance foyer wasn't large, but a wall of glass bricks facing the street gave it spaciousness. The floor was tiled in black marble, the walls sponged in a rich cream color with a high sheen. Joanna pointed to a corridor that ran beside the hardwood staircase. "The guest bedroom and bathroom are down there." She began to walk upstairs. "Coffee's this way."

At the top of the stairs, Fiona found herself in a large living room, with a kitchen off to one side. Huge windows gave a stunning view of the city skyline, alive with colorful flashing signs, buildings glittering with lights. Two butter-colored sofas were on either side of a low oak coffee table. An antique roll-top desk stood against one wall. The furnishings and color scheme were perfectly coordinated, the furniture comfortable-looking and well designed. The effect was understated with a beauty and style that, effortlessly, demanded attention. Just like Joanna, Fiona thought, watching her slip off her jacket and drape it over the back of a French antique chair.

The house had a strangely unlived-in feeling, though. There was an air of transience. By contrast, there was an intensity in Joanna's presence. Her gaze was focused on Fiona as she unbuttoned her shirt cuffs and neatly folded them back. With a sudden, weakening tremor, Fiona remembered those hands on her body, the urgency in those arms that held her. She averted her eyes, taking in the city through the windows. "It's a great place. I love the view."

"Thanks." Joanna headed into the kitchen. Fiona sat on a sofa. Joanna was in sight, surrounded by gleaming white tiles and stainless steel as she filled the coffee maker. "It's better since I had it re-decorated last year. It was all stark white when I bought it." She grinned. "A friend, an ex-client, is an interior designer. She suggested the color scheme, and was quite put out when I complimented her on the warm, cream color. 'It's fucking *banana*, darling!' she said, mortified, 'not bloody cream!'" They both laughed.

Fiona wondered whether they had also been lovers. More than likely, she thought, annoyed with herself that she found the idea discomforting. Suddenly, she noticed a framed photo lying face-up on the coffee table. With a jolt, she saw Joanna in the stranger's face. Examining it, she saw the same full, sensual mouth, dark complexion and hair. The almond-shaped eyes, with Joanna's long black lashes, were brown instead of hazel-green. Whereas Joanna possessed a strong, raw beauty, this woman's face was more delicate, pretty.

Joanna came in and set a tray down on the table. "My mother," she said casually as she sat on the opposite sofa. "Do you like this?" she asked, holding a bottle of Dom Bénédictine. "Or would you prefer something else?"

"Thanks, that's fine," Fiona said. Joanna poured the liqueur and coffee. "She's beautiful. You're obviously the cute baby."

Joanna smiled and sipped her liqueur. "I grabbed it from my father's house yesterday. Don't know why."

As Fiona reached for her cup, she noticed a letter that had been lying under the photo. In generous, sweeping letters, it was signed, "Isabella." Taken aback, Fiona said, "She sent you a letter? When?"

Joanna gave a little shrug. "When I turned eighteen. For some reason I kept it. Last night I dug it out of a suitcase full of junk. I hadn't read it for sixteen years. It doesn't give anything away, though. Read it if you like."

Intrigued, Fiona read the letter:

My dearest Joanna,

While I've missed you dreadfully all these years and regret not being able to watch you grow up, I'm relieved that at last, now you've turned eighteen, I can contact you.

I sincerely hope that you'll want to see me too. There's so much to talk about, to explain. I look forward to your reply. I can't wait to be with you again.

> *Your loving mother,*
> *Isabella*

Tears sprang to Fiona's eyes. It wasn't the kind of letter she would expect from a woman who had carelessly abandoned her small child. "What did you do about this?" she asked softly.

"I wrote back and told her to keep away from me." Joanna's elbows were resting on her knees. She stared into the glass that she was twirling in her hands. Her shoulders looked tense. She swallowed hard, and the muscle in her cheek flexed.

"Why?"

Joanna gulped down her drink, then continued staring into the empty glass. "By that time I'd written her off. Learned to live without her. I'd gotten over it all, you know."

"But it seems that she was *kept* away from you. It doesn't sound like it was her choice. Weren't you curious?"

Joanna shook her head. "Not then."

Fiona's throat tightened. In spite of Joanna's attempts to appear unconcerned, it was clear that the unresolved past still seriously bothered her. Wanting to hold her, comfort her, but afraid of releasing her emotions, Fiona concentrated on fighting back her tears. She wished she wasn't so easily upset. There was a long silence.

"When I was very little, I thought I was pretty worthless," Joanna continued in a low voice. "Had to be, I figured, for my mother to just walk out, stay away forever. But by the time I was eighteen, I'd come to terms with it. I no longer gave a damn about why she left, or how she could be forced to stay away. If she'd really wanted me, she wouldn't have allowed that. You can't suddenly erase everything and get all excited when they decide to waltz back into your life." She looked up at Fiona, a pained expression in her eyes. "That letter shook me up for a while. I wanted to forget her again as soon as I could." She paused. Fiona caught the glint of tears in her eyes. "You don't

103

know what it's like," she murmured, quickly averting her gaze.

Oh, God, Fiona thought. The more she knew about Joanna, the more she cared. And the more she cared, the more she wanted her. Agitated, she stood and went to the window, gazing outside, her back to Joanna.

She heard Joanna put her glass on the table, stand and walk over to her. Suddenly, Joanna's arms slipped around her waist and a flash like a spark to a wick made Fiona gasp. "Don't be upset," Joanna whispered. "It's not that important." Fiona trembled. Joanna's body was pressing against her. "God," Joanna breathed, then she kissed her neck.

At lightning speed the flame raced through Fiona's body. She had to leave straightaway or there would be no turning back. "I have to go," she murmured.

Gently, Joanna turned Fiona around to face her. Joanna's eyes were blazing. "Kiss me good-bye," she demanded, her voice husky. "Then you can go."

Helpless, like last time, Fiona just gazed into her eyes, looked longingly at her mouth. Joanna's hand glided down her thigh, found the split in her dress and slid inside. Fiona moaned softly. Joanna's hand moved higher, stroking. Suddenly, the fire engulfed Fiona and she threw her arms around Joanna's shoulders, kissing her passionately. Both Joanna's hands were under the dress, stroking her hips. Joanna was trembling. Fiona felt herself sway.

"We'd better lie down," Joanna whispered.

A street lamp cast a pale light through the bedroom window; leafy patterns danced on the walls as trees moved in the breeze. With Joanna holding her, while they devoured each other with kisses, Fiona slowly sank down onto the bed, onto her back. Leaning over her, Joanna softly kissed her throat.

Then, her actions purposeful, Joanna took two pillows and gently placed them beneath Fiona's head and shoulders. Her expression tense, she knelt beside the bed at Fiona's knees. She slid Fiona's shoes off, then reached under her dress and in a single fluid movement, peeled off her stockings and panties. Holding Fiona's gaze, moving her legs apart, Joanna began to lick the sensitive skin inside her thighs. Slowly, inch by inch, Joanna pushed the dress higher as she licked, her tongue like fire, all the way up both Fiona's thighs.

Fiona was quivering, gasping at the sight of Joanna before her, on her knees as if worshipful. She gave a low groan, realizing that Joanna had carefully placed the pillows so that Fiona could watch this erotic ritual. The crisp cotton of her shirt grazed Fiona's skin, the sensation an electrifying contrast with the soft wet strokes of her tongue.

Fiona's heart raced as Joanna's mouth moved closer to her core. Pausing, Joanna pushed the dress up around Fiona's waist, spread her legs wide and gazed at her. "Oh, baby," she breathed as she brought her mouth to her. In long deep strokes, she licked between her thighs. Shaking, Fiona's mind went blank. Then Joanna's strokes became tiny, accurately placed, ice-hot pinpoints and her fingers slid inside her. Teasing, her fingers moved slowly, just inside, then suddenly thrust deeply, once, and withdrew to tease again. It was a magical rhythm. Soon, in a powerful surge, Fiona was swept to her peak. Crying out in ecstasy, her body shook with heavenly tremors.

Taking her in her arms, Joanna held her tightly, kissing her face, her throat, murmuring sweetly. With tears trickling down her cheeks, Fiona felt her heart slip away.

Gradually, her body calmed while Joanna gently caressed her. As Fiona lay still, her body like liquid, Joanna unzipped her dress, slid it off over her hips and removed her bra. She kissed Fiona's breasts and stomach. Trailing her fingers over the starched cotton, stroking Joanna's back, Fiona could feel the tension in Joanna's body. Then Joanna got up and stood beside the bed. Her eyes dark, she held Fiona's gaze as she began to undress. She pulled her shirt out of her pants and unbuttoned it. Not needing a bra, she was naked underneath. Fiona glimpsed her breasts, the hard nipples prominent against the fabric. Joanna unbuckled her belt. With a groan, Fiona sat up, wrapped her arms around Joanna's hips and pulled her against her mouth. She inhaled the delicious scent of Joanna's desire as she unzipped the pants. They dropped to the floor. Joanna was wearing brief black satin panties, and quickly she slid them off. She began to take off her shirt.

Fiona put out her hand to stop her. "I like the shirt," she whispered. She lay down again as Joanna knelt over her, kissing her. Joanna moved her mouth to Fiona's breasts, circling her tongue around her nipples before taking one into her mouth and gently sucking it. Fiona gasped. Her hands under the shirt, she caressed Joanna's back and hips. Trailing her fingers around to her thighs, she reached between her legs. Joanna groaned. She was soaking, the inside of her thighs wet and slippery. Her heart pounding, Fiona stroked, then slid the tips of her fingers inside her. Wanting more of her, she drew Joanna close. With a sigh, Joanna's arms gave way, and Fiona plunged her fingers deeply into her.

Joanna was shaking, her breathing ragged as she lay in Fiona's arms. Pushing the shirt aside, Fiona kissed her shoulder, stroked her hair. "God . . ." she murmured as Joanna's tiny contractions began to grip her fingers. Remaining inside her, she turned Joanna onto her back and watched her. Joanna's eyes began to fill with tears, and Fiona kissed her. Suddenly, Joanna arched her hips and, groaning, convulsed with powerful contractions.

Joanna's skin was dewy with perspiration as Fiona kissed her way down her body. On fire, kissing and stroking between Joanna's thighs, Fiona nuzzled into her. With tears in her eyes, she anointed her face with Joanna's passion. She had fallen in love with Joanna, just as she knew she would.

When Joanna awoke the next morning, she was lying on her stomach, her body warm and still tingling. She sighed, focusing on the bedside clock. It was five minutes to seven. Reaching out, she switched off the alarm, which she had set for seven o'clock.

Fiona hadn't stirred. At the sight of her beautiful, peaceful face, her perfect, golden body, Joanna's heart turned over. Still wearing her diamond earrings and gold bracelet, she was on her back, her hair tangled around her shoulders. Her breasts seemed to be demanding Joanna's kisses; her legs were apart, inviting Joanna's mouth.

Like a shadow behind her lust, anxiety hovered.

This wanting was too much. Last night she had felt a kind of passion she hadn't known before. Giving herself up completely, she had lost control. Lost herself. The weight in her chest that, lately, she was often aware of, had moved painfully, like a rock was rolling around in there. More than once, tears had filled her eyes, run down her face. She didn't do that sort of thing.

Fiona stirred. She sighed, shifting her body a little, moving her head. A wave of desire overwhelmed other thoughts, and gently Joanna kissed her stomach. Fiona jumped slightly, then moaned. Her eyes remained closed, a smile forming on her lips as Joanna's mouth moved to her breasts, softly sucking, licking. Fiona writhed and gasped. Drawing Joanna to her, she looked into her eyes and kissed her deeply. She gave one of those tiny growls and Joanna began to shake. With a sudden urgency, Joanna moved between her legs, parting her thighs, opening Fiona fully to her mouth. She was already amazingly wet and Joanna felt flooded with her. Fiona groaned as Joanna's tongue flickered over her, slipped inside her. Fiona's fingers clenched in Joanna's hair.

Joanna didn't normally do things like this, either. Only occasionally moved to be so intimate with her lovers, Joanna had certainly never feasted like this. But Fiona was different. Joanna knew she was already addicted to the taste of her. Joanna held her hips firmly as Fiona shuddered and cried out, her body rippling with tremors.

Her arms around Fiona, kissing her shoulders and throat, hiding her face in Fiona's perfumed hair, Joanna fought against the tears that welled again in her eyes. Biting her lip, she told herself she had to pull back from all this before she tipped over the edge. She was lacking her usual self-control, she decided, because her worries about the past had weakened her. The sooner she sorted out that problem, the sooner she would be back to her old self. In the meantime, she had to cool things down with Fiona.

"Darling . . ." Fiona breathed in her sexy voice. Joanna shuddered. The rock shifted in her chest again. Fiona's hands were gliding down Joanna's body. Suddenly afraid, resisting the fire in Fiona's searching fingers, Joanna sharply withdrew from her arms.

Her eyes averted, Joanna shook her head. "I can't." She felt tears on her cheeks and hoped Fiona hadn't noticed them. Pulling on a long T-shirt, she stole a quick glance at her. Fiona looked stunned. "I've got to go to work . . . you know." Trying to sound bright and casual, she added, "I'll make us some coffee." Without a backward glance, she headed out to the kitchen.

A knot gripped her stomach as she filled the coffee machine. The last thing she wanted to do was hurt Fiona. But if they didn't keep this affair in perspective, they'd both be hurt when it ended. Fiona should know that, Joanna thought, setting out the cups. She had been through it all with Diane, maybe others before her. Fiona *did* know that. She had warned Joanna about things getting difficult.

Joanna got the milk out of the fridge. But how do you tell a gorgeous woman you care about, who has just taken you to paradise, that you shouldn't see too much of each other? Joanna had never been in the position of having to articulate such things. She sighed. You don't say anything, she decided. You're both grown-ups — you just know.

"I won't stay for coffee." Joanna jumped at Fiona's low voice. In her beautiful black dress, hair brushed, lipstick on, she was composed, her face impassive. Car keys tinkled in her hand.

Whatever Fiona might be thinking, her cool expression plainly showed that she wasn't happy. Joanna suddenly felt as cold as death. She wanted to see the fire in those soft gray eyes and that sexy smile.

Fiona swallowed and glanced away. "I've got things to do," she added.

Her throat tightening, Joanna went to her, took Fiona in her arms and kissed her. Fiona, as before, melted into her, passionately returning the kiss. Instantly, Joanna's body glowed. Then Fiona tensed. Drawing back, she took a deep breath. She ran her hand distractedly through her hair, avoiding Joanna's eyes. "Must go . . ." she murmured, heading for the stairs.

"I'll show you to the door."

"No. I'm fine. Good-bye." Fiona quickly disappeared down the stairs.

"I'll phone you," Joanna called after her, but there was no reply. Her heart pounding, she stood listening to the cutting echo of spiked heels on marble. The front door closed with a dull thud. In the silence that followed, Joanna shivered. It had to be this way, she told herself. No matter what they allowed to develop between them, no matter how long it took, inevitably the day would come when Fiona would walk out that door for the last time. Joanna was determined that she wouldn't be overly bothered when that day came.

She turned on the radio. Fiona probably hadn't been upset, she thought hopefully. Like herself, Fiona was probably only showing some restraint. Joanna poured her coffee and stirred in some sugar. She would call Fiona in a few days. They could have dinner, maybe meet some friends for a drink or something. They would have some fun and any awkwardness they felt this morning would be behind them. Joanna gulped down her coffee. Then they'd spend the night together. Everything would be fine.

Her mobile was lying on the counter. She switched it on in readiness for the usual Saturday morning barrage of calls, then turned her attention to the day's work ahead.

CHAPTER NINE

Monday morning was warm when Fiona arrived at work at eight-thirty. A few patients were sitting in the waiting room, reading magazines. Sally, the receptionist, was organizing the day's patient files for each doctor.

"Hi," Sally said with a bright smile. "Your first one's due in fifteen minutes, but I just had a panic call from Penny Watts." Fiona nodded. She had seen Penny and her new baby a few times, just for checkups. "She said the baby keeps crying. She's worried there's something wrong with him."

Hopefully only colic, Fiona thought. "Did you tell her to come down straightaway?"

"Yeah, she's on her way."

"Good. Thanks." Sally handed her the file and Fiona headed for her consulting room. Sue was showing a patient into the massage room at the end of the corridor and gave Fiona a wave.

Fiona closed her door, dropped the file on her desk and sank onto the chair. She sighed wearily. The appointments were already overlapping and the day hadn't even begun. It was going to be one of those difficult days. She had been determined, this morning, to shake off the despondency she had felt all weekend. But she couldn't get Joanna out of her mind. So much for learning lessons, becoming wiser, she chastised herself. She had forgiven herself for being blind and stupid with Diane. Diane had, after all, made promises that Fiona had chosen to believe. Joanna, on the other hand, had made her position perfectly clear. She hadn't lied, or misled her in any way. Fiona had allowed her judgment to be distorted by her own desire, and she couldn't excuse her own stupidity this time around.

There was a knock at her door, and Marie came in with two cups of coffee. "Hi, hon," she said. "It's going to be a hideous day. Thought we'd have a quiet coffee together before the shit hits the fan." She put the cups down on the desk and sat on the patients' chair.

"Good idea," Fiona said, accepting the coffee gratefully.

"So, how was dinner with Jo on Friday night?" Marie's bright blue eyes were sparkling with curiosity.

Fiona's throat tightened. She gulped some coffee. "Nice," she said evenly, averting her eyes.

Marie's expression became concerned. She shook her shaggy fringe out of her eyes. "Then why do you look so miserable?"

Fiona couldn't prevent the tears that sprang to her eyes. "I stayed the night with her," she blurted, glad to get it off her chest. "I knew I shouldn't, but at the last moment, I ignored my instincts. I've never wanted anyone so much." She took a deep breath. "Now I'm in love with a woman who, it seems, can turn her emotions on and off like a tap."

Marie put her arm around her and kissed her cheek. "Don't be so hard on yourself. It was inevitable that something would start between you two," she said gently. "And you were probably falling in love with her from the start. I know you pretty well, and I have to say, it seemed that way to me." Marie looked at her searchingly. Obviously trying to make her feel better, she added, "I'm sure Jo feels more for you than you think."

Fiona remembered gazing into Joanna's eyes just before that first kiss. She had believed she saw something deeper than ordinary lust, and that feeling had intensified as the night wore on. For Fiona, there was a special, powerful, erotic intimacy between them. As she held Joanna, trembling in her arms, kissed away her tears, she had been sure that Joanna felt the same way.

Fiona impatiently wiped the tears from her face. She had to pull herself together. This whole situation was her own fault and she had to get over it. "It wouldn't have been inevitable if I hadn't gone out with her. I was fooling myself that we could simply be friends. But I couldn't resist being with her." She sighed. "On Friday night, it seemed like she cared too, but if she did, she certainly hid it well the next morning." With a shudder, she recalled her shock when Joanna suddenly pulled away and got out of bed. It felt like a bucket of ice water had been thrown over her. "She switched from hot to cold in an instant. I haven't heard from her since."

Absent-mindedly, Marie took a pen from the pocket of her shirt and chewed the end of it. "It was clear to Louise and me, that night at your place, that you'd made a big impression on her. We talked about the way she looked at you, how good you looked together. Sounds like she's doing her best to cover her feelings, if you ask me. If she wasn't emotionally caught up herself, she would've phoned the next day to organize a repeat performance. That'd be Jo's usual style." She paused, sipping her coffee, looking thoughtful. "It's odd that she hasn't called you. Maybe she's just sorting out her feelings." She looked up. "Jo's a really nice person, honestly. I know she'll call."

Fiona smiled and rolled her eyes. "There's no point in either of us guessing what she really feels. If she's going to maintain her casual attitude, then it's academic, isn't it? You and I both know that Joanna never gets in too deep. I'm in too deep, and I simply can't see her alone again." She picked up a pencil and began doodling on her notepad. "I know she'll call when she's ready. I know she'll want us to get together again. And I'll just say no, that's all. Then that'll be the end of it."

Marie nodded but looked unconvinced. The phone

rang. It was Sally letting Fiona know that Penny had arrived with her baby. They both headed for the door. "We'll have lunch together if there's time," Marie said.

Fiona smiled warmly. "Yeah, that'd be good." Marie went off to her own consulting room.

As Fiona headed out to reception to meet her patient, she felt back in charge. Talking with Marie had made things seem less complicated. Marie was right. She couldn't help her feelings. There was nothing stupid about falling in love with Joanna, only unfortunate, and there was no point in being angry with herself. But she could control the way events proceeded with Joanna, and without question, she was bailing out before she got really hurt.

"Rough day, Jo?" Steve asked as Joanna slumped down on a barstool. Her splitting headache must be showing on the outside.

"Yeah," she said with a grin. "A strong espresso would help, I think." She rummaged around in her briefcase for some pain killers. She could feel the tightness in her temples loosening a little, just from the wonderful aroma as the coffee machine steamed and hissed. Steve put a glass of ice water on the bar beside the small cup of thick, foaming coffee. "Thanks," Joanna murmured as she gulped some water, swallowing the tablets.

It was four o'clock on Wednesday. Five days since she had seen or spoken with Fiona. Joanna had been waiting until she could think of Fiona without being swamped by desire. But instead of abating, the wanting had grown stronger. Like a watermark, the image of Fiona floated behind every thought. At cricket on Saturday, Joanna had spent half her time scanning the spectators for her. On Saturday night, at a bar in the city, while trying to enjoy a drink and conversation with Bev and Sandy and some other friends, she had kept wondering what Fiona was doing, wishing they were together.

Joanna sipped her coffee. Linda had been at the bar, flirting overtly with her. At one point, Joanna had gazed at her, trying, wanting to see the attraction she once found in Linda's pretty face, but Fiona's image pervaded. It was as though Fiona's striking beauty, cool elegance, powerful sexuality, made Joanna's past sexual encounters look like mere dress rehearsals for the real thing. Feeling jumpy, she had left early. On Sunday, she had wanted to call her, and Monday and yesterday, but didn't.

Joanna sighed. Apart from a couple of men at a table down the back, the café was empty. It was a hot day, but the fans spinning overhead created a pleasant breeze. Sizzling sounds and delicious cooking fragrances wafted from the kitchen. But Joanna had little appetite. She wouldn't stay around for dinner, as she often did. A toasted sandwich at home would be enough, she thought. Steve came out of the kitchen and Joanna ordered another coffee. She had been dragging her feet the last few days, finding her work unusually tedious. There were some ads she had to write and drop off at the office this evening. She would leave them on Karen's desk after everyone had gone home, she decided. On Saturday morning, Cathie had asked her how dinner went on Friday night, and Joanna had been evasive. If Fiona had said anything at the clinic, Cathie would probably know by now, via

Sue, that things had progressed beyond dinner. She wasn't in the mood for Cathie's analysis and advice about Fiona.

Joanna took her coffee over to a table and grabbed her phone from her briefcase. It scared her that she so desperately wanted to call Fiona, hear her voice, but she couldn't put it off any longer. She had to arrange to see her. She hesitated, fingering the keypad. How was Fiona going to respond? Joanna had been trying to convince herself that Fiona would appreciate and understand her delayed call. But her chest wasn't convinced. Heavy, aching, it made her remember the cold, hurt expression on Fiona's face on Saturday morning. You don't have sex like that with a woman like her then not call for five days. It wasn't decent.

Joanna gulped some coffee, took a deep breath, and dialed the North Melbourne Clinic. With her free hand, she massaged her temples while the receptionist put her on hold.

She heard a click, then, "Hello, Joanna." Fiona's tone was even.

Joanna gripped the phone tightly as a melting heat rippled through her. "I've been thinking about you."

There was a long pause before Fiona responded. "Yes?"

Oh, God. She *was* angry. "I'm sorry I haven't called before. I've been busy . . . and, you know. I meant to, but —"

"I assure you, Joanna, that if I'd wanted to see you in the last few days, *I* would've called *you*." Her voice was decidedly cool.

Joanna closed her eyes and inwardly groaned. You idiot, she chastised herself. She had been so preoccupied with her own strategy that she hadn't considered Fiona's intentions. Thoughtlessly, Joanna had implied that it was up to her to call all the shots. Fiona would not have liked that at all. "Of course, I didn't mean . . ." She cleared her throat. "I've missed you. I want to see you." There was another long pause. When Fiona spoke again, her voice was softer, lower.

"I don't want us to see each other alone again."

Joanna's heart began to pound. Pulling back was one thing, cutting off completely was an overreaction. "But I *have* to see you!" she blurted. "Are you mad at me? Because I didn't call?" She felt breathless, panicky. "I was only trying to be, you know . . . I wanted to take things easy!"

"Joanna . . ." Her voice was whispery, soft as a kiss. Joanna's skin tingled, tears stung her eyes. "I'm not mad at you. It's just that after the other night, things didn't end up the way I would've liked." Joanna thought she heard a tiny crack in her voice. There was silence for a moment. "You and I expect different things, want different things . . . it's best to leave it."

Joanna ground her knuckles into her temple, vaguely wondering when the pain killers would kick in. She felt at a loss. She hadn't considered for one moment that Fiona would want to call it all off when their affair had barely begun. "So . . . that's it?" she murmured.

"We'll bump into each other, here and there." Fiona cleared her throat. "Look, I've got a patient waiting. I have to go." There was another pause. Joanna listened to Fiona's soft breathing. "Good-bye."

Completely off-balance, Joanna couldn't think of anything else to say. "I'll see you around, then."

Fiona hung up.

Joanna drank the rest of her coffee. It was cold and bitter. The tension in her shoulders was creeping up her neck, gripping her muscles like steel fingers. Stretching, trying to loosen up, she composed herself. Fiona was probably right. It was best to leave it. After all, no matter how hard Joanna tried to see this affair as being just like any other, it wasn't. And she didn't want this obsession.

Steve came over. She ordered another coffee and a shot of black Sambuca to go with it. She had to take control of this desire before it took control of her. It was a shame that she and Fiona couldn't get it together, have a good time for a while. But, albeit sooner than she had expected, Joanna would simply have to move on, like she always did.

Taking a file and a notepad from her briefcase, Joanna focused her attention on the ads she had to write.

The following Friday evening, Joanna pushed open the glass door of the office at six o'clock. As usual for that time on a Friday, the place was virtually abandoned. She could hear Cathie's voice wafting down the corridor.

Joanna jumped as a head popped up from behind the reception desk. It was the owner of the company and managing director, old Harry Allcock. "Afternoon, Harry," Joanna said with a smile. He blinked at her, a vacuous expression on his face. Mumbling to himself, he began rifling through papers on Karen's desk. Seeming to avoid the staff, Harry was a rare sight around the office. His son, another Harry, was the general manager and ran the business. Joanna usually only saw old Harry at the quarterly sales meetings, where he sat in silence at the end of the boardroom table, looking bewildered, dipping biscuits into his tea.

Joanna headed to her office. Nathan had phoned earlier, wanting to see her urgently, and she had arranged to meet him at Café Q at six-thirty. No doubt he wanted to change his brief again in his endless battle to find something to please Robert. Karen had phoned to tell her that some new brochures promoting three different apartments had arrived from the printer's yesterday, and Joanna wanted to pick up a copy of each to show Nathan.

Cathie, on the phone, gave her a smile as Joanna went into her office. Karen had left the brochures on her desk. Carefully examining them, she was pleased and impressed. She stacked a dozen of each one into her briefcase. She would need plenty for tomorrow morning's inspections too. A shadow loomed in her doorway and she looked up to see Harry drifting past along the corridor. As usual, with his head down, muttering, he was tugging on his lower lip. A gaping split in his silvery comb-over betrayed him in a big, pink grin across his head. It was no wonder he was weird, Joanna thought. A name like Allcock would be quite a burden to carry through life. She was grateful, though, that he'd had the sensitivity not to name the company after himself.

Cathie hung up and swiveled her chair around to face Joanna. "I was just about to phone you. Where've you fucking been all week?"

"I've dropped in late a couple of times. I've been around. How've you been?"

Cathie was scrutinizing her. Without taking her eyes off Joanna, she reached out, picked up a cigarette and lit it. She clearly had something on her mind. "Do you want to join us tonight at Café Q? We're meeting for drinks at seven. Might stay for dinner."

"Yeah, great. I have to meet a client there anyway, so I'll join you after that."

Cathie got out her makeup purse and spread the contents over her desk. Compact in hand, she began touching up her eyeliner. Joanna prepared some notes to leave for Karen. She had viewed and valued a house that morning, and the usual follow-up company letter, including the proposed advertising campaign, schedule and auction date, had to be prepared and sent to the client. Cathie was unusually quiet. Harry's shadow reappeared as he crept past again, heading back toward reception.

"So, what's going on with Fiona?" Cathie suddenly blurted loudly across the corridor. Joanna glanced at Cathie's profile. She was gazing into her compact, applying her lipstick.

Joanna was annoyed to feel her chest tightening. "Nothing."

Cathie's compact closed with a piercing snap. "I heard that you two were lovers."

Out of sight, but obviously close by, Harry shuffled softly on the white vinyl tiles. Cathie was always doing that — yelling across the corridor, broadcasting Joanna's business to the whole office. Prickling with irritation, she got up and went to Cathie's doorway. "For Christ's sake!" she hissed. "Will you keep it down."

Unperturbed, Cathie sprayed on her perfume. The sweet scent filled the air. "Oh, you don't have to

worry about old Harry. He's in a world of his own."
She lit another cigarette. "Poor old thing wouldn't
know someone was up him till he felt hot breath on
the back of his neck."

Joanna shot a quick, anxious glance in Harry's
direction and was relieved to see him stepping out
through the front door. A sudden gust of wind caught
his hair, lifting his comb-over in an alarming erection
that seemed to say, "Up yours," as he mooched, head
down, past the display window.

Cathie switched off her computer and tidied the
files on her desk. Or rather, rearranged the clutter.
"So, what's going on? I heard Fiona's upset with you."

Joanna turned and went back to her office. A knot
was coiling up in her stomach. She hated to think
she'd upset Fiona. In truth, she was ashamed of her
behavior — not calling her for days — but what else
could she have done? Anyway, Fiona was the one who
had brought their affair to an abrupt halt. "I would've
thought they'd have more important things to talk
about at the clinic. Like people dying and things," she
said in a tight voice. She put her notes in a folder to
leave on Karen's desk.

Cathie sounded a little terse as she said, "Sue was
concerned that Fiona seemed down, you know. Marie
told her that things had heated up between you and
Fiona on Friday night and cooled off very quickly
afterwards."

Joanna shrugged. "We spent the night together.
She doesn't want a nice, uncomplicated affair. Doesn't
want to take it any further. No big deal."

Cathie sighed. "Oh, Joanna. How can you let her
go? You know she's special — not one of your usual
good-time girls. I can't fucking believe you!"

Joanna felt herself slipping. An unfamiliar anger unfolded in her chest. "I am what I am, all right! I don't get involved! She knows that, and you should know that too by now!"

"Don't give me that shit, Jo," Cathie said flatly. "You're bloody crazy about her. That night at dinner, I saw the way you were with her. I've never seen you like that before." She stubbed out her cigarette. "I thought maybe, at last, you might get serious with someone. She's perfect for you."

Suddenly, Joanna lost her grip. "What do you expect from me?" she shouted. Cathie looked stunned. "Yeah, Fiona's special! So, what am I supposed to do? Get a fucking personality transplant?" Her chest hurt so much it was hard to breathe. She tossed her stapler into her desk drawer and slammed it closed. "And what's this fixation you have, for Christ's sake, with getting serious. It's a bloody fantasy! How many 'this is it, I'll love you forever' relationships have you had? What's Sue? Number five? Six?"

Cathie gasped. Joanna never lost her temper. She was shocked at herself. It was as though someone else had spat out those angry words. God! What was the matter with her? Slowly, tears filled Cathie's eyes and Joanna crumbled. She got up and went to her.

"I'm sorry. I didn't mean it."

Cathie pushed past her and stormed down the corridor to the ladies' room. Joanna followed her. The door slammed in her face.

"Come on, Cathie," Joanna urged, staring at the closed door.

"What do I care if you waste the rest of your life screwing around!" Cathie's indignant voice echoed. "I hope Fiona finds a *real* woman soon! Who fucking knows what it's all about!"

Joanna rolled her eyes and sighed. "I'm going to meet my client. I'll see you at the bar," she said wearily.

Returning to her office, she packed up her things, and after dropping the file on Karen's desk, left to meet Nathan.

A small crowd had already gathered around the bar when Joanna arrived ten minutes later. Nathan was sitting at the bar, staring into his glass, gripping it with both hands. It didn't look like he was having a terrific day either.

She slid onto a barstool beside him. "Hi," she said with a smile.

Nathan glanced at her and gave a weak smile before staring back at his glass.

"Barbados, Jo?" Steve asked.

Joanna nodded. "Thanks. And whatever Nathan's having." Steve fixed her drink, then topped up Nathan's glass with wine. Joanna swallowed half her rum at a gulp and waited for Nathan to speak.

Eventually, he took a deep, ragged breath. "It's all off," he said. "We won't be buying a bloody house." He sighed. "Robert's got himself a new lover. He's left me." Nathan's shoulders slumped and he began to sob quietly.

Joanna wasn't surprised but felt sympathetic. "I'm sorry to hear that," she said gently.

"He promised me, you know? We had an understanding." Nathan drained his glass.

"Yeah. Happens all the time, though." Especially

with little bastards like Robert, she thought. She gave Steve the nod and he refilled Nathan's glass.

"We both agreed that if we ever met anyone really cute, we'd bring him home. And he goes and fucking falls in love!"

Joanna was confused. "Bring him home?"

Nathan turned to her tearfully. "Share him!"

She caught Steve's eye and he grinned. "Oh, right. I see," she murmured. Another glorious example of true love. Sniffling, Nathan leaned over his glass again. Christ, she thought. She really wasn't in the mood to sit watching Nathan crying into his Chardonnay. She finished her drink.

"Anyway, thanks for being so nice, showing us all those places," Nathan said, getting off his barstool.

"You're welcome," she said with a smile. "I hope everything works out okay." They said good-bye and Nathan left.

Joanna ordered another Barbados just as Sue and Cathie walked in.

"Hi, Jo." Sue gave her a hug. Cathie averted her eyes and stood with her back half turned to Joanna. "She said you yelled at her," Sue said. "I told her she's got to stop trying to marry everyone off, but . . ." She shrugged helplessly and grinned. "You know . . ."

Joanna put her arm around Cathie's shoulders. "I'm really sorry I lost my temper. You can't stay mad at me. I couldn't bear it." Cathie stole a quick glance at her. Joanna smiled and kissed her cheek. "How about a glass of Champagne."

Cathie gave a reluctant smile. "Möet," she said. "And I'll forgive you because you're lovesick."

Joanna blinked at "lovesick" but knew better than to argue. She turned to Steve and ordered a bottle.

Sue chuckled, slipping her arm around Cathie's waist. "Don't make a habit of getting cross with her. It could get very expensive."

Joanna shook her head. "I don't know what got into me."

"Here comes Fiona," Cathie said, taking the glass of Champagne off the bar. She smiled at Joanna, fluttering her eyelashes, feigning innocence. "I forgot to mention that she was coming with Marie and Louise."

She turned to the door just as Fiona walked in with the others. Joanna's pulse quickened. A melting heat flooded her body. She had made up her mind since their phone conversation on Wednesday that she would be ready for this, that she would be cool and collected the next time she saw Fiona. But she wasn't feeling cool at all. The rest of the room became a blur as she watched Fiona approach the bar. She was wearing a tight, deep-pink linen pencil skirt that finished just above the knee, with a matching fitted sleeveless top and black high heels. The color accentuated her radiant complexion. In response to something Louise whispered to her, Fiona dropped one of her stunning smiles and swept back her hair. Then she looked up and saw Joanna. Unease flitted across her eyes, just for a split second.

Joanna was distracted for a few moments while she said hello to Marie and Louise. When she turned back to Fiona, she was smiling calmly. "Hello, Joanna." Her smoky voice made Joanna tingle.

Joanna adopted a casual smile. "Good to see you."

"Let's grab a table," Marie said. Joanna couldn't take her eyes off Fiona as the others all moved away. Fiona held her gaze with an intimacy that made

Joanna's throat tighten. Then, with a perfunctory smile, she turned to join the others.

"Wait," Joanna said. "Have a drink with me first."

Fiona hesitated for a moment. Then she nodded. "Okay." She sat down on a barstool, and leaned an elbow casually on the bar. Her skirt inched up. Joanna's heart raced as she focused on her exposed thigh. That perfect, silky, honey-sweet thigh that Joanna had licked like candy. "I'll have a sloe gin and tonic, thanks."

As she ordered the drinks, Joanna wondered if beneath that perfect poise Fiona was churning up like she was. She desperately tried to think of some small talk, anything that would keep Fiona there for a while. Fiona swallowed and glanced around the room. She fidgeted with the hem of her skirt. Gazing at her manicured hand, Joanna remembered those glossy, painted nails softly raking her back. She trembled. Christ! she thought. There *had* to be some way they could get together, some understanding they could reach.

Joanna handed Fiona her drink. "I should make a time to show you those other properties I mentioned."

"I think I'll leave that for a while." Fiona was obviously determined that they wouldn't be alone again. Fiona sipped her drink. "Have you been to see your father?"

The issue of confronting him had been compounding Joanna's anxiety in recent days. "No, but I'm going on Sunday."

"Good. I hope it goes well." Fiona stood. Averting her eyes, fingering a fine gold chain at her throat, she said, "Um . . . I think I'll go and join the others. Are you coming?"

Suddenly, Joanna's composure completely evaporated. She couldn't bear to leave things unresolved. Except when their eyes met, they were behaving like strangers. Jumping to her feet, she grabbed Fiona's arm. "Don't do this, baby," she said in a low voice. Fiona was clearly taken aback. "For God's sake, this is crazy." She could feel Fiona quiver and desperately wanted to kiss her. "Come home with me," Joanna breathed. Tears suddenly glinted in Fiona's eyes; the tension in Joanna's chest increased its grip. Fiona glanced away, biting her lip, as she allowed Joanna to draw her closer. Joanna began to shake as she brushed her lips against Fiona's hair. "I can't leave it," she whispered. "We can't ignore this." Fiona gazed, through her tears, into Joanna's eyes.

"Hi, Joanna," a voice purred beside her.

Fiona's attention shifted abruptly to the woman beside Joanna. Fiona stiffened. In an instant, her expression turned to stone. Horrified, Joanna turned. It was Tina. She dropped a coquettish smile.

"I've been hoping I'd run into you somewhere. You haven't called. Maybe you'll have a drink with me later?" Disoriented, Joanna hesitated for a second, then before she could respond, Tina gave Fiona a cursory smile and continued on her way to the back of the bar.

Fiona pulled her arm away. Her eyes flashed. Her tone was terse. "Don't waste my time, Joanna." She quickly walked over to the table and sat down with the others.

Joanna slumped down on the barstool and gulped the rest of her drink. Fiona had almost said yes, and the opportunity had been destroyed by Tina. Tina! She couldn't care less about bloody Tina. Was it her fault that Tina had bad manners and even worse timing? But maybe, she thought, that was a clue to Fiona's refusal to continue their affair. She might think Joanna wanted to date other women too, and Fiona would hate that. God! That was the last thing Fiona had to worry about! Joanna only ever dated one woman at a time, and her obsession with Fiona had made other women virtually invisible. Perhaps if she got the chance, she could reassure Fiona about that. It might make a big difference.

She watched Fiona laughing and talking. She'd apparently relaxed. Joanna sighed. Fiona wasn't a woman to be pushed. Once again, Joanna would wait. Cathie and Sue were having a party next Saturday night to celebrate the end of the cricket season. Fiona would certainly have been invited. Maybe then, Joanna thought, they'd have a chance to talk.

The bar was becoming crowded, the music growing louder. A waiter was at their table taking their dinner order. Cathie looked up and waved Joanna over. With a smile, Joanna shook her head. It would be impossible to sit there beside Fiona without constantly gazing at her, wanting to touch her. Opting for a quiet night at home, Joanna left.

CHAPTER TEN

Bracing herself for a confrontation with her father, Joanna drove into the parking area beside Golden Oaks Nursing Home. Sometimes she doubted the wisdom of her urge to unearth the past, but it was too late to turn back. As though she were on a one-way street, she had to push forward until she came to the end of it. It was ridiculous that she had actually felt afraid to meet Beatrice after all those years. She still despised the old bitch but had realized once she faced Beatrice that her fear was merely a habit left over from her childhood.

Joanna walked down the path to the entrance. It would be the same with him, once she faced him, she told herself. She had always regarded him with some contempt and shown him little respect, but when she was a small child, his awesome power had been impressed upon her. In dragging Joanna from her mother's arms, throwing Isabella out of the house, it was clear that he alone was in charge of everyone's life. Joanna had to admit, that impression had persisted in her mind. She had rebelled against him, though, and all of his allies, including Beatrice and the nannies he hired.

She smiled, remembering the one time he brought a woman home. Joanna had been seven or eight. The nanny, Rosa, had dressed Joanna for dinner in a pretty blue dress with a satin sash that tied in a bow at the back. Joanna disliked the dress, didn't want to meet the woman, but tried to endure the performance. They sat down to dinner — her father, the blond woman and Joanna — with candles flickering in the candelabra, and soft music playing. Her father fawned over the woman. She gushed and fluttered, her look-at-me laughter like crockery smashing on concrete. By the time Lucy brought in dessert, Joanna couldn't stand it any longer. Picking up the shiny, shivery lime jelly in the shape of a heart that Lucy had made especially for her, Joanna hurled it at the woman. In what seemed to be slow motion, it dribbled off her startled face onto her ample, well-exposed cleavage. Her father got up, dragged Joanna from her chair, shook her and shouted for Rosa, who came running to escort Joanna to her room. Upstairs, Joanna tore off her dress and tossed it out of her window. It caught in the branches of the birch tree where it flapped around like a victory flag for a week. Finally the gardener had climbed up on a ladder and taken it down.

But, she thought, her tantrums as a child and off-hand attitude as an adolescent had all been acts of bravado. She had only really felt in charge of her own life when she walked out on him that last time. The old anger and apprehension still lurked underneath, however, and had caught up with her, thrown her off-balance. Those dreams, the way tears that she had virtually forgotten could now spring to her eyes at any time, and the way that rock rolled in her chest whenever she thought about Fiona all showed her that. Even the earth under her feet didn't feel as solid as it used to. There was a sponginess to it, she thought, looking down at the footpath, as though beneath the neat paving, a murky swamp was rising.

As long as her father held the secrets of a past that had so profoundly affected her, it seemed he still held some power over her. Confronting him at last, demanding an explanation, would dissipate the vestiges of that power.

A smiling young nurse in a white uniform directed her to the garden. "You'll find Mr. Kingston sitting near the fountain. Just follow the path."

Automatic glass doors opened with a whisper, and Joanna went outside. To her right, the grounds stretched out in gentle curves of green velvety lawns, broken in places by symmetrical flower beds of yellow, red and white petunias. To the left of the path was a tall hedge of English box. The smell of freshly mown grass was in the air; birds were singing in the oak trees.

She tried to imagine his reaction, not just to her unannounced appearance, but also to her questions.

133

Her clearest images of him were his departures and arrivals. Shiny leather suitcases, perfectly cut business suits, white designer shirts. Housekeepers and nannies rushing around, his deep voice resonating throughout the house as he left his instructions. A hand in Joanna's back, shoving her forward to receive a farewell pat on the head or a homecoming gift of a Javanese shadow puppet or jade carving.

The hedge ended and the path took a sharp turn to the left. An expanse of lawn opened out before her, and a large fountain, complete with Romanesque lions spouting water from their mouths, stood in the center. The path led to the fountain and a paved area around it. Suddenly, in the shade of a tree beside the fountain, a person came into view. Joanna froze. Huddled in a wheelchair, a red rug across his knees, sat a wizened old man. Shocked, her heart pounding, she could hardly believe he was her father.

Slowly, she approached him. He didn't respond to her as she stood gazing at him. His once-thick dark hair, salted with gray, had become wispy and white. A gray cardigan was draped over his shoulders, once broad and proud, now stooped and bony. Joanna sank down onto the garden seat beside him. She struggled to find the words to begin.

"I've come to visit you . . . ask you some things." He continued to stare into the distance. Only his hand trembled slightly. She cleared her throat. "About Isabella."

Slowly, he turned and looked at her. His eyes, at one time piercing and intelligent, seemed unfocused. "Isabella," he breathed.

A lump formed in Joanna's throat. She swallowed. "Why did you send her away?"

To Joanna's horror, tears filled his eyes and slowly trickled down his cheeks. His withered skin absorbed them like parched earth soaking up rain. "She was the only one I ever loved," he whispered.

Joanna's contempt began to seep away. It was impossible to not feel sorry for this pathetic shell of the man she once knew. Perhaps, all along, his quiet tyranny had only been a mask disguising his bitterness, she thought, his show of strength only bluff hiding his sadness. Perhaps she had learned the cover-up game from him. "Why didn't she take me with her? Why didn't she come back?"

A trembling hand reached out and touched her face, a tentative caress that shocked her. His voice was low, his breath raspy. "She was no good, as it turned out. She was leaving me anyway. I just stopped her from taking you too." Shaking, he wiped at the tears on his face. "I couldn't let her have everything, leave me with nothing." He shook his head slowly, gazing off into the trees. "I made sure of that . . . you were all I had left of her . . ." he mumbled. "Didn't let her come back . . . kept her away."

Joanna blinked away her tears, rubbing at the ache in her chest. She had expected him to be reluctant to answer her questions, even refuse to do so. She had been prepared for a cold exchange, not this exposure of a heart he wasn't supposed to have, not this spilling of tears as though his ice-blue eyes were melting. In her mind, it was a given that her father had harshly sent Isabella away after discovering some infidelity, and Isabella, because of weakness or lack of interest, had stayed away. Joanna's view of the world was set on that foundation. Gazing at the trees, she concentrated on their solid reality. She wouldn't have been overly surprised, at that moment, to see them anchored to the earth by their branches, roots in the air.

So, if Isabella planned to leave him anyway, almost certainly it would have been with a lover. And, furious, his pride in tatters, her father would have done his utmost to prevent Isabella taking her child too. But if Isabella had truly wanted to take Joanna with her, why didn't she fight him? Why did she give up?

"I'll just take him inside now, for his medication and afternoon tea."

Joanna jumped. She hadn't noticed the nurse's arrival. She gave Joanna a smile, straightened his rug, and began to wheel him away along a path cut through the lawn, into a glass conservatory attached to the beautiful Victorian building. He didn't look back. Through the potted palms, hanging baskets of pink azaleas and nodding fuchsias, Joanna glimpsed gray heads dipping into white, china cups.

Slowly, Joanna got up and walked back past the fountain, heading for her car. Unsure whether her unexpected compassion for him was easier to handle than her habitual contempt, she knew, at least, that there was no point in coming back. They had nothing more to say to each other. He had never moved on from that disappointment and anger. But she was moving on. Now the mystery all lay with Isabella. She had no choice but to go and see Thelma.

CHAPTER ELEVEN

All week, Joanna had looked forward to Cathie's and Sue's party. Her casual inquiry of Cathie, during the week, about whether Fiona was going, had been met with a delighted smile, and Cathie assured her Fiona would be there. Joanna had given up trying to conceal from Cathie her preoccupation with Fiona. Her concern was concentrated on whether Fiona would eventually yield to their desire for each other. Waiting and wanting. Joanna had never waited for anyone or wanted for anything, but suddenly, her life pivoted on the whim of one woman. She couldn't help it and had given up trying to stop it.

She sprayed on her perfume, then pulled on her shimmery silver sleeveless silk top, tucking it into slouchy, black linen pants. It would be different if she had reason to think Fiona's feelings had changed, but at the café last week, they clearly hadn't. For two long weeks, Joanna had been burning up. Hopefully, so had Fiona.

Apart from that, Joanna wanted to talk with her, tell her about the visit with her father, ask what she thought about it all. That was odd too. Normally, she preferred to retain some privacy where personal matters were concerned. Still, she thought, lots of odd things were going on lately. All of a sudden, she wasn't directing the events that affected her life, but was being forced to pause, to watch things unfold.

It was a clear, mild night, perfect for a party. At eight o'clock, Joanna got into her car and headed off.

"Wild Thing" was pulsing in the background as Joanna rang the doorbell, twenty minutes later. Cathie loved Sixties music.

"Hi, sweetie," Cathie said with a smile. She kissed Joanna's lips. "We're in the garden." Joanna followed her to the kitchen. Cathie took a Heineken from the fridge and handed it to Joanna, then added the finishing touches to a platter of smoked salmon canapés.

"They look good," Joanna said.

Cathie grinned. "You'd better test them." She handed one to Joanna, then went to the oven and took out a tray of golden pastry triangles. "Spinach and ricotta," Cathie said, giving them a prod.

"Mmm . . . great." Joanna was only half paying

attention. She kept glancing outside through the screen door, at the thirty or so women gathered in the large terra-cotta-paved courtyard. It was softly lit by lights tucked away in the garden borders. The members of the entire cricket team seemed to be there with their partners, plus a few others. But she couldn't see Fiona. Then a group of women directly in Joanna's view dispersed, and suddenly she saw her. Joanna thought her knees would give way.

"Sexy dress," Cathie said, following her gaze.

Her heart racing, Joanna watched Fiona chatting with Marie and Louise. The dress was deep emerald-green leather, which smoothly followed the curve of her waist, hips and thighs. Just short of knee-length, it had thin shoulder straps, a plain round neckline and a small side-split. In black high heels, her long legs looked gorgeous. Trembling, Joanna remembered the last time she saw Fiona in a dress with a split, how she used it, how Fiona had loved it.

Impatient to speak with her, create a chance to sweep her into her arms again, Joanna pushed open the door.

"Joanna!" Cathie's voice had a warning tone. Joanna hesitated. Cathie averted her eyes and re-arranged the garnish on the platters. "Fiona's not alone." Joanna's skin prickled. "She rang this morning to ask if it was okay if she brought someone with her." Cathie cleared her throat. "Someone from Sydney."

Joanna felt a sudden chill deep in her stomach. "Who?"

"Um . . . Diane."

Christ! Joanna swung around to the window, just in time to see a tall, good-looking blond stroll across the courtyard and stand beside Fiona. So this was sweet Diane! Leaning close to Fiona, saying something, Diane put her hand on Fiona's back.

A rage suddenly gripped Joanna. "What the fuck is Fiona doing with her?"

Cathie took her arm gently and said quietly, "I don't know. Probably nothing." Cathie picked up the platters from the counter. "Diane's only here for a few days, apparently. She seems quite nice." Joanna held the door open for her as Cathie carried the platters outside. Sweet *and* nice, for Christ's sake! Joanna's teeth were on edge as she crossed the courtyard.

Joanna greeted Marie and Louise, kissing them hello, then she turned to Fiona with a confident smile. "Hi."

Fiona gave a tiny gasp as Joanna kissed her cheek. Her fragrance had Joanna's head swimming in erotic memories. Almost imperceptibly, like a breath on a pool of water, there was a ripple in Fiona's poise. She held Joanna's gaze for a beat too long. She cleared her throat, then introduced Joanna to Diane. They both smiled and shook hands.

There was an awkward silence for a moment. Marie's blue eyes were watchful behind her fringe, Fiona stared into her empty glass, and Diane slid one hand into her jeans pocket and the other around Fiona's waist. Joanna clenched her teeth, her heart thumping. Louise's crunch into her canapé was deafening. Fiona moved away from Diane, placing her glass on a nearby iron-lace table.

"I'll get you another drink," Diane said to Fiona. With relief, Joanna watched her take the glass and head inside to the kitchen.

"We'll just go and say hi to Wendy," Marie said,

grabbing Louise's arm and dragging her off to join a group of women nearby.

Fiona sighed and avoided Joanna's eyes.

"We have to talk," Joanna said quietly.

"There's no point."

Sue was tidying up the table, gathering empty glasses. She gave Joanna a quick glance.

"There is a point," Joanna said in a low, urgent tone. "Last week I think you wanted to talk. We were interrupted . . . you misunderstood —"

"I think *you* misunderstood." Fiona looked shaken.

"What's wrong?" Diane suddenly appeared at Fiona's side with the glass of wine. Glaring at Joanna, her manner toward Fiona was definitely proprietorial.

Fiona wouldn't have taken Diane back, would she? The chill in her stomach had turned into a lead weight. Holding onto her self-control, Joanna said in a quiet, even tone, "I was speaking privately with Fiona."

Cathie, wandering around among her guests with a platter of food, paused, staring at them. From the corner of her eye, Joanna saw Marie, Louise and Wendy freeze, watching.

"Doesn't seem like she's interested," Diane said bluntly, a smug expression on her arrogant face.

Fiona took a deep breath, glancing around as if considering making a run for it. Never having felt before that anything or anyone was worth fighting over, Joanna had always avoided confrontations like this. Normally, long before a situation had gotten this far, Joanna would have smiled, shrugged and walked away. But she wasn't going to walk away from Fiona, and she wasn't going to have this smart-arsed bitch telling her who she could talk to, either.

The heavy glass platter Cathie was holding tilted. Taking a swig of her beer, Joanna distractedly watched a succulent pink prawn slither off the end of it. Sassy, the cat, instantly pounced on it and tore off under a rhododendron.

Adopting a casual tone, Joanna said, "I wasn't aware that you were Fiona's personal bodyguard. You're not wearing a badge."

"For God's sake!" Fiona swept back her hair and turned to Joanna, her eyes flashing. "Inside!" she hissed. Without waiting for a response, she marched across the courtyard to the door. Taking care not to catch anyone's eye, Joanna casually put her bottle down on the table, slid her hands into her pockets and strolled off after her.

Fiona was waiting for her in the living room. There was no one else in the house. Her arms crossed, she was fuming. "What's the matter with you?" Her voice was tight and frighteningly low.

Gazing at her, Joanna was mesmerized. Fiona was so beautiful, and they were so alone. Fiona's gray eyes were blazing, her glossy lips luscious and inviting. Her icy anger was awful, but the heat of Joanna's desire was overwhelming.

Fiona was waiting for an answer. "I've never been so embarrassed in my —"

Joanna grabbed her and kissed her. A fire ignited inside her. Her head swam. She thought she'd collapse. Fiona's body was tense with resistance, for a moment. Then, with a moan, she relaxed, slid her arms around Joanna's shoulders and returned the kiss hungrily. Joanna's hands glided over Fiona's back and hips, the leather soft and buttery. Fiona's mouth was consuming her, then Fiona groaned — one of those tiny, throaty growls. Burning up, Joanna pressed her up against the wall and, still kissing her, slid her hand inside that split, beneath the fine, warm leather.

Trailing her fingers up her thigh, Joanna murmured against her lips, "Does she make you do that?" They kissed again. "That little groan?"

Suddenly, Fiona's body tensed again and she withdrew from the kiss. Her breathing ragged, her eyes moist, she gazed at Joanna as if disoriented. "What?" she whispered.

"Are you back with her? That's not possible! Not after what she did! And not when you feel this way about me."

Fiona took a deep breath, disengaged herself and walked over to the window. With her back to Joanna, she ran her hand through her hair. A lamp on a side table threw her reflection onto the glass, the black hulking shapes of trees in the background. "I don't have to explain to you what I'm doing with Diane, or anyone else." There was a pack of cigarettes and a lighter on the mantelpiece. She took a cigarette and lit it. Turning to Joanna, she exhaled slowly, then added, "All you have to know is that there's nothing happening with you and me."

"Could have fooled me."

Fiona drew on the cigarette. "Can you tell me why on earth I'd be interested in continuing this thing with you?" She was terse, impatient. "I don't know what you think of me, but I assure you that I have absolutely no interest in your idea of an affair. Dinner, or whatever, followed by sex, at intervals that you deign to be acceptable? And for a period of time that you feel is sufficient?" She stepped over to the coffee table to use the ashtray.

Joanna's mind was a mess. Fiona was candidly articulating what Joanna had never really considered. Why don't you just forget all this? she asked herself. You can't give her what she wants. You don't see things the way she does. Walk! she told herself. But she was riveted to the spot. Her chest ached. She couldn't prevent tears from filling her eyes. She bit her lip as Fiona glared at her.

"I'm a grown woman, Joanna. Not a bloody teenager! Affairs involve some obligation, some emotional investment. For most of us, that's the whole point. Sometimes affairs work out, lead to heaven. And, okay, sometimes they lead to hell and someone gets hurt, but that's the way it is with grown-ups! We go along with these things."

Joanna didn't believe in heaven and knew all about hell. She had been trying to protect them both from that. Why did a woman as smart as Fiona want to take risks that could be avoided?

Fiona took another drag of the cigarette. A door slammed and they both jumped. Fiona turned to the window again. A dark form shot quickly down the path to the gate. A moment later, a car started and took off with a screech. "There goes Diane," she said in a flat, tired tone.

Joanna swallowed and found her voice. "You'd rather be with her? A cheat and a liar? I don't cheat or lie."

Fiona looked at her, rolled her eyes and sighed. She stubbed out her cigarette. "Maybe not, but you do share one significant trait with Diane. You both seem to be blind to the fact that I have other options apart from *either* of you."

No, Joanna thought. She wasn't blind to that, at all. She had seen the way women looked at her, lots of them. Fiona could take her pick.

Fiona began to leave the room. Pausing in the doorway, her voice low and restrained, she said, "You've ruined tonight for me. Don't *ever* behave like that with me again — make a fool of me." Joanna couldn't bear Fiona's contempt, or the terrible realization that she had really lost her. Tears glinted in Fiona's eyes. Agitated, she fiddled with her hair. "Like I said to you before. Just leave it, Joanna. Stop wasting my time."

Panicking, not caring that the shameful tears had spilled from her eyes, Joanna caught her arm. "What about the way we feel? I can't forget, baby," she whispered. Tears slowly trickled down Fiona's cheeks. Impatiently, she wiped them away, gave Joanna a burning look, then left.

The Rolling Stones' "Satisfaction" began throbbing from the speakers under the eaves at the back of the house. Her mind in turmoil, Joanna slumped down on the sofa, sank her face into her hands and gave herself up to her tears.

A few minutes later, she heard the front door close, then Cathie burst into the room. "What's going on? It's like fucking *Days Of Our Lives* out there!" Joanna quickly wiped her face. Cathie's expression softened. "Oh, sweetie," she said gently. She sat beside Joanna, put her arm around her and kissed her cheek. "I can't believe this. First Diane storms off in a rage, taking Fiona's car, then Fiona comes back outside, tears in her eyes, all shaken up. Marie's just taken her home." She shook her head and stroked Joanna's cheek. "And look at you." She got up and opened the sideboard. Taking out a bottle of scotch and two glasses, she poured them both a drink.

Joanna accepted it gratefully and drank it in one gulp. "It's all gotten out of hand," she said as Cathie refilled her glass. "I can't believe it either. I've never lost it like this. Never had a woman mad at me like she is." Cathie got a cigarette from the mantelpiece, lit it and inhaled, studying Joanna as if she could hardly believe her eyes. "I want this longing to stop," Joanna continued softly. "Wanting her and not being able to be with her, having her starting to hate me. It's too hard."

"Hate you?" Cathie smiled. "Can't you see she's in love with you?"

Shocked, Joanna's heart began to pound. "Of course she isn't!"

Cathie shrugged. "Looks like it to me."

Joanna stood and paced across the room. "Why would she love me? We barely got anything happening."

"Doesn't take long. There's that cozy kind of love that grows on people slowly. That's okay for a while. But in my experience, the *real* thing, like what happened with Sue and me, well, it just hits you like a truck."

"So, what about Diane?" Joanna asked breathlessly.

Cathie sipped her drink. "Diane doesn't mean anything to her. You can tell. Fiona doesn't look at her, you know. And she's not crazy about Diane's touching her." She tapped the ash off her cigarette. "I was watching."

"Oh, right. Diane's sleeping on the sofa, is she?"

"I don't know, but what's interesting is that you care so much. You're jealous, sweetie."

Joanna didn't bother trying to deny that. It was a new experience, but she was well aware that the feeling of razor blades grinding around in her chest, cutting her up, was jealousy. "Well, if Fiona's into recycling her lovers, that's her problem. There's nothing I can do about it." Joanna slid her hands into her pockets, and leaned against the doorframe. "She doesn't love me, she just wants a certain kind of relationship, and I can't give her what she wants."

"If you could stop pretending that you don't care, drop the tough bad-girl act, there's nothing you couldn't give her."

Suddenly, Aunt Beatrice's voice reverberated in Joanna's head. Through the study door, she had heard Beatrice tell her father, "She's got bad blood, that girl. You should send her away to a boarding school where she'll get it knocked out of her. Bad blood, just like her mother." Trembling, eight-year-old Joanna had wondered, terrified, what "bad blood" meant, and at thirty-four, she wondered if it were possible to inherit an inability to love.

Cathie finished her drink, then smiled. "You're adorable, you know that? It's no wonder she's in love with you. And you're in love with her, too."

Joanna shook her head. The idea was ridiculous. "I just haven't been myself lately. I've allowed myself to become obsessed with her, nearly fainting every time I think of her, wondering what she's doing every bloody minute." She ran her hand through her hair and sighed. "Lost perspective, that's all."

Cathie chuckled. "What do you bloody think love

is? Something else?" She went to Joanna and hugged her. "Don't lose your chance, sweetie," she whispered. Her gentleness made tears sting Joanna's eyes again. "Come on, let's go back to the party."

Joanna shook her head, swallowing the lump in her throat. "I don't think I'd be good company tonight."

She kissed Cathie, said goodnight and headed for home.

CHAPTER TWELVE

In the tiny cubicle behind the waiting room at the Crisis Center, Fiona poured herself a cup of coffee. It had been made hours ago and tasted stale, but she hoped the caffeine might boost her energy level. It was eleven p.m. on Tuesday, and it had been a busy night. Two other doctors would arrive in half an hour to take over the last shift until the Center closed at three a.m.

Glad for the lull in patient traffic, she sat at the desk, gazing through the one-way glass window overlooking the waiting room and entrance. Marie was with a patient in one of the consulting rooms, stitching up cuts on his face and arm. The patient report sheet would state that he fell over. But it was obvious to Fiona and Marie that the injuries were consistent with his having been in a fight. For fear of reprisals and police interrogation, the patients never admitted to involvement in street fights.

Fiona sighed. Since the party on Saturday night, she had felt miserable. Her usual enthusiasm for work was subdued, and the Crisis Center, which demanded a positive attitude and quick thinking, had been hard work tonight.

She had thought she could deal with her feelings for Joanna. After their meeting at Café Q, she had believed Joanna would lose interest in her. Then, without Joanna's enticement, Fiona's love for her could die away. On the night of the party, she had been determined that when she saw Joanna she would be warm and friendly. But when Joanna simply kissed her cheek, Fiona felt herself begin to unravel. The private scene with Joanna proved to them both that Fiona's feelings were as powerful as ever. Fiona was shocked and disturbed by the hunger in Joanna's kiss, her display of emotion. Fiona had ached to hold her, kiss her again, go home with her, make love with her. But the pattern would repeat itself. Joanna would continue alternating from hot to cold, keeping Fiona at a distance. Being in love with her made that a too-painful option. Her mind constantly shimmered with the image of Joanna's beautiful face, the tears in her eyes as she whispered, "I can't forget, baby." Fiona closed her eyes and shuddered. She wished Joanna *would* forget, let her forget too.

In the waiting room, a faulty fluorescent light

flickered depressingly above the drab olive-green floor and gray vinyl seats placed rigidly around the walls. The Crisis Center was jointly funded by the state and local governments. Few of the patients presented health cards, usually having lost them, not bothering to apply for new ones, so the cost of the health care had to be borne by the Center. Therefore, the facilities' basic comfort for either doctors or patients was not a consideration. On one of the hard seats, an old man was curled up asleep in a drunken stupor. Near the entrance, a teenage boy sat fidgeting with a grubby dog-eared magazine. Nervously, he kept glancing toward the door as if hiding from someone. Earlier, Fiona had asked him if he needed any help. He had shyly shaken his head but accepted a cup of coffee.

Marie's patient, bandaged, clutching a prescription, emerged from the consulting room and shuffled toward the door. Suddenly, there was a commotion outside. Raised, frightened voices were arguing. Fiona stood as five teenagers burst in, three boys and two girls. They were carrying the limp body of another young girl.

Fiona raced out to the waiting room as they dumped the girl on the floor and fled. "Wait!" Fiona yelled. A girl hesitated. "What happened?"

"Smack," the girl said before she took off after the others.

The girl on the floor looked to be no more than about fourteen. She had no pulse and was turning blue. A rush of adrenaline made Fiona's pulse race as she began heart massage. "Marie!" she called. "Narcan, quick!" The massage wasn't working, the girl's color was getting worse.

Marie tore over to her with a syringe. Fiona pushed up the girl's dirty sleeve and with dismay saw that her arm was scarred with needle marks. "Here," Marie said, handing her a pair of surgical gloves. Fiona quickly pulled them on, found a vein and cautiously injected half of the Narcan. Instinctively, Marie moved back and Fiona leaned away from the girl. Once the drug worked, the victim usually flailed around violently. Nothing happened, so Fiona injected the rest of the drug. The girl's body jerked, then she jumped to her feet, delivering an accidental blow to Fiona's face with the back of her hand. She stood looking around, wild-eyed, panting. Rubbing her cheek, Fiona breathed a sigh of relief. Then the girl charged toward the door. Marie grabbed her arm. "Hang on, hon," she said gently. "We want to check you over, make sure you're okay."

Looking scared, the girl shook her head. "At least take this," Fiona said. She took a plastic bag from a rack just inside the door, packed with condoms and sterile syringes. The girl snatched it and took off.

"Good job," Marie said with a smile. Fiona began to tremble, tears welling in her eyes. "Hey, what's wrong?" Marie put her arm around her. Fiona shrugged and bit her lip. "I think we should go for a drink at the dive on the corner after we finish here. Okay?"

Fiona nodded. She was faced with similar situations every week at the Center, but in her present mood, the girl's obvious poor health, drug abuse and the fact she was so very young had gotten to her.

Right on time, the two relieving doctors walked in. Fiona packed up her things while Marie handed over the case notes and filled them in on the night's activities. Then they both signed off and headed to the bar.

Apart from a few men perched on stools at the bar, nursing large glasses of beer, the place was empty. The strong, stale smell of cigarette smoke and spilt beer became unnoticeable after a few minutes; adjusting to the shock of the lime-green, tangerine and purple swirly patterned carpet took slightly longer. The dingy lighting helped. They ordered their drinks at the bar, then sat at a table by the window overlooking the street. Houses, their paint peeling, crouched at the edge of the sidewalk. The few shops still in business were caged behind iron grills; others gaped, windowless and gutted. A sheet of corrugated iron covered the missing window of a house opposite. Red spray paint adorned it with the succinct message, "fuck youse all."

It was only after a particularly frantic or satisfying night's work, when they were feeling hyped-up, that they dropped into this bar for a drink. With a twinge of guilt, Fiona thought how keen she usually was after her shift to jump into her comfortable BMW and head for the city as fast as possible, leaving the squalor behind her. Her spirits always rose as trees, parks, beautiful homes, bright lights, theaters and boutiques came into view. Content with the thought that she had done her duty, she put this other world out of her mind until the following week. But tonight, the deprivation clung to her. She could feel it seeping into her skin.

The bar attendant brought their glasses of Cognac and a pack of cigarettes that Fiona had ordered. Marie watched Fiona's hands as she peeled off the cellophane wrapping and took out a cigarette. Grabbing a book of matches from the next table, she lit it and inhaled with pleasure.

Marie took a quick gulp of her drink, eyeing the pack. With a sharp jerk of her head, she shook her fringe out of her eyes, as if also shaking temptation from her mind. She focused on Fiona. "You look like you just killed someone, instead of saving a life."

"Saved her for some more abuse, for a few more years. Some, you know, will make it." Fiona took a sip of her drink. "She won't."

Marie's eyes clouded; she toyed with the cigarette pack. "I can't deal with that. We can only patch them up, try to point them in the right direction. Most of those people would be worse off without the Center." Fiona drew on her cigarette and stared out of the window. "You're usually full of good news stories after a night at the Center. It's not like you to be negative." Marie took a cigarette and stuck it in the corner of her mouth. "It's Joanna, isn't it? All you've told me since Saturday night is that Diane's gone home. What's going on?"

Fiona sighed. "Yeah, that's something I can thank Joanna for. Diane's out of my life for good. She'd been okay for a while. You know, she'd stopped phoning me to bitch and moan. I thought it was safe to be on friendly terms with her. So when she rang last week, asking if she could come and stay for a few days, I agreed." Marie rolled her eyes and slowly shook her head. "The clinic where she works has downsized. She lost her job. She was feeling depressed, you know."

"For Christ's sake," Marie mumbled impatiently.

"I have to admit, I was glad to have the distraction. Been having trouble dealing with my feelings for Joanna." Fiona looked up at the barman and signaled for more drinks. She drew on the cigarette. "Anyway, after you drove me home on Saturday night, Diane flew into a rage about Joanna. It turns out she was still harboring the ridiculous fantasy of us getting back together. She seemed to be totally stunned by the idea that I could be attracted to someone else. I think she actually believed that there was some special place in my heart for her, and she could always, whenever she wanted, pick up where she left off."

"She arrived a couple of days before the party. How'd you get on then? Did you give her any reason to think you were still interested?"

The drinks arrived, and Fiona took a gulp. "Well, the night before . . ." She shook her head. "She was being nice and amusing. You know how she can be."

"Nope. I never saw nice. Only conceited smart-arse."

Fiona smiled. "Her street persona. And she wasn't always like that, anyway. Most people really like her."

"And that night, she showed you her bedroom persona."

Fiona nodded. "I wasn't thinking. I was upset about Joanna."

"And hot for Joanna."

Fiona gave a shrug. "Well, I don't know about Diane, but it didn't do a lot for me. You know when you have sex for some stupid, needy, pathetic reason? Not because you feel real hot-blooded lust, or love. You feel like shit afterwards." She exhaled slowly, staring at the ceiling. "I hate that."

"Oh, fuck it!" Marie suddenly blurted. Snatching up the matches, she lit her cigarette and took a deep drag. She closed her eyes and seemed to shudder slightly. "Oh, God," she murmured. "There's nothing like that zap in your brain and that fantastic feeling of your arteries constricting." Marie took another drag.

"I love that." They both chuckled. "Well, you may have seen the last of Diane, but I doubt you've seen the last of Joanna."

Fiona shook her head. "I made myself very clear. I can't accept her terms for an affair and she can't even *understand* mine."

"Won't make any difference. After I drove you home and Joanna left, Cathie, Sue and Louise sat around talking about it." Fiona rolled her eyes and grinned. "You can't blame them! None of us has ever seen Joanna do anything like that. Not Ms. Cool! According to Cathie — the recognized expert on matters of the heart — Joanna's completely gone. In love with you."

Fiona's pulse quickened. Just the words sent a heavenly ripple through her body. Again, she recalled the passion Joanna displayed that night, the longing in her voice, but still Joanna hadn't moved an inch. Joanna didn't do love. Fiona shook her head in disbelief and gulped the rest of her Cognac.

An ear-splitting crash coming from the street, made them jump. An alarm began ringing. "Sounds like a shop's being done over," Marie said flatly.

Suddenly Fiona felt very tired and craved sleep. "Let's call it a night."

Cautiously stepping out onto the street, they went to their cars parked behind the Crisis Center, and as police cars shot past, sirens wailing, they both headed for home.

CHAPTER THIRTEEN

Joanna turned up the volume of the CD player as the opening chords of Tracy Chapman's "Give Me A Reason" began to beat through the car speakers. Joanna was on the highway heading north to visit Thelma. It was Saturday afternoon, two weeks since the party — two weeks without seeing Fiona. The turnoff to Fiona's house was coming up on the left. Fiona would almost certainly be there. Joanna wondered what she would be doing. Swimming in her crystal clear dam in that tiny, sexy bikini? Playing music? Cooking? Sitting on the veranda reading?

Would anyone be with her? At least it wouldn't be sweet-and-nice Diane. Cathie had told her that Diane took off after the party, back to Sydney for good.

Ignoring the sign post, Joanna focused on the road ahead and planted her foot on the accelerator. Some kilometers past the turnoff, she glanced at the speedometer and was surprised to see she was doing one hundred and forty. Dropping back her speed, she peered nervously into the trees on either side of the highway, watchful for police cars, radar guns hanging out of the windows. All those cylinders under the hood seemed to be pushing for a good workout, but if caught doing that speed, she would probably lose her license. Life was complicated enough without that.

Of course, Fiona would meet someone else soon. She would meet a woman who could give her what she wanted, and Fiona deserved to have everything she wanted. But the idea of giving her up was becoming harder every day. Ever since the party, Joanna had replayed that kiss over and over. She wanted to forget, but when she was alone, she couldn't help closing her eyes and reliving the night they spent together. She could feel Fiona in her arms, feel her body move against her own. She could smell her and taste her and feel her presence as though Fiona was still a part of her, as she had been that night. But when she reminded herself it was finished, her longing gave way to an empty ache, the heat in her body quickly growing cold.

It was March, and in the last couple of weeks the first autumn rains had fallen. The yellow paddocks had turned green, shimmering with shiny new grass. Fluffy with new, pure-white wool, the sheep looked like clover flowers sprinkled over the hills.

Thelma had sounded delighted to hear from her, thrilled that she was coming up for a visit. With a pang of guilt, Joanna wished that she was paying the visit without an ulterior motive. She wondered what Thelma's reaction would be to her questions about Isabella. And wondered whether she would be happier knowing the story. Her father's meager revelations had only made her more confused. She hoped Thelma would be able to fill in the gaps without too many surprises.

Half an hour later, Joanna arrived at the 800-acre farm. It was a diversified business of wool and wheat. Cypress trees thickly lined the wide, sealed road leading to the homestead. Two kilometers farther on, she came to a gate on her right. After closing it behind her, she followed the winding driveway through five acres of landscaped garden, then parked in a bay beside the house. A traditional design, the farmhouse was painted cream with dark-green trims and had a red iron roof with a bull-nosed veranda on all sides. Bursting with early autumn blooms in apricot and yellow, rose bushes filled the deep garden beds across the front of the house. Blue Canterbury bells clustered at the front of the borders.

As she got out of the car, Joanna grabbed the large bouquet of bright-pink gerberas that she had brought for Thelma. The hinges on the screen door whined as Thelma came out onto the veranda. Beaming, she was wiping her floury hands on her floral apron. "Hello, darling," she said warmly as Joanna picked her way up the front steps between clucking, scattering hens. A rooster let out an ear-splitting crow as Joanna hugged Thelma and kissed her cheek. Thelma couldn't bear to leave the hens in their run all day, so after they'd finished laying each morning, she let them loose. For as long as Joanna could remember, instead of ranging over the expansive lawns and garden beds, they had always made a beeline for the house, spending the day staring in through the screen door and getting under everyone's feet.

The kitchen smelled appetizingly of freshly baked orange cake. A large cake, frosty with butter icing, was on a stand on the pine kitchen table. Thelma filled the kettle to make coffee, then arranged Joanna's flowers in a tall vase. Joanna hadn't realized her shoulder muscles were tight until she relaxed in a chair at the table and felt the tension melt away. Through the sliding glass door leading onto the back veranda, Joanna admired Thelma's kitchen garden. Surrounded by a white picket fence to keep out the hens, it had a luxuriant thyme lawn between long rectangular beds of herbs and vegetables. Joanna remembered rolling in that thyme when she was little, heady with its savory scent. An orange tree laden with fruit took up one corner; a lemon tree filled another. French beans tumbled from stick teepees, tomatoes spilled from wooden stakes, black and orange butterflies paused to feed on the pollen of the yellow zucchini flowers. On the horizon, a cloud of dust and the low rumble of an engine told Joanna that Ted was harvesting the wheat.

Thelma put the cups, milk jug and sugar on the table. "I've got a box of fruit and vegetables ready for you to take home. You're eating properly, aren't you?" she asked.

Joanna smiled. "Yeah."

"I know you won't cook anything, so I've given

you things you can eat raw or put into salads. You always liked raw vegetables."

"I still do. Thanks."

In her mid-sixties, Thelma was still looking fit and robust; her blue eyes twinkled in good humor, as always. But, perhaps because her father's sudden decline had shocked her, Joanna was acutely conscious that Thelma was growing old. Her hair was completely gray and there was a slight stiffness in some of her movements. Joanna regretted that she hadn't visited more often, spent more time with her. The years had just slipped away.

"Have you heard Adrian's news?" Thelma poured boiling water into the coffeepot.

"About his new boyfriend? Yeah, we had a long chat on the phone about two months ago."

Thelma sighed. "I hope it works out this time. I worry about his being on his own."

Joanna grinned. Adrian fell in love every five minutes with five men at a time. He was never alone. "Oh, he's okay. You don't have to worry about him." At the sound of a high-pitched motorbike engine, Joanna looked up to see Ted coming over the hill toward the house on the three-wheeled farm bike.

Thelma glanced out through the door as she poured the coffee. "Ted's been looking forward to seeing you."

With a smile, Joanna got up as Ted walked in. They hugged each other and, as usual, he smelled of wheat and grass and petrol. "How are you, love?" he asked, beaming. A sharp line cut across his forehead from the hat he always wore outside — his skin was white above and ruddy brown below. He ran his hand through his hair as he sat down at the table. White hair. With a pang, Joanna realized the day wasn't far off when they would have to sell the farm. They had no one to hand it over to. She remembered following him around as he performed various tasks on the farm. She carried the tools while he repaired fences, and he let her hammer in the nails. Always patiently answering her questions, he made her feel clever and capable.

Once, when she was six or seven, when he had picked her up from the railway station, he said, "I've got a surprise for you when we get home." When they arrived, he took her hand and led her to one of the sheds not far from the house, where he nurtured his breeding sheep and their offspring. A shaft of light, hazy with straw dust, beamed through a window onto one of his prize-winning Merino sheep, suckling a newborn lamb. Barely a day old, the lamb was wobbly on its spindly legs, and in stark contrast to its creamy-white mother, its fluffy, curly fleece was chocolate-brown. Ted dragged off his hat and scratched his head. "Seems like one of Thelma's pet rams got through the fence," he said. Grinning, he tousled Joanna's curly hair. "Anyway, she's a little dark beauty and she reminded me of you. I thought, when she's weaned, you might like her for your own pet."

Gazing at the lamb, Joanna's throat tightened. She wanted to scoop it up into her arms and hold it right away. Blinking back tears, biting her lip, Joanna just nodded. Within a week, she had been allowed to hold the lamb. Joanna could still recall the feel of its tiny quivering body in her arms and the sweet, milky smell of its wool. She had adored it, naming her Bessie. For five years, until Bessie died, she had always come to Joanna when she called.

Thelma served them generous slices of the orange cake. They chatted about the farm, Joanna's job and Adrian for a half-hour or so, until Ted had to get back to work. He kissed her good-bye, went outside and, pulling on his battered hat, retreated out of the back gate.

"More coffee?" Thelma asked.

"Yeah, you sit down, I'll make it." Joanna got up and filled the kettle to make a fresh pot. She was wondering how to broach the subject of Isabella. She cleared her throat. "I, um . . . was wanting to ask you about something." Thelma nodded, cutting more cake. "About my mother."

Thelma's head jerked up. She gazed at Joanna in astonishment, the color draining from her face. "I'd given up hope of ever hearing you say that," she said softly. She swallowed. "I tried so hard when you were little, to keep you interested in her. Showed you photos . . ."

Joanna gave a wry grin. "Until I cut them all up one day."

Thelma nodded. "I realized then that it was best to leave the subject alone. I was sure that when you got older your anger would fade away. I was so disappointed when you got that letter and refused to contact her." Tears suddenly glinted in her eyes. "I think that broke Isabella's heart all over again."

Joanna's skin prickled. "What do you mean? Broke her bloody heart! I don't hear a word from her all of those years? Then I get a bloody letter!" She brought the pot to the table and sat down. "None of this makes any sense. The other week, I went to see my father, to ask him about it all. He tells me that she wanted to take me away with her. Why did she let him stop her?"

Thelma sighed and stirred sugar into her coffee. "Those were dreadful days," she murmured. "Richard used the law to keep her away — made a case that she was an unfit mother."

"What did she do? Have orgies while he was away or something? Was she an alcoholic, a drug addict?"

Thelma rolled her eyes. "Not long after the divorce, she moved to Sydney. But all the time you were growing up, she stayed in contact with me, asking about you, checking on you. I sent her photos, copies of things you did at school." Joanna's heart started pounding. This didn't fit with her picture of Isabella at all. More black and white assumptions were fusing into gray. "By the time you were in your early teens, you came here less often, I had less to tell her, and she drifted out of contact. Until that letter came for you."

"But what did she do? What was wrong with her?"

Thelma shook her head. "You have to get the whole story from Isabella. But she wasn't an alcoholic or a drug addict." She smiled. "And I never heard about any orgies."

Joanna shook her head vehemently. "I don't want to talk to her, and I don't want her to know I'm asking questions, either."

"I haven't heard from her in ten years, not since I got a Christmas card giving me her new address in case I ever needed to contact her about you. Or, I guess, in case you ever changed your mind. She moved to Queensland." Thelma swept cake crumbs from the table into her hand and dropped them onto her plate.

"I only know the basic facts — the blow-up with Richard, her leaving. I never got to know her very well, and I don't know the details of the story. I'm not going to color your thinking, or let you off the hook by telling you the little I do know." She stood up and took the plates to the sink. "You should talk to her. She'd be thrilled to hear from you. I have no doubt about that."

God! Joanna thought. Why did it have to be so complicated? Just the bloody facts would be enough. Then she could forget all this nonsense. "Well, she must have taken off with someone." Joanna looked at Thelma, but she busied herself at the sink and didn't answer. "We're talking about an affair here. My father said she broke his heart."

"Oh, yes, she did. And he made her pay for it dearly. Took away her baby." When Thelma turned back to Joanna, drying her hands on her apron, her eyes were filled with tears.

Joanna's throat tightened; tears suddenly sprang to her eyes. Blinking them away, she took a deep breath. "So, did she marry the guy? Or did she leave him too, after a while?"

Thelma looked at her for a long moment. "The last I heard was that Isabella and Chris were still together." She headed out of the room. "I'm going to dig out that card. I know where it is." A few minutes later, she returned with it and copied out the address and phone number onto a piece of notepaper.

Joanna read the card. It didn't say much, but was signed off with: *Please be sure to contact me if there's anything concerning Joanna that I should know. I hope she's well and happy. Best wishes, Chris and Bella.*

Joanna's head swam. It had never occurred to her that for all those years Isabella had thought about her. But thinking about her wasn't good enough, Joanna reminded herself. They were only words.

Thelma handed her the note. "You have to decide what to do."

Her chest tightening, Joanna folded the note and shoved it into her pocket. She gave a little shrug. "I'll think about it."

It was time to go. Thelma handed her the box of fruit and vegetables and came out onto the front veranda with her. Hens scattered as she opened the door. Joanna hugged her tightly. "I'm sorry I haven't been to see you in so long. Missing Christmas and everything." Adrian had missed last Christmas with them, too. Joanna had accepted his invitation to spend it with him and some mutual friends in Sydney. They'd partied and had a great time, but suddenly, Joanna pictured Ted and Thelma having Christmas alone and her heart ached with guilt and sadness.

Thelma gave a good-natured smile and shrugged. "Oh, that's all right. I know you're busy."

"I'll call you in few weeks and arrange to come up for a couple of days. Or maybe Ted can take some time off after the harvest is finished, and you can come to Melbourne. You can stay at my place and I'll take you out to dinner and a show."

Thelma chuckled. "That sounds good." She kissed Joanna's cheek. "Drive carefully, and look after yourself."

Thelma was framed in the rearview mirror as Joanna drove down the driveway. She was waving, smiling, the hens jostling around her legs anticipating a shower of grain from her yellow-daisied apron. The rooster crowed as if in farewell, and the scene was swallowed by the canopy of trees.

Like snapshots, still frames flashed through Joanna's mind — of times on the farm, times with Isabella before she vanished. Life could have turned in any number of directions, but decisions had been made by others before Joanna was old enough to have a say. When, at eighteen, she had a choice, she had stuck to the course that she knew. There was another opportunity now, to alter that course. That opportunity was folded in her pocket and felt like a stick of dynamite. She could defuse it — throw it away before it blew up in her face. Did she really want to hear Isabella tell her that it was easier to stay away, that Joanna hadn't been worth fighting for? Did she really need to relive those fears, to remember how she cried every night for a mother who never came? For months, without Isabella, she had lost all sense of her own existence. She had felt, literally, invisible, surprised when anyone looked at her or spoke to her directly. For months she barely spoke. Over time, she had reconstructed her sense of self and it had excluded Isabella. Her mother had been buried in the dark recesses of Joanna's mind for so long that it was difficult to make a new space for her, to see her in a different light.

The turnoff to Fiona's house was coming up. Suddenly Joanna felt panicky. Fiona had told her plainly to stay away, but her body, her eyes, her kiss . . . they all told another story. Joanna ached whenever she thought of her. The intimacy between them during that night they spent together had scared her then and scared her still, but the emptiness without her was worse. Joanna had thought she knew all about sex, but Fiona showed her there was much more to know. She had felt an extraordinary connection with Fiona. Her body, mind and emotions seemed to be woven together by silken threads, floating in another erotic dimension that she hadn't experienced before.

It was only the physical thrills that Joanna had ever known. She knew the bedroom games to play, the roles to act, the fantasies to fulfill — techniques learned as a teenager, streamlined as an adult. Fiona had referred to emotional investment, grown-up sex. No doubt she meant intimacy. But it must be possible to have all that without losing your head.

The signpost was visible in the distance.

Complete! she thought. That was how Fiona made her feel. The signpost looming was another opportunity. If she drove past, it would be the end. She would bury her desire, gather up those mental pictures of Fiona and pack them away like a photo album in her memory. Like she did with Isabella. She would learn to live with the empty space that Fiona had created. But the wanting was consuming her, and Fiona's desire beckoned. The price was high, the risk had to be calculated, but Joanna hungered for that connection again.

A quick glance in the rearview mirror revealed the road was clear. Quickly, barely reducing her speed, Joanna swung the wheel to the right and headed down the road toward Fiona's house. The evening was warm, the wind on her face and arms caressed her like satin-gloved hands. The gum trees on either side of the narrow road were glowing pink in the setting sun. Still dark shapes under the trees suddenly shifted, and a pair of grazing kangaroos bounded away across the paddocks as she sped past. Her knuckles white, she clutched the steering wheel, her heart pounding. What would she say to Fiona? Would she slam the door in her face? Joanna recalled their last meeting and the way Fiona's anger had dissolved while her body melted in Joanna's arms. It reassured her. Fiona was strong, but so was her desire. Another kiss like the last one, and they would be in each other's arms all night long.

Slowly crunching along the gravel driveway, Joanna approached the house. Maybe Fiona wasn't there. Breathless with anticipation, carefully watching out for the horses, she considered the embarrassment of finding that Fiona was entertaining friends. Her chest tightening, she imagined the horror of discovering another lover. The trees gradually cleared. The expanse of grass around the house was washed pink, the house framed by a sky the color of crushed raspberries. Blood-red arrows of light shot off the window-glass, piercing her eyes. Crickets cried; frogs moaned. Fiona's car was in the open garage.

As she got out of the car, Joanna glanced down at her white tank top and faded jeans, worn through and frayed at the knees. If she had planned this visit, she would have dressed to impress. But more important than her clothes, she thought, approaching the front door, was trying to appear casual, relaxed and in control. She took a deep breath and knocked on the door.

After what felt like an eternity, the door opened. Looking directly into Joanna's eyes, her expression stony, Fiona stood bathed in pink. Her eyes blazed, her hair, tumbling around her shoulders, shimmered. Wearing only a black silky tank top with bikini bottom that was little more than a g-string, she looked so sexy that Joanna felt momentarily dizzy. It was difficult to breathe in that pink air.

After another eternity, Fiona said in her smoky voice, "What are you doing here?"

Joanna gave a little shrug and slipped her hands into her pockets. "I, um . . . wanted to apologize for the other week, you know . . . upsetting you at the party."

Fiona looked past her, tears suddenly forming tiny pools in her eyes. In an irate gesture, she swept back her hair and swallowed hard as if trying to compose herself. Then her gaze roved slowly over Joanna's body. When she looked up into Joanna's eyes, her expression showed repressed anger. "Don't give me that shit," she said, her voice husky. "That's not why you're here." Suddenly, she grabbed the front of Joanna's tank top and yanked Joanna against her with one impressively strong, rough jerk. "This is why you're here," she breathed against Joanna's lips. Then she kissed Joanna with a savage passion.

A searing heat erupted inside Joanna; white-hot, it streamed through her body turning her legs to jelly. Her mind went blank. Intoxicated with Fiona's perfume, she slid her hands over Fiona's hips. With a gasp, Fiona withdrew from her arms, moving back into the entrance hall. Joanna stepped inside and Fiona closed the door. Joanna reached for her again, but Fiona slipped out of her reach. Raspberry light spilled through the glass pane above the door, staining the polished floor, splashing up the walls. In a flicker of black lightning, Fiona whisked off her top and dropped it on the floor. Breathless, Joanna gazed at her beautiful body.

"Come on," Fiona said in a low, clipped voice. She

turned and walked down the hallway into her bedroom.

Joanna's mind was spinning. Underneath the fire, a chill, biting deep in the pit of her stomach, told her something was terribly wrong.

The half-drawn curtains, creating a muted floral backdrop of pale yellow, reflected the fabric of the quilt cover. Fiona, in a wildflower meadow, sat on the side of the bed. Her legs apart, she was leaning back on her hands, her hair cascading down her back. Her expression was composed, but her eyes blazed. She seemed to seethe with an underlying passion, scorching Joanna with its powerful heat, stinging with its icy restraint.

"Come here," Fiona said coolly.

Barely trusting her legs for support, Joanna went and stood before her. Her heart pounding, Joanna stared at the ceiling, then closed her eyes. She heard Fiona's ragged breath, felt the tugging as Fiona unbuckled her belt, unzipped her jeans and pulled them open. When Fiona gave a little moan, Joanna began to shake, and when she felt the warm wetness of Fiona's tongue on her stomach, she couldn't stand the agony any longer.

Grasping Fiona by the shoulders she pressed her down onto her back. Quickly stepping out of her jeans, she straddled her. On her knees, she leaned down and kissed her, savoring her mouth. Fiona, arching her body against Joanna's, her fingers under Joanna's top raking her back, gave her low sexy growl. Passion swelled at the sound that told Joanna Fiona was hers. Fiona's body, trembling, anticipating her touch, was Joanna's again. Kissing softly, teasing, licking with the tip of her tongue, she moved her mouth to Fiona's throat, shoulders and down to her breasts. Fiona was gasping as Joanna took first one taut nipple then the other into her mouth. Fiona's hands were in her hair as Joanna trailed her kisses down to her hips. Joanna groaned as she traced her tongue along the band of the tiny satiny panties that just barely concealed Fiona's essence. Heady with the heavenly scent of Fiona's desire, she was desperate to taste her, to take her with her mouth. The narrow strip of fabric between her legs was soaking — dark and glistening. Quivering, Joanna ran her tongue over it. Fiona whimpered, her hips writhing. Joanna pulled the fabric aside. "God . . ." she breathed, sinking her tongue inside her.

The fingers in her hair suddenly tightened. Fiona was pulling her head away. "Fuck me," she said bluntly.

The words struck Joanna like a slap in the face. Shocked, she looked at Fiona, but her eyes were closed. She was breathing quickly, her face expressionless. The rock rolled around painfully in Joanna's chest. Why did those words bother her? When other women had said that, it had turned her on. Then, like a tide breaking through a sea wall, tears began to seep from Fiona's closed eyes.

Her throat tightening, her own tears suddenly welling, Joanna kissed her softly. "What's wrong, baby?" she whispered.

Fiona didn't answer. She pushed Joanna's hand between her legs. Gazing into her closed face, watching the tears trickle slowly down her cheeks, Joanna slid her fingers inside Fiona, moving them gently.

"Hard," Fiona hissed.

Her chest aching, the terrible loss dawning on her,

Joanna did what Fiona demanded. She watched Fiona's impassive face until her tears blurred her vision. Stifling the sobs that rose to her throat, she hid her face in Fiona's breasts, listening to Fiona's heart pounding, rocking with Fiona's body.

It was gone, the connection. They weren't as one, this time. Fiona wasn't allowing it. Like every other woman Joanna had ever known, Fiona was taking what she wanted and, no doubt, in turn would give what she wanted. Other women had always playfully pushed, nudged, urged. "Fuck me, Joanna," they often said, and pleased, smiling down into their flushed faces, Joanna would, in her own good time, give them what they wanted.

But Fiona wasn't like them. Last time, she hadn't wanted Joanna's performance; she had purely wanted Joanna. Unlike the others, Fiona had given while she took. Powerful herself, Fiona had made Joanna feel strong even while she lay trembling, like a lamb, in Fiona's arms.

Fiona began to shudder. Joanna gazed longingly into her exquisite face. Her eyes remained closed, her lashes wet with tears. *Look at me.* The chill deep inside Joanna began to creep like icy tentacles through her body, merging with the fire. Fiona arched her hips and groaned, shaking with tremors, her contractions gripping Joanna deeply inside her. *Look at me.* Joanna held Fiona tightly, fighting back her tears.

Fiona's body stilled, and she sighed. She opened her eyes and gazed into Joanna's for a long moment. Drawing Joanna down to her, she kissed her gently with a slow, sensual passion. Powerfully, the fire ignited again. Joanna began to shake. Fiona's hand glided down her back, along her inside thigh, then through her panties to caress between her thighs. Joanna groaned. Then she caught Fiona's hand, stopping her. She shook her head. The lump in her throat straining her voice, she said, "Not like this."

"It's what you want," Fiona said quietly. "And right now, it's what I want too. It's why you're here."

Joanna couldn't understand the game Fiona seemed to be playing. All she knew was that Fiona was hurting her in a way that no one ever had before — at least, not in her adult memory — and she couldn't understand how or why. Biting her lip, she shook her head again.

Fiona stroked Joanna's face, wiping away the traces of her tears. Then she sat up, kissed her cheek, got off the bed and left the room.

Shivering with tension, Joanna ground her balled fist into her chest, trying to ease the ache of that shifting weight. More tears threatened and she blinked them back. Strains of music floated from the living room down the hall. The third movement of Beethoven's *The Tempest*. Maybe Fiona would explain all this, she thought. Maybe something could be saved. She got dressed and wandered down the hallway.

She leaned against the living room doorframe. It was dark outside, and the apricot-colored Austrian blinds were drawn. Polished rosewood arms of tapestry-covered antique chairs shone in the soft lamplight. Fiona, wearing the camisole retrieved from the floor, was standing at the magnificent, mirrored Victorian sideboard, pouring a glass of Cognac. She was holding a cigarette. Catching Joanna's reflection, she turned to her. "Cognac?"

Joanna nodded and slowly crossed the room toward

her. Fiona held her gaze as she handed her the balloon-shaped crystal glass. Joanna tingled as their fingers touched. Then Fiona went to stand in front of the large fireplace and leaned an elbow on the white marble mantelpiece. Gazing across the room, she drew on her cigarette and exhaled slowly. Tearing her eyes away from Fiona's gorgeous legs, Joanna swallowed the Cognac in a single gulp. Her throat burning, she poured herself another. She sat down on the sofa. The music swelled then calmed.

Joanna cleared her throat. "So, what's going on?" Fiona sipped her drink. Except for the music, there was a long silence. Fiona wasn't helping her. "You were acting like you wanted me to stay and like you wanted to kill me at the same time." Fiona drew on her cigarette. "What does it mean?" Obviously set on repeat, *The Tempest* ended, then began again. The piano notes were melancholy, mysterious and fast.

Fiona ran her hand through her hair, then stubbed out her cigarette in an ashtray on the mantelpiece. "Simply that I want you so much, I can't resist you." Warm, melting waves rippled through Joanna's body. Fiona lit another cigarette. "But I was trying to hold on to myself, protect myself. I'm sorry if it seemed like I was so angry that I wanted to kill you." She smiled weakly. "That's the last thing I would want to do." Joanna picked up a maroon velvet cushion and hugged it, absent-mindedly playing with its silky tassels. "I can't afford to give you everything and receive so little in return."

Joanna was baffled. "But last time . . ." she blurted. "It was different last time . . ."

Fiona went to the sideboard and poured herself

another drink. She took a sip and, with her back to Joanna, said softly, "Last time I fell in love with you." Joanna felt faint. "And do you know why?" She turned to Joanna with tears in her eyes. "Because you showed me something. You took me inside yourself. Inside your skin — your beautiful, sexy, sophisticated skin — and you showed me another woman. She was filled with love and warmth and depth and had no fear. She set the very core of me on fire."

Joanna was shaking. For a moment, her mind shimmered with happiness at the thought that Fiona could possibly really love her. But it was quickly dulled by an accompanying sense of responsibility, settling on her chest like a ton weight. Worse than any fear of *allowing* herself to love Fiona was the horrible realization that she didn't know *how* to love her.

Back at the mantelpiece, Fiona gazed at the ceiling, exhaling a silvery misty stream of smoke. "That other woman whispered to me with your mouth, looked at me through your eyes, but the next day she vanished. Each time I've seen you since then, I've glimpsed her and watched her slip away. Even tonight . . . when I didn't want to see —"

The connection, Joanna thought, her heart thudding. That was what Fiona was talking about. That was when the "other woman" presented herself — when Joanna let go, when she lost herself in that other erotic dimension.

The piano notes were quiet but building rapidly. Fiona put her glass down on the mantelpiece. "I think you should go now," she said softly. Joanna looked at her searchingly, hoping to find the words to express her longing and confusion, but none came. Fiona headed out into the hallway. Slowly, Joanna rose and followed her.

The wailing of the crickets and frogs roared through the front door that Fiona was holding open. The night was thick and black. Aching to hold her, to kiss her, Joanna hesitated, then went past her out onto the doorstep. Composed, Fiona held her gaze, the smoke from her cigarette curling languidly, hanging in the still air.

"I'm sorry," Joanna murmured.

"It's not your fault that I love you. It's mine," Fiona said calmly.

It couldn't be the end! It couldn't end like this! Joanna's body grew cold in the balmy night air. "But I can't bear this. I have to see you again."

Fiona gave a slight shrug. "Like this?"

No, Joanna thought. Not like this! But what could she offer that would make any difference? Without another word, she turned, crossed the veranda and headed for her car. Suddenly, she was breathless. The night was smothering her like a heavy black velvet shroud. Disoriented, she gulped deep breaths of the fibrous air. In the light, Fiona stood in silhouette, looking out into the darkness as if trying to see Joanna. Then she closed the door.

For a terrifying moment, Joanna felt herself being swallowed by the darkness — becoming invisible. "Fuck this!" she yelled at the sky. The sound of her own voice was reassuring. "Fuck it!" she yelled again, kicking the car door hard, the sickening crunch of the pristine metal a distracting relief. The gutsy rumble of the engine was comfortingly real. The headlights beamed on the silent, impassive audience of ghostly trees. Taking a deep breath, Joanna turned and headed for home.

CHAPTER FOURTEEN

"Your father's dead," Thelma had said. There were other things she added when she phoned with the news yesterday morning, like when he died — Sunday — the time — around eight p.m. She had mentioned a memorial service for sometime next week, and offered unsure murmurings of condolence. But on Tuesday afternoon as Joanna folded and packed a few last things into a suitcase, it was those words, "Your father's dead," that boomed in her head.

Suddenly, the significance of the fleeting nature of time, and of opportunities taken, created or lost, hit her. Three weeks ago she had seen her father for the first time in ten years and it was as if she were seeing him for the first time in her life. She had never considered his feelings for Isabella, but with his defenses abandoned due to age and illness, he had revealed another side of himself. It had shaken her, and now he was dead. What if she hadn't gone to see him when she did?

Joanna went into the bathroom, gathered up her toiletries and perfume, returned to her bedroom and placed the small bag in the suitcase. Maybe, if she hadn't been so taken aback, she could have found a few words of comfort to offer him. But he probably wouldn't have been interested. Joanna had been the currency he chose to make his wife pay for her sins, and as an adult, her usefulness to him was long gone.

Another stroke killed him, they said, but Joanna imagined it was his bitterness that caused it. A broken heart that he would not allow to heal. His anger had probably fortified him all those years, while unnoticed, it ate away at him slowly, like a fallen log on a forest floor rotting from the inside out.

She and her father had been more alike than was comfortable to admit. Hadn't she, her heart broken like his, closed the door on Isabella just as surely as he had? She would like to think that in his position she would have behaved differently — been more generous — but when she reflected honestly on the hard-line attitude she had adopted for most of her life, she doubted it.

Joanna gazed out of the window at the leaden sky. Heavy rain beat against the glass. A few leaves on the trees had turned golden, taking an early plunge into autumn. It looked like the rain had settled in, a good time to leave Melbourne for a few days. It was cool outside, so she pulled on a cotton-knit V-neck black sweater over a white sleeveless top.

Since Saturday night, she had walked around as if comatose, numb with confusion about her feelings for Fiona. The image of her in the light on the veranda, closing the door, was frozen in her mind, draining the warmth from her body, making her shiver. She couldn't bear to not see Fiona again, but she felt helpless to alter the situation. She realized the importance of the depth of her desire but felt ill-equipped to handle it.

After she finally fell into an exhausted sleep last night, decisions seemed to have been made in her subconscious. She had awoken this morning with a clear head. It was ironic, she thought, when she'd had so little to do with her father, that it had taken his illness to unearth her past, propelling her, albeit reluctantly, in a new direction, and his death to galvanize her to action. She accepted that she had changed. She was open to emotions that she had always denied herself, to the vulnerability that she had never permitted. And it was all focused on her desire for Fiona. Joanna couldn't retrace her steps and return to her old ways. It was too late, and she didn't want to go back. But she couldn't go forward while her past stood before her like a solid stone wall.

She was going to face Isabella.

Not knowing what she would discover, or whether after all the angst it would make much difference, worried her. Maybe taking this final step would rid her of entrenched fears. Maybe it would confirm them.

Or perhaps she was just made that way and could never really love anyone. Perhaps with Fiona it was too late anyway.

Joanna zipped the suitcase closed and took it out to the living room, then redirected her phone and mobile phone to the office. She had gone into the office early and met briefly with her boss, young Harry, to arrange some time off and organized with Peter, the other senior sales consultant, who looked after commercial properties, to take over her clients while she was gone. Then she sat down in Cathie's office with the door closed and filled her in on her father's death, her recent inquiries about her mother and her planned trip. Cathie threw her arms around her and broke down. "You poor baby, no bloody wonder you've been so fucking grumpy lately," she said, sobbing. Between hugs and kisses, she chastised Joanna for not telling her all this before. "And what about Fiona?" she asked anxiously. "What's happening with her?" Joanna had said she didn't know.

Joanna glanced at her watch. It was two o'clock. Opening her roll-top desk, she picked up the note containing Isabella's address, folded it and pushed it into her pocket. She had checked with the phone company and confirmed the name and address were still current. It might have been smarter to phone, make arrangements to meet with her, make sure she was home, but the thought of calling her, of saying what she had to say without seeing her face, filled Joanna with dread. She preferred to take her chances, look around, size up the situation. If a meeting didn't eventuate this time around, a few days in the tropics getting her head together wouldn't hurt anyway.

Grabbing her suitcase, she headed downstairs to the car. Her flight to Cairns was leaving in forty minutes.

At around six o'clock that evening, Joanna stepped out of the cool air conditioning of the Cairns airport terminal and gasped in the heat. The wet season was virtually over, but the air was still excessively steamy. She pulled off her sweater and tied it around her waist, regretting that she hadn't changed out of the leather pants she wore into the office that morning. They'd be welded to her legs by the time she got to the hotel, she thought. She headed across to the car park to pick up her hire car. Tossing her suitcase into the back of the four-wheel-drive Subaru, she headed for the city.

Last time she had visited Cairns, four years ago, it was with Rebecca — a girl Joanna had met in a bar one night. A cute, blue-eyed blond, Rebecca was an exchange student from Canada, keen to travel. They spent a pleasant week together before Rebecca moved on to her next destination, and Joanna had returned home. Her hair had been short and spiky, Joanna remembered, but she couldn't clearly recall Rebecca's face.

With a jolt, Joanna realized that Isabella would have lived here then. You could have passed her on the street, she thought, or on the beach. May have been within a few feet of her. Isabella would have changed, but Joanna felt sure she would still have recognized her. It was the wrong time then, she decided, and wasn't meant to be.

A steamy heat haze hung over the city as she approached it coming down from the hills. It was eighty-five degrees, the humidity ninety percent, according to the weather report on the radio. Set in a basin with bush-covered hills on three sides, Cairns squatted beside the ocean. Driving along the beachfront highway lined with date palms and umbrella trees, Joanna bypassed the city. She was heading for Palm Cove, an area filled with luxury homes, hotels and a large resort, half an hour out of the city. She had booked a room in a hotel that was right on the beach.

Soon, the tropical vegetation took over. She reduced her speed and turned off the radio. A mixed chorus of birds reverberated from the rain forest, the fecund scent of growth and decay filling the air. Tall trees of enormous girth dominated, but saplings jostling for the light rose from the thick mosses and ferns covering the forest floor. In the green steam, she glimpsed flashes of red, pink and yellow wild orchids threading their way through the trees. Closer to the road, they draped over tall guinea grass, their beauty concealing the thick, spiky blades of grass that were sharp enough to slice off inquisitive fingers. She crossed over a few estuaries filled with mangroves, then suddenly, the ocean appeared on her right — clear, sparkling turquoise edged with pure-white talcum-powder sand and stands of coconut palms.

What kind of life did Isabella have in this place? Joanna's memories of her were as limited as a child's world — Isabella kneeling beside the back garden beds, weeding and planting; tucking Joanna into bed at night; or bustling about in the kitchen, cooking something at the stove. Knots gripped Joanna's stomach at the thought of confronting her. She would have to figure out her approach, her line of questioning, and ensure that she appeared in control.

The sun was beginning to set by the time she arrived at the hotel. Once in her room, she quickly peeled off her leather pants, then opened the double bifold doors leading onto the veranda. She grabbed a bottle of light beer from the fridge and sank down onto a cane chair outside. The hotel garden spread out before her, lush and green, dotted with red-flowering Poinciana trees. The lawn ended where the sand began, and the sea extended into the distance. A gentle sea breeze and the sound of the lapping waves were comforting.

If things weren't so complicated, Fiona could be with her, she thought. A gentle warmth moved through her like melted honey as she remembered the last time they were together. Joanna had taken for granted that their desire for each other guaranteed the dimension of ecstasy they had shared before. But Fiona had shown her that it had to be given and could easily be taken away.

She sighed and sipped her beer. It was almost dark. A restaurant on the beach, surrounded by timber decking and yellow umbrellas, suddenly lit up, like a fairyland, with tiny lights. It looked like a good place to try for dinner, she thought. She gulped down the rest of her beer, then went inside to shower and change.

There were few other people in the restaurant, and Joanna chose a table where she could gaze out at the sea. Moonlight glimmered on the waves as they heaved onto the beach, then collapsed with a sigh into a carpet of white froth. The tranquillity of the place was beginning to penetrate. Sipping her ice-cold Chablis, she watched the seagulls gathering around the restaurant's deck. Obviously used to being fed by diners, they were patrolling up and down, chests puffed out, occasionally pecking at their competition. Some threw tantrums, squawking, flapping their wings and stamping their feet.

The waiter brought her dinner of mudcrab simmered in coconut milk, mild spices and lime leaves, cooked in a clay pot with transparent noodles. From time to time, she glanced down the beach in the direction of Isabella's house. She knew it was a little farther down the highway, past Palm Cove. Tomorrow, after a swim, maybe after lunch, she might take a drive down there, she thought. Might just look at her house. Like the clothes people wore, their houses could tell you things about them, even from the outside. She tried to settle her nerves by reminding herself that when she knocked on that door, she would have the advantage. Isabella would have had no time to prepare herself — put on a good act, get her story ready. Hopefully, if she was still with the partner Thelma had mentioned, he wouldn't be there when Joanna arrived. She would feel more confident if she and Isabella were alone.

With a sigh, she turned her attention back to the view. That was a problem to deal with tomorrow.

On Wednesday morning, Fiona sat at her desk in her consulting room and gazed out of the window at the pouring rain. In a ten-minute break between patients, she finally gave herself up to the tears she had been fighting back. Sue had come in earlier and told her about the death of Joanna's father and her visit to Cairns to see her mother. Why, Fiona wondered, when every other aspect of life had always seemed easy to negotiate, did she always screw up where love was concerned? Her decision to stay away from Joanna was undoubtedly sensible. But being wise didn't feel very good.

A split in the rain gutter above her window had torn open under the weight of the rain, and it gushed in a torrent that drummed on the black asphalt. Knowing how hard it would be for Joanna to see her mother, how exposed she would feel, made Fiona worry terribly for her. She had long suspected that Joanna's distrust of intimacy stemmed from her unresolved past, but knowing the reason did not alter the reality. Joanna would not allow herself to accept Fiona's love, much less give any in return. Joanna was an intelligent woman. She made her choices and lived her life the way she wanted. Fiona wiped away her tears and sipped her lukewarm coffee.

But what made Joanna's attitude so hard to accept was that Fiona felt instinctively that Joanna loved her too. She thought she had seen it in Joanna, the first night they were together. Then, the other day, Joanna's behavior seemed to confirm that Fiona's instincts had been right. Fiona's throat tightened, picturing Joanna's face as she was leaving. Tears had glimmered in her eyes, her expression perplexed as she gazed for an agonizing moment at Fiona. Then she turned away and had been quickly swallowed up by the darkness. Inside, Fiona poured another drink, lit another cigarette. Turning up the CD player, she hoped *The Tempest* would transcend the storm inside her and swamp the crushing image of Joanna's car driving away. In emotionally withdrawing from Joanna, she had thought she could conquer the love she felt, protect herself from being hurt any further, but it hadn't worked.

Fiona ran her hands through her hair and sighed. The constant sound of the rain splattering on the ground was irritating. The weather was probably fine in Cairns. She hoped Joanna's meeting with Isabella would go well. Joanna would be feeling shaky about her father's death, despite their bad relationship, and a poor reception from her mother would be too much.

During the last few days, thinking about Saturday night, Fiona's perspective had shifted. Being forced, under the circumstances, to tell Joanna that she loved her made further resistance seem pointless. She had come to realize that she would feel happier allowing herself to love Joanna, accepting for a brief time whatever Joanna was prepared to give. It couldn't be much worse than the pain she felt already. She had been determined from the start not to allow Joanna to hurt and make a fool of her as Diane had done. But she had overlooked something. With both women, Fiona had concerned herself more with what she guessed was in *their* hearts and hadn't listened to her own. With Diane, Fiona had stayed, given Diane more chances because her head told her she should try harder, although her heart told her to leave. And she had never in her life wanted a woman as much as she wanted Joanna, but she had once again allowed reason to overrule her feelings. Her heart told her to stay. Her instincts rarely let her down, if only she would listen to them. She loved Joanna absolutely, whether

Joanna loved her or not. To try to destroy that was to destroy a part of herself.

Fiona took a deep breath. Her ears ringing with the monotonous rain, she went to the washbasin and wiped her face with a moist paper towel. She had left a message for Joanna to call her when she returned. Hopefully, Joanna would still want to see her. Fiona touched up her lipstick and prepared herself for her next patient.

CHAPTER FIFTEEN

Joanna drove slowly along Ocean Grove, past exquisite homes half-hidden by luxuriant tropical gardens. Hot pink bougainvillea festooned front fences of brush or picket. Built on the side of a hill, standing tall on stilts — typical of Queensland dwellings — the houses all had a spectacular view of the glittering ocean spread out before them, so breathtakingly blue it hurt the eyes.

Her heart pounding, Joanna rolled the car to a stop opposite number ten and stared. So this was Isabella's house. It was a classic Queenslander, but in the grand style. All white, its deep verandas were enclosed with fixed shutters, the broad louvers half-closed like sleepy eyes against the hot late-afternoon sun. Projecting out from the center of the house, a gracious wooden portico, decorated in Federation-style fretwork with carved posts, covered the entrance porch. Two flights of steps set parallel with the house led to either side of the entrance. Both ends of the house were dominated by beautiful, open-sided octagonal rotundas with domed roofs. They were also trimmed with fretwork, but scalloped, accentuating the divisions of the eight sides.

"Christ..." Joanna breathed. She loved this style of architecture, which could only be found in the tropics, and it was one of the best examples she had ever seen. Set on a large allotment, thick green lawns were edged by garden beds overflowing with ferns of all kinds, frangipani trees sporting waxy, creamy-lemon blooms, and tall droopy northern bangalow palms. The steamy air throbbed with the hum of insects. Occasionally Joanna's skin was touched by a cool, salty breath from the sea. The house had the solid, timeless air of a place where nobody rushed about. Around this time of day, when the sun was starting to think about changing into something pretty and going out for the night, you would wander onto one of the rotundas, Joanna thought. You would gaze at the Pacific ocean while you sipped a long gin and tonic, with a dash of bitters, of course, and wonder lazily what you might have for dinner ... later ... when you could be bothered.

With a pang, Joanna suddenly imagined being in a house like this, in a place like this with Fiona. Joanna would spread something comfortable on the floor of the rotunda and make love to her under the melon-colored sky, and continue making love to her in the balmy, perfumed air while darkness dripped all around them, not caring that the moon was watching. Joanna turned and gazed at the ocean. She blinked away tears that had sprung to her eyes, her longing churning in her body in rhythm with the waves below, lapping the beach.

God. Unless she could find a way to make Fiona satisfied, she would have to get used to life without her. She had to get a grip on this elusive love or Fiona wouldn't want her again. It was difficult to imagine, though, how a confrontation with the woman who had left her was going to help.

It was six-thirty. At the end of the long driveway lined with macadamia and mango trees, stood a white Range Rover. Joanna swallowed. Somebody was home. What was she going to do? Stare at the lovely house until it was dark? Go back to the hotel and think about it some more, tossing back Barbados rum until she *couldn't* think anymore? Or have some bloody guts and go and knock on the front door?

Joanna got out of the car. The ground had that squishy feel to it again as she crossed the road, opened the gate and made her way up the stone steps through the garden. She jumped as a lime green parrot squealed and shot out of a shrub in front of her. Somewhere, a dog started barking. Her pulse pounded in her ears as she climbed the wooden front steps to the porch.

The screen door offered a dim, hazy view to the veranda, which looked to be at least twelve feet deep. Across the polished hardwood floor, a double-width doorway led into the house. Near the door, a huge terra cotta urn was bulging with tall yellow lilies. Farther down the veranda, rattan chairs nestled around a cane coffee table. On it sat two tall glasses, empty, as far as she could tell, and an ashtray which looked half-full. Soft music was playing — Sarah Vaughan. A woman laughed in the background. A rich, throaty, happy laugh. Slowly, like icy fingertips beneath her black silk tank top, sweat trickled down between her breasts. Goosebumps rose on her skin as she reached out and pressed the doorbell.

Footsteps approached. A woman strolled through the double doorway toward the screen door. Wearing a white T-shirt — the sleeves rolled up to expose her tanned muscled arms and shoulders — and faded jeans that fitted snugly to her lean hips, the woman had short dark-blond hair, touched with gray. Joanna guessed she was in her fifties. Her smile was bright and friendly until she got right up to the screen door and saw Joanna. Then her eyes seemed to widen; the smile began to fade. She was clearly a dyke, and her expression suggested that she had picked Joanna for a dyke too. You don't get any prizes for that, Joanna thought. And although in conservative Far North Queensland the chances of having an unknown dyke suddenly knock on your door would be slim, the woman's shocked expression seemed a bit excessive.

Joanna wasn't sure if she was disappointed or relieved. But it seemed there had been a mistake. The woman could be a friend of Isabella's, but more likely it was simply the wrong address.

Joanna cleared her throat. "I'm sorry to disturb you. I think I've come to the wrong place." The woman took a ragged breath and, almost imperceptibly, shook her head. Joanna shivered slightly.

"No, you haven't," the woman said, her voice low and husky.

"Darling?" another woman called from inside the house. "Who is it?"

Joanna began to tremble. From somewhere deep in her mind, she sensed that she knew that voice. Or was it her imagination? Footsteps came closer. Then she appeared in the light of the doorway and paused. Even from there in the gloom, Joanna knew her. She knew her stance, the tilt of her head. Slowly, she approached the door and her face came into focus. Isabella. Joanna felt faint. The blond woman looked disoriented, almost scared, as she grabbed Isabella's hand. But Isabella's beautiful, deep brown eyes never left Joanna's face. Suddenly, they brimmed full of tears.

"Joanna . . ." she breathed.

The world around Joanna started to spin. Blue, green, yellow, dark and light all merged, losing definition. Somehow, her legs carried her inside as the blond woman opened the door and took her arm. "I'm Chris," she murmured. "You mightn't remember me." Only half-listening, Joanna had no idea what she meant.

Isabella, the same height as Joanna, continued to stare at her with a mixture of wonder, pleasure and disbelief. Tears spilled down her cheeks and Joanna felt her own tears stinging her eyes. Then Isabella smiled. A smile so warm and gentle that Joanna felt the rock tilt in her chest. "I knew you'd come one day," she said quietly.

Chris ran a nervous hand through her hair and cleared her throat. "Well, come on inside and sit down."

As they crossed the veranda into the living room, Joanna saw, from the corner of her eye, Chris stroke Isabella's hair and quickly kiss her cheek. Her mother was a dyke! For Christ's sake! She could hardly take it all in.

The living room was large. The diffused light, tinted pink by the setting sun, was beginning to seep through the veranda louvers. Fine pieces of cane furniture mingled attractively with white calico-covered sofas that were, Joanna discovered, deep and comfortable. Through a doorway across the room, she glimpsed timber cupboards and the corner of a granite countertop. At the far end of the room, another double-width doorway revealed a dining room with glass French doors leading to a back garden shady with palm trees. The high ceiling supported white, wooden fans that turned slowly.

"What would you like to drink?" Chris asked with a smile. She was looking calmer and much more in control than Joanna felt.

"You wouldn't have a Barbados, would you? With ice?"

"Sure do." Isabella had sat down in a cane armchair opposite Joanna. Chris touched her shoulder. "A scotch, darling?" Isabella nodded. Chris left them and went into the kitchen.

Feeling shell-shocked, Joanna's mind wouldn't clear. Thelma had said she presumed her mother was still with Chris. Pity she hadn't mentioned that Chris was a woman! But how long had they been together? It had to be at least ten years, but these two women in their mid-fifties acted like young lovers. Joanna could feel Isabella's scrutiny and was afraid to raise her eyes and look at her. She focused on the tiled floor. The tiles were large, laid diagonally, and were a pale, milky, matte terra cotta. They were a perfect complement to the indoor-outdoor style of the house. Joanna cleared her throat. "French terra cotta?"

"Yes. I understand you're interested in architecture and interiors." Joanna looked up at her, surprised. Isabella smiled. "Thelma told me years ago. Are you still in real estate?"

"Umm . . . yeah."

"She told me you were very successful."

Joanna shrugged. She suddenly felt very young and awkward. It was strange having her mother know things about her. "Oh, okay, I guess."

Joanna felt a wave of relief when Chris returned with their drinks. She was pleased that the glass Chris handed her was large and full. Hoping it would soon calm her nerves, she gulped down half of it at once. Chris and Isabella both lit cigarettes and sipped their scotch.

Isabella was still remarkably beautiful. Her dark hair was shoulder length, with a soft curl. Her olive skin was tanned; there were few lines on her face. Long, dark lashes framed eyes still wet with tears. Her full, gentle mouth was glossy with light-pink lipstick. Dressed in fitted, white cotton pants with a long matching sleeveless top, she was trim and fit.

"You look well, Joanna," she said. "And you've become a beautiful woman." Isabella drew on her cigarette. "We saw that in the last photo we got from Thelma, about ten years ago. But we weren't surprised." She smiled. "You were an extremely cute little girl." With a start, Joanna realized they had been staring at each other. Embarrassed, she glanced away. "Thank you for coming," Isabella added.

"Um . . . I'm sorry I just barged in. I've given you both a shock." Joanna took another gulp of her drink. "I, you know . . . couldn't do it any other way," she mumbled.

"There was no other way," Isabella said softly. Turning to Chris, she added with a smile, "See, darling? I knew our daughter would come. I just knew it."

Joanna's heart began to pound with anxiety and confusion. Looking shaken, Chris rubbed the back of her neck and glanced at Joanna before she put her hand over her eyes. Joanna caught the glint of her tears.

"What do you mean," Joanna asked Isabella breathlessly, "*our* daughter?"

Isabella exhaled a long stream of smoke. "Chris and I were in a relationship before I married Richard, and after a short break, we resumed it. She was there when you were born, and we always considered you to be our daughter."

Joanna's head swam. Her mother had *always* been a dyke? Then comprehension began to flood her brain. A sudden heat prickled her skin, and her heart raced. "Fucking Christ!" she sputtered. "He found out! That's why he got rid of you . . . kept you away forever."

Isabella nodded. Chris quickly wiped at her eyes and guzzled her scotch.

"He's dead, by the way," Joanna blurted. "Last Sunday. A stroke." Isabella seemed to shudder slightly. Chris took a deep breath and nodded slowly, her expression impassive.

Isabella cleared her throat. "Are you feeling okay about that?"

Joanna gave a little shrug. "I never got on with him, so I can't say I'll miss him much. It was just a bit of a shock, that's all. The end of lots of things, you know." She gulped down the rest of her drink. Strangely, the alcohol was helping her to see more clearly. She shook her head. "Of all the reasons I imagined for his throwing you out, I never thought of that. *I'm* a bloody dyke! Why wouldn't I think of that!"

Chris reached over from her chair and touched Joanna's arm. "Unless they'd been given any hints, no one would ever guess their estranged mother was a dyke. Don't blame yourself."

"When I sent you that letter sixteen years ago, I had no idea that you were a lesbian too," Isabella said. "If Thelma knew, she didn't mention it to me. The last thing I was going to confess in a letter to a presumably straight, eighteen-year-old daughter was that I was a lesbian. Thelma obviously chose not to tell you about me, either."

Joanna slowly shook her head. Absent-mindedly, she twisted her ear stud around. "I wish she had."

"I'll get some more drinks," Chris said, gathering up the glasses and heading to the kitchen.

"Thelma knew I wanted to explain everything to you when you were grown up. It wasn't something she could explain when you were little, and by the time you were old enough to be told, you refused to hear a word about me, according to Thelma. She's a wonderful woman, very open-minded, but we were never close. There wasn't the opportunity. You were all we had in common. She never even met Chris. She only knew that a lesbian relationship had caused the whole catastrophe, and I'm sure that rather than holding out on you, she would have been anxious for you to get the full story directly from me." Isabella lit another cigarette. "Chris and I met at Melbourne University when I was eighteen; she was twenty-one. You know my parents were Spanish?" Joanna nodded. "They were both killed in a boating accident when you were a baby. I used to show you pictures of them. Anyway, I was their only child, and all their hopes for a prosperous future in Australia were pinned on me. I was studying to become an architect, and they were very proud."

Chris returned with the drinks and sat down. "Bella was the most beautiful girl I'd ever seen. I was gone the first moment I set eyes on her. I was doing an arts degree, to become a teacher. We met at a women's social group on campus in nineteen sixty-two."

Isabella chuckled. "I was a wide-eyed virgin with a very strict Catholic background. I'd never even thought about boys sexually, and there I was, at the first meeting I'd attended, mesmerized by this gorgeous, brazen woman smiling at me." She gave Chris an adoring glance. "Very sexy in tight black pants, black shirt open at the neck with a loosely knotted white tie, and a long, broad-shouldered, tweed coat."

Chris laughed. "I loved that coat. Pity it wore out."

Scrutinizing Chris, still a very good-looking woman, Joanna could easily picture her in the outfit. Joanna admired her style.

Isabella ran her hand through her hair and sighed. "But some stupid young man who was interested in me and wouldn't take no for an answer was suspicious of our relationship and kept an eye on us. He caught us kissing behind the lockers one day and reported it to my parents."

Frowning, Chris rubbed the back of her neck. "I told Bella to not worry about it. I had big plans of us running away together. We could go to university in another state, I said." She looked across at Isabella with soft, warm eyes. "But you were scared out of your wits, weren't you, baby?"

Isabella nodded. "My parents went mad. I couldn't imagine how two women could realistically make a life together, and I allowed myself to be convinced that I was committing a terrible sin, you know the sort of crap." She gave a helpless shrug. "I was too young and hadn't developed any sense of my own power."

Joanna shook her head in disbelief. She couldn't imagine being bothered by the incident. In the same position at that age, she would have laughed in the boy's face and told her father to mind his own damn business. But she was forced to admit that 1962 was a very different time. Plus, she hadn't been brought up stuffed full of Catholic shame.

"I was nineteen by then. I told myself that my love for Chris was an aberration, and to prove it I ran into the arms of the first man who showed a keen interest. Richard Kingston. He was a lecturer in engineering at the university and a successful engineer working for a big international company. He was around twenty years older than me and seemed stable and kind. If he'd ever heard the rumors about Chris and me, he obviously disbelieved them." Ice cubes rattled as she finished her drink and put the glass on the table. "Almost straightaway I got pregnant and we got married." She gave a rueful smile. "Even though he wasn't Catholic, my parents were very relieved."

"But I wouldn't stay away from her," Chris said with a grin. "Soon we were lovers again, and it was made fairly easy by the fact that Richard was in Indonesia for weeks, even months at a time." Her smile faded as she gazed off across the room, drawing on her cigarette. "We knew we couldn't go on like that forever."

"We didn't really know what to do," Isabella said. "Simply running away wasn't an option. I didn't want you to lose contact with your father. And although it didn't take Richard long to realize that I didn't love him and the marriage had been a mistake, I knew he still loved me. But I was terrified of losing you if I was completely honest and came out to him about Chris." She paused and sipped her drink.

"Anyway," Chris continued, "by the time you were getting close to five, we knew we had to make a decision and turn our dreams of the three of us living together into concrete plans. Then we got discovered again, early one Sunday morning, by Beatrice. Richard was away and I'd been staying for a week. We didn't know she had a key to the house." She stared at the floor. "Couldn't have been worse. We were sitting up in bed drinking coffee, you were tucked in between us drinking milk out of one of those funny little cups with a spout thing. I was reading you a story, and Bella was reading the paper."

Tears suddenly filled Joanna's eyes. Everything she had assumed for thirty years couldn't have been more wrong. Unable to control her tears, she sank her face into her hands, giving herself up to them like she hadn't since she was a child. All that she had suffered, that Isabella and apparently Chris too had suffered, was simply because of Isabella's love for another woman. A love that had already lasted thirty-six years and was still, clearly, powerful and romantic. And Joanna had believed that romantic love couldn't last.

The wasted time, the unnecessary heartache, the horror of feeling unwanted, lost and terrified was all because of a love that her father would not allow. That the whole world, back then, would not allow. The weight in Joanna's chest, heavy as lead, swelled fit to burst. She could have ended the pain for them all, sixteen years earlier, if she hadn't been so afraid and so angry and so stubborn like her father.

Bent over, her head almost on her knees, not caring about the shame, she cried silently and thought her heart would break all over again.

Arms wrapped around her and held her tightly. A cool soft hand stroked her cheek. "But it's all over now," Isabella whispered. Fingers gently smoothed back her hair. "You've still got a bit of curl, I see." She kissed Joanna's cheek.

Some part of Joanna seemed to step out of her body and watch from a distance. She saw a small child being soothed by her mother, and every touch, every kiss was dissipating the years. The stone wall was shaking, the rock in her chest shrinking. There was the sense of losing herself, relinquishing control like she had with Fiona. But the hair-raising, hovering shadow of fear that had always tracked her, kept her in check, was dwindling in her mind's eye.

With a sigh, Joanna raised her head. Chris quickly passed her a handful of tissues. Joanna dried her eyes and blew her nose. "I never do this," she mumbled self-consciously.

Isabella, sitting beside her on the sofa, smiled and

stroked Joanna's face. "I've been doing it for years. I'm happy to say I can stop now." She stood up. Her voice sounded lighter, her gestures more relaxed. "I think it's close to dinnertime. You'll stay for dinner, won't you?"

Joanna nodded. "Thanks," she murmured.

"Why don't you show Joanna around, darling," Isabella said, "while I find something to cook?"

"Great." Chris bounced to her feet. Smiling, she seemed relieved that the painful moment had come to an end. "Come on, Jo, let's open up the veranda and set up for dinner in the rotunda."

Taking a deep breath, still feeling disoriented, Joanna got up and followed Chris while Isabella went into the kitchen.

Night was beginning to fall, and the diffused pink haze had deepened. The full sunset was bleeding through the down-turned louvers, forming crimson pools on the floor. Chris opened all the louvers to a full horizontal position, and her face glowed in the rich light. Ruby stripes swept across the veranda and into the living room. The heady, sweet perfume of the frangipanis pervaded the air. And, as if waiting to be allowed in, the breeze rushed through from the blushing-pink sapphire sea.

"This is a stunning house," Joanna said.

"Bella designed it. She continued with her studies while you were little and eventually qualified as an architect. We run a business together, working from here. She designs homes and renovations and I take care of the clients and accounts."

So maybe it was from Isabella that she got her own love for architecture, Joanna thought.

A contented half-smile on her face, apparently lost

in her thoughts, Chris gazed at the ocean. There was a serenity in her demeanor that Joanna admired. She was clearly a happy woman. Joanna wondered how that could be after all the troubles she had shared with Isabella. Joanna wanted to know her secret.

"Why did you stay with Isabella after she married my father? Why didn't you give up on her — find someone else?"

Chris chuckled softly. Her green eyes were gentle. "That never occurred to me. Isabella was all I wanted. I would've waited forever, gone anywhere with her, done anything for her." She shrugged. "I had no choice. No one else would be able to make me feel the way she does."

With a sharp ache, Joanna thought of Fiona. Desperately, she wished Fiona was with her. Everything else was tumbling into place but at the same time, the empty space inside her where Fiona belonged was becoming more clearly, painfully defined.

Joanna ran her fingers along one of the glossy white louvers. Smooth, satiny, it had been painted perfectly. "What is that feeling?" she asked quietly. "How does she make you feel?"

Chris looked thoughtful as she stared at the water. "God. Everything, I suppose . . ."

Joanna's heart beat a little faster, tears pricked at her eyes. "Complete?" she asked hopefully. Her throat constricted, her voice caught. "Is it complete?"

With a smile, Chris turned to her. "Yeah. That's it exactly. Complete. I wouldn't be whole without her." Joanna could feel the tears pricking her eyes. Chris's expression became concerned. "You must have a special girl in your life, or you wouldn't know about that."

Joanna blinked away her tears, toying with the louvers' shutter mechanism. "I used to think I knew everything. But I really don't know anything at all."

Chris put an arm around her shoulders. It felt completely natural and comfortable, and Joanna was moved by her kindness. "You're Bella's child," Chris said, "so you were born knowing things. You're deep and complicated like her. You were like that even when you were little." She smiled. "You know things or you wouldn't be here. You having trouble with this girl?"

Joanna swallowed the lump in her throat. "The only trouble is me. She, Fiona . . . well, she's amazing. I've never known anyone like her. I can hardly believe the way she makes me feel. She says she loves me but I've been, you know, hanging back, scared to go too far, scared that I'll let her down. I've never loved anyone before. But I can't stand being without her."

Chris gave her shoulders a little squeeze. "You had to clean up the mess behind you first, that's all. It's not going to be right if you're all in bits, feeling confused. You want to give her the best you can be. Then her love makes you even better and stronger, frees you up. Know what I mean?"

Joanna nodded. "Think so," she murmured.

Chris raised her head, sniffing the air. She beamed a smile. "We're in for a big treat. Bella's cooking paella — a recipe she learned from her mother. It's the best you've ever tasted." She headed toward the living room. "Let's find a couple of bottles of really good red to go with it."

"Chris." She stopped and looked questioningly at Joanna. Joanna took a deep breath. "I remember your reading me stories, and I remember the games we played." She paused, visualizing a much younger Chris, laughing, tumbling on the back lawn with her, pushing her on the swing, picking her up when she fell over and hugging her. Joanna swallowed the lump in her throat. "I remember you," she whispered.

Tears suddenly welled in Chris's eyes. She bit her lip. "Course you do." Her words were choked.

They returned to the living room, selected some wine, then piled up trays with glasses, china and cutlery and took them out onto the south rotunda to set the teak table for dinner.

A short time later Chris and Joanna were seated at the table waiting for Isabella. Chris opened a bottle of Shiraz and poured it into fine crystal glasses. Draped with a starched white damask cloth, the round table was the perfect shape to offset the octagonal half-walls of the rotunda and to take advantage of the panoramic view. The moon had risen; stars flecked the sky. The ocean was disappearing from sight, but the sound of it sighing contentedly was peaceful. Nina Simone crooned quietly from inside the house. A light set into the ceiling cast a soft warm glow. The atmosphere was enchanting. Joanna wanted to tell Fiona all about it, wanted her to meet these two wonderful women, wanted them to meet her.

Isabella arrived carrying a huge shallow cast iron pan, which she placed in the center of the table. It looked fabulous, and the spicy aroma from the dish of golden rice, chicken and seafood was mouth-watering. Isabella spooned a generous quantity onto Joanna's plate and offered her warm crusty bread.

Joanna sipped her wine. "What a great place to live. What made you come here?"

"Well," Chris said, "we had to get away from

Melbourne after the divorce. The court case was unbelievable. They had both of us up on the stand and portrayed us as depraved perverts. Your father had no trouble convincing the court that your lesbian mother should be kept away from you." Absent-mindedly, she scratched at the label on the wine bottle. "Afterwards, every night after work, I'd go to find Bella. She'd be perched somewhere in sight of your house or your kindergarten, watching for you, and after a while I couldn't stand it any more. So I took her away to Sydney. We had friends there, and soon Bella got a job, started to use her talents."

Joanna was watching Isabella buttering some bread. She looked up at Joanna and smiled. "We had a good life there, and I was happy to be not too far away from you. I kept in touch with Thelma and she told me everything she could about you, sent me photos and things. I was so grateful that you had someone looking after you who really loved you."

Joanna nodded. "I loved her, too."

"You see, I couldn't make personal contact with you. It would have meant making you keep very big secrets, tell lies, and I wasn't prepared to do that. Apart from the issue of corrupting you, there was the risk. If my contact with you had been discovered, Thelma, involved in the conspiracy, would have been denied access to you too, and I might have been imprisoned. It was better, as painful as it was, to accept the best option. I had to content myself with the knowledge that Thelma and Ted were watching over you. I'm sure your father loved you the best he could, but he wasn't one to show affection and he didn't have much time to spend with you."

Joanna suddenly pictured her father — old, crushed

and sad. It occurred to her that in the end he'd hurt himself more than anyone else. She was glad she'd seen him one last time, and that her newfound pity for him had replaced the burden of her old anger.

"And then," Chris said, "by the time you were about twenty-four, it looked pretty certain that you weren't going to contact Bella. It felt like time for another move."

Joanna, ashamed, stared down at her plate. "I'm sorry."

Isabella reached over and stroked her arm. Gently she said, "Don't be sorry. Not ever. You were the innocent one who should never have been put through all that. You have no apologies to make to me. I had great hopes that you would want to see me, but I completely understood why you didn't. You'd made your own life without me, created an identity without any influence from me. You were strong and I was proud of you. But there's a time for everything. You came when you were ready, and I'm proud of you now."

A sob caught in Joanna's throat, and with one hand she covered her eyes, hiding a fresh bout of tears.

"There's no need for any more sadness, sweetheart," Isabella said. Her voice was as soft as the tropical dew settling on the perfumed flowers in the garden below. "Although you're a full-grown woman, you're my baby still, and believe me, you were worth every minute of it."

Behind her hand, Joanna's tears flowed, but the sadness was a release of pent-up sorrow packed down inside her. The weight in her chest that had already begun to dissolve suddenly vaporized. She took a deep breath and her whole body felt as light as air. Aware once more of the moaning sea, the scent of salt and the warm air on her skin, she gazed into the star-filled sky. Suddenly, life held exciting promise that she had never imagined before. It brimmed with opportunities for happiness.

She wiped away her tears, then looked at Isabella and Chris. "You're right. There's no need for any more sadness. And I want to tell you something that I've just woken up to." Joanna grinned. "For the first time — and I know, as my friend Cathie would say, it's the *real* thing — I'm in love. With Fiona. The most gorgeous woman in the world."

Isabella and Chris smiled, looking delighted. "She's a very lucky girl," Isabella said.

"After dinner, I'm going to call her and tell her. I just hope, after I've messed her around so much, she'll still want me."

Chris chuckled. "Oh, she will. No doubt about it." She stood and topped up their glasses. "Relax, enjoy your dinner and spend the night in our guest room. There's a phone in there, and you can sweet-talk her until dawn."

Suddenly ravenous, Joanna helped herself to more paella. Excited, looking forward to speaking with Fiona later, Joanna settled in and enjoyed the rest of the evening while, with stories galore, they began to fill in the missing years.

It was one o'clock when Isabella showed her to her room. A large, airy room with French doors open to the veranda, it had a double bed with a white mosquito net bunched above it, to be dropped down if needed. The decor was white and cream. A door led to a private bathroom. "You'll find a toothbrush and anything else you need in there," Isabella said.

They looked at each other for a long moment, then Joanna hugged her. Isabella hugged her tightly in return. "Goodnight, sweetheart," she whispered. Then she left.

The cool night air wafted through the room. Outside, the flying foxes, squeaking, were busy at work in the mango trees. Joanna flopped down onto the bed. She gazed at the phone on the bedside table. It would be selfish to phone and wake her up, she thought. Fiona had to go to work tomorrow. But if Fiona felt the way Joanna did, she wouldn't mind being woken to be told that Joanna loved her. Anyway, Joanna couldn't wait. Pulling the phone down onto the bed beside her, she dialed the number.

It felt like an interminable time before she answered.

"Hello?" Fiona's voice was soft and sleepy. Joanna quivered as she remembered Fiona's sweet, sexy scent that one time when they had woken up together.

The lump in her throat made it difficult for Joanna to speak. "It's me — Joanna. I'm sorry I woke you."

"Joanna?" Fiona took a deep breath. "Are you all right? I've been terribly worried about you. I heard about your father and that you'd gone to find your mother and . . . and . . ." Her voice broke. Tears sprang to Joanna's eyes. Fiona was so soft-hearted, so easily upset by other people's problems. "I've been worried that I was too hard on you the other night. You had enough to deal with —"

"Baby," Joanna interrupted gently. "Everything's wonderful. Everything's changed. I've got so much to tell you, but the only thing I need to tell you right now is that I love you."

Joanna heard Fiona's sharp intake of breath. Her heart pounded. Fiona hadn't changed her mind, had she? "I couldn't deal with my feelings before I came up here. There were parts missing in me, but not anymore." Fiona was weeping softly, and Joanna desperately wished she could hold her. "I'm crazy in love with you, baby, and you've just got to still love me too."

"Oh, God, darling. I love you desperately. All I want is to be able to be with you — all the time."

The words penetrated deep into the heart of her, and Joanna's body tingled. "I'll come home tomorrow," she said breathlessly.

"I've got a better idea. I'll come to you," Fiona said, her smoky voice warm and seductive. "I know my schedule for Friday is light, and I'm sure Marie will fill in for me. Why don't I fly up there tomorrow afternoon? I'll leave early, shift appointments around. It's a special occasion, after all. We can spend a long weekend together while you tell me everything that's happened. We can make plans." Joanna heard a smile in her voice. "And other things."

A whole weekend making love with her! God! A whole lifetime of it! "Sounds like heaven," Joanna said.

Fiona agreed to call her the next day with her flight details, and after many goodnights, both of them reluctant to let go, Joanna eventually hung up. She lay back on the soft pillows and closed her eyes, imagining Fiona in her arms again. She felt the empty space inside her fill with a vibrant warmth. The connection with Fiona had returned. She was complete.

CHAPTER SIXTEEN

After the most peaceful night's sleep Joanna could remember in a long time, she enjoyed breakfast with Isabella and Chris on the rotunda. A light rain had fallen during the night. The trees, flowers and lawns glistened in the early-morning sun. The air was fragrant with flowers, fresh coffee and their delicious breakfast of omelets and bacon that Chris had cooked. Parrots, cockatoos and lorikeets flashed crimson, purple, electric-blue and yellow between the trees and shrubs. Insects droned. Joanna sipped her coffee, gazing into the distance. It felt like they were floating above the teal-colored sea. As the sun climbed higher in the sky, steam rose from the garden beneath them.

Joanna was meeting Fiona's plane at six o'clock that evening, and although she was reluctant to leave Isabella's and Chris's company, she was anxious to get back to the hotel to make arrangements for Fiona's arrival.

In response to their enthusiastic invitation, Joanna promised to bring Fiona over to dinner the following night. Then, late in the morning, after thanking them for everything, Joanna kissed them both good-bye.

Impatiently, Joanna waited in the arrival lounge at Cairns airport. An amplified voice announced that Fiona's Qantas flight had landed, and Joanna jumped up. Earlier in the day, she had swapped her hotel room for a luxury suite and arranged for it to be filled with creamy-yellow roses. She had ordered a bottle of Champagne to be delivered to the room by the time they returned. The rest of the day had been spent swimming, lying on the beach and checking her watch.

The passengers began to trickle through the arrivals door. Joanna shifted her weight from one foot to the other. The passengers were congregating, their numbers swelling. With her heart pounding, Joanna scanned the milling crowd. Christ! What if she hadn't made the flight? What if something was wrong?

Suddenly, Fiona appeared. Joanna's heart nearly leapt out of her chest. In a red, clingy jersey dress, low-cut with shoestring straps, and black high heels, Fiona stood holding an overnight bag. Running her free hand through her hair, she looked around anxiously.

Joanna raced over to her. "I'm here, baby," she called.

Fiona's face lit up in a beaming smile. She dropped the bag onto the floor as Joanna swept her into her arms, hugging her tightly. "God," Joanna murmured. "You're so beautiful. Are you really mine?"

Fiona gazed into her eyes seductively. "Oh, yes," she breathed, and then, to Joanna's amazement and delight, she slid her arms around Joanna's shoulders and kissed her passionately.

A fire swept through Joanna and at the sound of Fiona's little growl, she thought she'd faint.

Calmly, with a little smile, Fiona wiped the traces of her lipstick from Joanna's mouth with her thumb. The blur of Joanna's surroundings came slowly back into focus. This was Far North Queensland, after all, and they had attracted a lot of attention. It was easy to pick out the locals. The southern tourists from Melbourne and Sydney just glanced at them, a few shook their heads as they passed by, but the locals were standing frozen, staring, open-mouthed, their eyes nearly popping out of their heads.

Joanna looked at Fiona and chuckled. She picked up her bag, firmly clasped her hand and, her heart bursting with pride, strode with her outside into the sun.

On the top floor of the hotel, their suite had a deep balcony overlooking the sea. The sun was just beginning to set over the water.

Fiona gazed around at the large, beautiful living room and the adjoining luxurious bedroom complete with a king-size bed. The rooms were scented with roses spilling from deep round bowls on cherry wood sideboards and bedside tables. Tears filled her eyes. "It's all so lovely," she said.

Joanna kissed her cheek. "I wanted it to be special." She grinned. "I got us the honeymoon suite."

Fiona smiled and kissed her. "Perfect."

On the coffee table, beside a dish of tropical fruit, stood an ice bucket containing the Champagne. Two crystal flutes glittered on the silver tray. Fiona raised her eyebrows appreciatively. "The Krug was a nice touch, darling."

Joanna took her into her arms and gazed into her eyes. "And I've ordered dinner to be delivered later. A banquet. The chef's choice."

"Well," Fiona murmured, "I hope it's a lot later, 'cause I've got more urgent things on my mind." With the tip of her tongue, she licked Joanna's throat, then began to unbutton Joanna's white satin vest that covered her white, silk camisole.

The white tulle curtains, gathered on either side of the open balcony doors, shivered gently in the balmy breeze. The salmon-colored light of the sky filtered through the bedroom.

Enraptured, Joanna gave herself up to Fiona's magical hands. Fiona, taking obvious delight in the process, undressed her, then undressed herself.

Joanna quivered as Fiona ran her fingers over Joanna's nipples and gently squeezed them between her fingers. She pressed Joanna down onto the bed. "I want to make up for last time," she whispered.

Joanna gazed in wonder at Fiona kneeling astride her. Her body was perfect, glossy and golden. Fiona placed a feathery kiss on Joanna's throat, then trailed the tip of her tongue down to her breasts, circling her nipples. Joanna gasped. Fiona positioned her knees between Joanna's, pushing them wide apart. Kissing her passionately, Fiona reached between Joanna's thighs and stroked her. Joanna whimpered helplessly. With tiny strokes of her tongue, Fiona kissed her way down Joanna's stomach to her hips.

With every touch, Joanna's skin burned. Her insides felt like molten silver. She was dissolving. Fiona's moans were her own. Fiona's every gasping breath was hers.

Then — her mouth hot, wet, electric — Fiona took her. Joanna gave a long, low groan. She was floating. Her body on fire, her mind soaring, she looked down at Fiona, whose honey-brown hair spilled over her shoulders, across Joanna's thighs.

Tears filled Joanna's eyes. Surrender. Oh, God. It was so sweet. That was the secret of their connection — what made them complete. Tenderly, she ran her fingers through Fiona's soft hair. Surrender. It was that simple. And it was all she had ever had to do.

LOOKING FOR NAIAD?

Buy our books at
www.naiadpress.com

or call our toll-free number
1-800-533-1973

or by fax (24 hours a day)
1-850-539-9731

WATERMARK by Karin Kallmaker. 256 pp. One burning
question . . . how to lead her back to love?   ISBN 1-56280-235-6 $11.95

THE OTHER WOMAN by Ann O'Leary. 240 pp. Her roguish
way draws women like a magnet.   ISBN 1-56280-234-8   11.95

SILVER THREADS by Lyn Denison.208 pp. Finding her way
back to love . . .   ISBN 1-56280-231-3   11.95

CHIMNEY ROCK BLUES by Janet McClellan. 224 pp. 4th Tru
North mystery.   ISBN 1-56280-233-X   11.95

OMAHA'S BELL by Penny Hayes. 208 pp. Orphaned Keeley
Delaney woos the lovely Prudence Morris.   ISBN 1-56280-232-1   11.95

SIXTH SENSE by Kate Calloway. 224 pp. 6th Cassidy James
mystery.   ISBN 1-56280-228-3   11.95

DAWN OF THE DANCE by Marianne K. Martin. 224 pp. A dance
with an old friend, nothing more . . . yeah!   ISBN 1-56280-229-1   11.95

WEDDING BELL BLUES by Julia Watts. 240 pp. Love, family,
and a recipe for success.   ISBN 1-56280-230-5   11.95

THOSE WHO WAIT by Peggy J. Herring. 160 pp. Two
sisters . . . in love with the same woman.   ISBN 1-56280-223-2   11.95

WHISPERS IN THE WIND by Frankie J. Jones. 192 pp. "If you
don't want this," she whispered, "all you have to say is 'stop.'"
    ISBN 1-56280-226-7   11.95

WHEN SOME BODY DISAPPEARS by Therese Szymanski.
192 pp. 3rd Brett Higgins mystery.   ISBN 1-56280-227-5   11.95

THE WAY LIFE SHOULD BE by Diana Braund. 240 pp. Which
one will teach her the true meaning of love?   ISBN 1-56280-221-6   11.95

UNTIL THE END by Kaye Davis. 256pp. 3rd Maris Middleton
mystery.   ISBN 1-56280-222-4   11.95

FIFTH WHEEL by Kate Calloway. 224 pp. 5th Cassidy James
mystery.   ISBN 1-56280-218-6   11.95

JUST YESTERDAY by Linda Hill. 176 pp. Reliving all the
passion of yesterday.   ISBN 1-56280-219-4   11.95

THE TOUCH OF YOUR HAND edited by Barbara Grier and
Christine Cassidy. 304 pp. Erotic love stories by Naiad Press
authors.   ISBN 1-56280-220-8   14.95

WINDROW GARDEN by Janet McClellan. 192 pp. They discover
a passion they never dreamed possible.   ISBN 1-56280-216-X   11.95

PAST DUE by Claire McNab. 224 pp. 10th Carol Ashton
mystery.   ISBN 1-56280-217-8   11.95

CHRISTABEL by Laura Adams. 224 pp. Two captive hearts and
the passion that will set them free.   ISBN 1-56280-214-3   11.95

PRIVATE PASSIONS by Laura DeHart Young. 192 pp. An
unforgettable new portrait of lesbian love . . .   ISBN 1-56280-215-1   11.95

BAD MOON RISING by Barbara Johnson. 208 pp. 2nd Colleen
Fitzgerald mystery.   ISBN 1-56280-211-9   11.95

RIVER QUAY by Janet McClellan. 208 pp. 3rd Tru North
mystery.   ISBN 1-56280-212-7   11.95

ENDLESS LOVE by Lisa Shapiro. 272 pp. To believe, once
again, that love can be forever.   ISBN 1-56280-213-5   11.95

FALLEN FROM GRACE by Pat Welch. 256 pp. 6th Helen Black
mystery.   ISBN 1-56280-209-7   11.95

THE NAKED EYE by Catherine Ennis. 208 pp. Her lover in the
camera's eye . . .   ISBN 1-56280-210-0   11.95

OVER THE LINE by Tracey Richardson. 176 pp. 2nd Stevie
Houston mystery.   ISBN 1-56280-202-X   11.95

JULIA'S SONG by Ann O'Leary. 208 pp. Strangely
disturbing . . . strangely exciting.   ISBN 1-56280-197-X   11.95

LOVE IN THE BALANCE by Marianne K. Martin. 256 pp.
Weighing the costs of love . . .   ISBN 1-56280-199-6   11.95

PIECE OF MY HEART by Julia Watts. 208 pp. All the
stuff that dreams are made of —   ISBN 1-56280-206-2   11.95

MAKING UP FOR LOST TIME by Karin Kallmaker. 240 pp.
Nobody does it better . . .   ISBN 1-56280-196-1   11.95

GOLD FEVER by Lyn Denison. 224 pp. By author of *Dream
Lover.*   ISBN 1-56280-201-1   11.95

WHEN THE DEAD SPEAK by Therese Szymanski. 224 pp. 2nd
Brett Higgins mystery.   ISBN 1-56280-198-8   11.95

FOURTH DOWN by Kate Calloway. 240 pp. 4th Cassidy James
mystery.   ISBN 1-56280-205-4   11.95

A MOMENT'S INDISCRETION by Peggy J. Herring. 176 pp.
There's a fine line between love and lust . . .   ISBN 1-56280-194-5   11.95

CITY LIGHTS/COUNTRY CANDLES by Penny Hayes. 208 pp.
About the women she has known . . .   ISBN 1-56280-195-3   11.95

POSSESSIONS by Kaye Davis. 240 pp. 2nd Maris Middleton
mystery.   ISBN 1-56280-192-9   11.95

A QUESTION OF LOVE by Saxon Bennett. 208 pp. Every
woman is granted one great love.   ISBN 1-56280-205-4   11.95

RHYTHM TIDE by Frankie J. Jones. 160 pp. . . . to desire
passionately and be passionately desired.   ISBN 1-56280-189-9   11.95

PENN VALLEY PHOENIX by Janet McClellan. 208 pp. 2nd
Tru North Mystery.   ISBN 1-56280-200-3   11.95

BY RESERVATION ONLY by Jackie Calhoun. 240 pp. A
chance for true happiness.   ISBN 1-56280-191-0   11.95

OLD BLACK MAGIC by Jaye Maiman. 272 pp. 9th Robin
Miller mystery.   ISBN 1-56280-175-9   11.95

LEGACY OF LOVE by Marianne K. Martin. 240 pp. Women
will do anything for her . . .   ISBN 1-56280-184-8   11.95

LETTING GO by Ann O'Leary. 160 pp. Laura, at 39, in love
with 23-year-old Kate.   ISBN 1-56280-183-X   11.95

LADY BE GOOD edited by Barbara Grier and Christine Cassidy.
288 pp. Erotic stories by Naiad Press authors.   ISBN 1-56280-180-5   14.95

CHAIN LETTER by Claire McNab. 288 pp. 9th Carol Ashton
mystery.   ISBN 1-56280-181-3   11.95

NIGHT VISION by Laura Adams. 256 pp. Erotic fantasy romance
by "famous" author.   ISBN 1-56280-182-1   11.95

SEA TO SHINING SEA by Lisa Shapiro. 256 pp. Unable to resist
the raging passion . . .   ISBN 1-56280-177-5   11.95

THIRD DEGREE by Kate Calloway. 224 pp. 3rd Cassidy James
mystery.   ISBN 1-56280-185-6   11.95

WHEN THE DANCING STOPS by Therese Szymanski. 272 pp.
1st Brett Higgins mystery.   ISBN 1-56280-186-4   11.95

PHASES OF THE MOON by Julia Watts. 192 pp. . . . . . hungry
for everything life has to offer.   ISBN 1-56280-176-7   11.95

BABY IT'S COLD by Jaye Maiman. 256 pp. 5th Robin Miller
mystery.   ISBN 1-56280-156-2   10.95

CLASS REUNION by Linda Hill. 176 pp. The girl from her
past . . .   ISBN 1-56280-178-3   11.95

DREAM LOVER by Lyn Denison. 224 pp. A soft, sensuous,
romantic fantasy.   ISBN 1-56280-173-1   11.95

FORTY LOVE by Diana Simmonds. 288 pp. Joyous, heart-
warming romance.   ISBN 1-56280-171-6   11.95

IN THE MOOD by Robbi Sommers. 160 pp. The queen of
erotic tension!   ISBN 1-56280-172-4   11.95

SWIMMING CAT COVE by Lauren Douglas. 192 pp. 2nd
Allison O'Neil Mystery.   ISBN 1-56280-168-6   11.95

THE LOVING LESBIAN by Claire McNab and Sharon Gedan.
240 pp. Explore the experiences that make lesbian love unique.
                                           ISBN 1-56280-169-4   14.95

COURTED by Celia Cohen. 160 pp. Sparkling romantic
encounter.   ISBN 1-56280-166-X   11.95

SEASONS OF THE HEART by Jackie Calhoun. 240 pp. Romance
through the years.   ISBN 1-56280-167-8   11.95

K. C. BOMBER by Janet McClellan. 208 pp. 1st Tru North
mystery.   ISBN 1-56280-157-0   11.95

LAST RITES by Tracey Richardson. 192 pp. 1st Stevie Houston
mystery.   ISBN 1-56280-164-3   11.95

EMBRACE IN MOTION by Karin Kallmaker. 256 pp. A whirlwind
love affair.   ISBN 1-56280-165-1   11.95

HOT CHECK by Peggy J. Herring. 192 pp. Will workaholic Alice
fall for guitarist Ricky?   ISBN 1-56280-163-5   11.95

OLD TIES by Saxon Bennett. 176 pp. Can Cleo surrender to a
passionate new love?   ISBN 1-56280-159-7   11.95

LOVE ON THE LINE by Laura DeHart Young. 176 pp. Will Stef
win Kay's heart?   ISBN 1-56280-162-7   11.95

DEVIL'S LEG CROSSING by Kaye Davis. 192 pp. 1st Maris
Middleton mystery.   ISBN 1-56280-158-9   11.95

COSTA BRAVA by Marta Balletbo Coll. 144 pp. Read the book,
see the movie!   ISBN 1-56280-153-8   11.95

MEETING MAGDALENE & OTHER STORIES by
Marilyn Freeman. 144 pp. Read the book, see the movie!
                                           ISBN 1-56280-170-8   11.95

SECOND FIDDLE by Kate 208 pp. 2nd P.I. Cassidy James
mystery.   ISBN 1-56280-169-6   11.95

LAUREL by Isabel Miller. 128 pp. By the author of the beloved
Patience and Sarah.   ISBN 1-56280-146-5   10.95

LOVE OR MONEY by Jackie Calhoun. 240 pp. The romance of
real life.   ISBN 1-56280-147-3   10.95

SMOKE AND MIRRORS by Pat Welch. 224 pp. 5th Helen Black
Mystery.   ISBN 1-56280-143-0   10.95

DANCING IN THE DARK edited by Barbara Grier & Christine
Cassidy. 272 pp. Erotic love stories by Naiad Press authors.
                                           ISBN 1-56280-144-9   14.95

TIME AND TIME AGAIN by Catherine Ennis. 176 pp. Passionate
love affair.   ISBN 1-56280-145-7   10.95

PAXTON COURT by Diane Salvatore. 256 pp. Erotic and wickedly funny contemporary tale about the business of learning to live together.   ISBN 1-56280-114-7   10.95

INNER CIRCLE by Claire McNab. 208 pp. 8th Carol Ashton Mystery.   ISBN 1-56280-135-X   11.95

LESBIAN SEX: AN ORAL HISTORY by Susan Johnson. 240 pp. Need we say more?   ISBN 1-56280-142-2   14.95

WILD THINGS by Karin Kallmaker. 240 pp. By the undisputed mistress of lesbian romance.   ISBN 1-56280-139-2   11.95

THE GIRL NEXT DOOR by Mindy Kaplan. 208 pp. Just what you d expect.   ISBN 1-56280-140-6   11.95

NOW AND THEN by Penny Hayes. 240 pp. Romance on the westward journey.   ISBN 1-56280-121-X   11.95

HEART ON FIRE by Diana Simmonds. 176 pp. The romantic and erotic rival of *Curious Wine*.   ISBN 1-56280-152-X   11.95

DEATH AT LAVENDER BAY by Lauren Wright Douglas. 208 pp. 1st Allison O'Neil Mystery.   ISBN 1-56280-085-X   11.95

YES I SAID YES I WILL by Judith McDaniel. 272 pp. Hot romance by famous author.   ISBN 1-56280-138-4   11.95

FORBIDDEN FIRES by Margaret C. Anderson. Edited by Mathilda Hills. 176 pp. Famous author's "unpublished" Lesbian romance.
                                                              ISBN 1-56280-123-6   21.95

SIDE TRACKS by Teresa Stores. 160 pp. Gender-bending Lesbians on the road.   ISBN 1-56280-122-8   10.95

WILDWOOD FLOWERS by Julia Watts. 208 pp. Hilarious and heart-warming tale of true love.   ISBN 1-56280-127-9   10.95

NEVER SAY NEVER by Linda Hill. 224 pp. Rule #1: Never get involved with . . .   ISBN 1-56280-126-0   11.95

THE WISH LIST by Saxon Bennett. 192 pp. Romance through the years.   ISBN 1-56280-125-2   10.95

OUT OF THE NIGHT by Kris Bruyer. 192 pp. Spine-tingling thriller.   ISBN 1-56280-120-1   10.95

LOVE'S HARVEST by Peggy J. Herring. 176 pp. by the author of *Once More With Feeling*.   ISBN 1-56280-117-1   10.95

THE COLOR OF WINTER by Lisa Shapiro. 208 pp. Romantic love beyond your wildest dreams.   ISBN 1-56280-116-3   10.95

FAMILY SECRETS by Laura DeHart Young. 208 pp. Enthralling romance and suspense.   ISBN 1-56280-119-8   10.95

INLAND PASSAGE by Jane Rule. 288 pp. Tales exploring conventional & unconventional relationships.   ISBN 0-930044-56-8   10.95

DOUBLE BLUFF by Claire McNab. 208 pp. 7th Carol Ashton Mystery.   ISBN 1-56280-096-5   10.95

BAR GIRLS by Lauran Hoffman. 176 pp. See the movie, read the book! ISBN 1-56280-115-5   10.95

THE FIRST TIME EVER edited by Barbara Grier & Christine Cassidy. 272 pp. Love stories by Naiad Press authors.
ISBN 1-56280-086-8   14.95

MISS PETTIBONE AND MISS McGRAW by Brenda Weathers. 208 pp. A charming ghostly love story. ISBN 1-56280-151-1   10.95

CHANGES by Jackie Calhoun. 208 pp. Involved romance and relationships. ISBN 1-56280-083-3   10.95

FAIR PLAY by Rose Beecham. 256 pp. An Amanda Valentine Mystery. ISBN 1-56280-081-7   10.95

PAYBACK by Celia Cohen. 176 pp. A gripping thriller of romance, revenge and betrayal. ISBN 1-56280-084-1   10.95

THE BEACH AFFAIR by Barbara Johnson. 224 pp. Sizzling summer romance/mystery/intrigue. ISBN 1-56280-090-6   10.95

GETTING THERE by Robbi Sommers. 192 pp. Nobody does it like Robbi! ISBN 1-56280-099-X   10.95

FINAL CUT by Lisa Haddock. 208 pp. 2nd Carmen Ramirez Mystery. ISBN 1-56280-088-4   10.95

FLASHPOINT by Katherine V. Forrest. 256 pp. A Lesbian blockbuster! ISBN 1-56280-079-5   10.95

CLAIRE OF THE MOON by Nicole Conn. Audio Book — Read by Marianne Hyatt. ISBN 1-56280-113-9   16.95

FOR LOVE AND FOR LIFE: INTIMATE PORTRAITS OF LESBIAN COUPLES by Susan Johnson. 224 pp.
ISBN 1-56280-091-4   14.95

DEVOTION by Mindy Kaplan. 192 pp. See the movie — read the book! ISBN 1-56280-093-0   10.95

SOMEONE TO WATCH by Jaye Maiman. 272 pp. 4th Robin Miller Mystery. ISBN 1-56280-095-7   10.95

GREENER THAN GRASS by Jennifer Fulton. 208 pp. A young woman — a stranger in her bed. ISBN 1-56280-092-2   10.95

TRAVELS WITH DIANA HUNTER by Regine Sands. Erotic lesbian romp. Audio Book (2 cassettes) ISBN 1-56280-107-4   16.95

CABIN FEVER by Carol Schmidt. 256 pp. Sizzling suspense and passion. ISBN 1-56280-089-1   10.95

THERE WILL BE NO GOODBYES by Laura DeHart Young. 192 pp. Romantic love, strength, and friendship. ISBN 1-56280-103-1   10.95

FAULTLINE by Sheila Ortiz Taylor. 144 pp. Joyous comic lesbian novel. ISBN 1-56280-108-2   9.95

OPEN HOUSE by Pat Welch. 176 pp. 4th Helen Black Mystery.
ISBN 1-56280-102-3   10.95

ONCE MORE WITH FEELING by Peggy J. Herring. 240 pp.
Lighthearted, loving romantic adventure.   ISBN 1-56280-089-2   11.95

FOREVER by Evelyn Kennedy. 224 pp. Passionate romance — love
overcoming all obstacles.   ISBN 1-56280-094-9   10.95

WHISPERS by Kris Bruyer. 176 pp. Romantic ghost story.
ISBN 1-56280-082-5   10.95

NIGHT SONGS by Penny Mickelbury. 224 pp. 2nd Gianna
Maglione Mystery.   ISBN 1-56280-097-3   10.95

GETTING TO THE POINT by Teresa Stores. 256 pp. Classic
southern Lesbian novel.   ISBN 1-56280-100-7   10.95

PAINTED MOON by Karin Kallmaker. 224 pp. Delicious
Kallmaker romance.   ISBN 1-56280-075-2   11.95

THE MYSTERIOUS NAIAD edited by Katherine V. Forrest &
Barbara Grier. 320 pp. Love stories by Naiad Press authors.
ISBN 1-56280-074-4   14.95

DAUGHTERS OF A CORAL DAWN by Katherine V. Forrest.
240 pp. Tenth Anniversay Edition.   ISBN 1-56280-104-X   11.95

BODY GUARD by Claire McNab. 208 pp. 6th Carol Ashton
Mystery.   ISBN 1-56280-073-6   11.95

CACTUS LOVE by Lee Lynch. 192 pp. Stories by the beloved
storyteller.   ISBN 1-56280-071-X   9.95

SECOND GUESS by Rose Beecham. 216 pp. An Amanda
Valentine Mystery.   ISBN 1-56280-069-8   9.95

A RAGE OF MAIDENS by Lauren Wright Douglas. 240 pp.
6th Caitlin Reece Mystery.   ISBN 1-56280-068-X   10.95

TRIPLE EXPOSURE by Jackie Calhoun. 224 pp. Romantic
drama involving many characters.   ISBN 1-56280-067-1   10.95

PERSONAL ADS by Robbi Sommers. 176 pp. Sizzling short
stories.   ISBN 1-56280-059-0   11.95

CROSSWORDS by Penny Sumner. 256 pp. 2nd Victoria Cross
Mystery.   ISBN 1-56280-064-7   9.95

SWEET CHERRY WINE by Carol Schmidt. 224 pp. A novel of
suspense.   ISBN 1-56280-063-9   9.95

CERTAIN SMILES by Dorothy Tell. 160 pp. Erotic short stories.
ISBN 1-56280-066-3   9.95

EDITED OUT by Lisa Haddock. 224 pp. 1st Carmen Ramirez
Mystery.   ISBN 1-56280-077-9   9.95

SMOKEY O by Celia Cohen. 176 pp. Relationships on the
playing field.   ISBN 1-56280-057-4   9.95

KATHLEEN O'DONALD by Penny Hayes. 256 pp. Rose and
Kathleen find each other and employment in 1909 NYC.
ISBN 1-56280-070-1   9.95

STAYING HOME by Elisabeth Nonas. 256 pp. Molly and Alix
want a baby . . . or do they?   ISBN 1-56280-076-0   10.95

TRUE LOVE by Jennifer Fulton. 240 pp. Six lesbians searching
for love in all the "right" places.   ISBN 1-56280-035-3   11.95

KEEPING SECRETS by Penny Mickelbury. 208 pp. 1st Gianna
Maglione Mystery.   ISBN 1-56280-052-3   9.95

THE ROMANTIC NAIAD edited by Katherine V. Forrest &
Barbara Grier. 336 pp. Love stories by Naiad Press authors.
                                         ISBN 1-56280-054-X   14.95

UNDER MY SKIN by Jaye Maiman. 336 pp. 3rd Robin Miller
Mystery.   ISBN 1-56280-049-3.   11.95

CAR POOL by Karin Kallmaker. 272pp. Lesbians on wheels
and then some!   ISBN 1-56280-048-5   11.95

NOT TELLING MOTHER: STORIES FROM A LIFE by Diane
Salvatore. 176 pp. Her 3rd novel.   ISBN 1-56280-044-2   9.95

GOBLIN MARKET by Lauren Wright Douglas. 240pp. 5th Caitlin
Reece Mystery.   ISBN 1-56280-047-7   10.95

FRIENDS AND LOVERS by Jackie Calhoun. 224 pp. Mid-
western Lesbian lives and loves.   ISBN 1-56280-041-8   11.95

BEHIND CLOSED DOORS by Robbi Sommers. 192 pp. Hot,
erotic short stories.   ISBN 1-56280-039-6   11.95

CLAIRE OF THE MOON by Nicole Conn. 192 pp. See the
movie — read the book!   ISBN 1-56280-038-8   11.95

SILENT HEART by Claire McNab. 192 pp. Exotic Lesbian
romance.   ISBN 1-56280-036-1   11.95

THE SPY IN QUESTION by Amanda Kyle Williams. 256 pp.
A Madison McGuire Mystery.   ISBN 1-56280-037-X   9.95

SAVING GRACE by Jennifer Fulton. 240 pp. Adventure and
romantic entanglement.   ISBN 1-56280-051-5   11.95

CURIOUS WINE by Katherine V. Forrest. 176 pp. Tenth Anniver-
sary Edition. The most popular contemporary Lesbian love story.
                                         ISBN 1-56280-053-1   11.95
     Audio Book (2 cassettes)   ISBN 1-56280-105-8   16.95

CHAUTAUQUA by Catherine Ennis. 192 pp. Exciting, romantic
adventure.   ISBN 1-56280-032-9   9.95

A PROPER BURIAL by Pat Welch. 192 pp. 3rd Helen Black
Mystery.   ISBN 1-56280-033-7   9.95

SILVERLAKE HEAT: A Novel of Suspense by Carol Schmidt.
240 pp. Rhonda is as hot as Laney's dreams.   ISBN 1-56280-031-0   9.95

LOVE, ZENA BETH by Diane Salvatore. 224 pp. The most talked
about lesbian novel of the nineties!   ISBN 1-56280-030-2   10.95

A DOORYARD FULL OF FLOWERS by Isabel Miller. 160 pp.
Stories incl. 2 sequels to *Patience and Sarah.*   ISBN 1-56280-029-9   9.95

MURDER BY TRADITION by Katherine V. Forrest. 288 pp. 4th
Kate Delafield Mystery.   ISBN 1-56280-002-7   11.95

THE EROTIC NAIAD edited by Katherine V. Forrest & Barbara
Grier. 224 pp. Love stories by Naiad Press authors.
                                            ISBN 1-56280-026-4   14.95

DEAD CERTAIN by Claire McNab. 224 pp. 5th Carol Ashton
Mystery.   ISBN 1-56280-027-2   9.95

CRAZY FOR LOVING by Jaye Maiman. 320 pp. 2nd Robin Miller
Mystery.   ISBN 1-56280-025-6   11.95

UNCERTAIN COMPANIONS by Robbi Sommers. 204 pp.
Steamy, erotic novel.   ISBN 1-56280-017-5   11.95

A TIGER'S HEART by Lauren W. Douglas. 240 pp. 4th Caitlin
Reece Mystery.   ISBN 1-56280-018-3   9.95

PAPERBACK ROMANCE by Karin Kallmaker. 256 pp. A
delicious romance.   ISBN 1-56280-019-1   10.95

THE LAVENDER HOUSE MURDER by Nikki Baker. 224 pp.
2nd Virginia Kelly Mystery.   ISBN 1-56280-012-4   9.95

PASSION BAY by Jennifer Fulton. 224 pp. Passionate romance,
virgin beaches, tropical skies.   ISBN 1-56280-028-0   10.95

STICKS AND STONES by Jackie Calhoun. 208 pp. Contemporary
lesbian lives and loves.   ISBN 1-56280-020-5   9.95
Audio Book (2 cassettes)   ISBN 1-56280-106-6   16.95

UNDER THE SOUTHERN CROSS by Claire McNab. 192 pp.
Romantic nights Down Under.   ISBN 1-56280-011-6   11.95

GRASSY FLATS by Penny Hayes. 256 pp. Lesbian romance in
the '30s.   ISBN 1-56280-010-8   9.95

THE END OF APRIL by Penny Sumner. 240 pp. 1st Victoria
Cross Mystery.   ISBN 1-56280-007-8   8.95

KISS AND TELL by Robbi Sommers. 192 pp. Scorching stories
by the author of *Pleasures.*   ISBN 1-56280-005-1   11.95

STILL WATERS by Pat Welch. 208 pp. 2nd Helen Black Mystery.
                                            ISBN 0-941483-97-5   9.95

TO LOVE AGAIN by Evelyn Kennedy. 208 pp. Wildly romantic
love story.   ISBN 0-941483-85-1   11.95

IN THE GAME by Nikki Baker. 192 pp. 1st Virginia Kelly
Mystery.   ISBN 1-56280-004-3   9.95

STRANDED by Camarin Grae. 320 pp. Entertaining, riveting
adventure.   ISBN 0-941483-99-1   9.95

THE DAUGHTERS OF ARTEMIS by Lauren Wright Douglas.
240 pp. 3rd Caitlin Reece Mystery.   ISBN 0-941483-95-9   9.95

CLEARWATER by Catherine Ennis. 176 pp. Romantic secrets
of a small Louisiana town.   ISBN 0-941483-65-7   8.95

THE HALLELUJAH MURDERS by Dorothy Tell. 176 pp. 2nd
Poppy Dillworth Mystery.   ISBN 0-941483-88-6   8.95

BENEDICTION by Diane Salvatore. 272 pp. Striking, contemporary romantic novel.   ISBN 0-941483-90-8   11.95

COP OUT by Claire McNab. 208 pp. 4th Carol Ashton Mystery.
                                         ISBN 0-941483-84-3   10.95

THE BEVERLY MALIBU by Katherine V. Forrest. 288 pp. 3rd
Kate Delafield Mystery.   ISBN 0-941483-48-7   11.95

THE PROVIDENCE FILE by Amanda Kyle Williams. 256 pp.
A Madison McGuire Mystery.   ISBN 0-941483-92-4   8.95

I LEFT MY HEART by Jaye Maiman. 320 pp. 1st Robin Miller
Mystery.   ISBN 0-941483-72-X   11.95

THE PRICE OF SALT by Patricia Highsmith (writing as Claire
Morgan). 288 pp. Classic lesbian novel, first issued in 1952 . . .
acknowledged by its author under her own, very famous, name.
                                         ISBN 1-56280-003-5   11.95

SIDE BY SIDE by Isabel Miller. 256 pp. From beloved author of
Patience and Sarah.   ISBN 0-941483-77-0   10.95

STAYING POWER: LONG TERM LESBIAN COUPLES by
Susan E. Johnson. 352 pp. Joys of coupledom. ISBN 0-941-483-75-4   14.95

SLICK by Camarin Grae. 304 pp. Exotic, erotic adventure.
                                         ISBN 0-941483-74-6   9.95

NINTH LIFE by Lauren Wright Douglas. 256 pp. 2nd Caitlin
Reece Mystery.   ISBN 0-941483-50-9   9.95

PLAYERS by Robbi Sommers. 192 pp. Sizzling, erotic novel.
                                         ISBN 0-941483-73-8   9.95

MURDER AT RED ROOK RANCH by Dorothy Tell. 224 pp.
1st Poppy Dillworth Mystery.   ISBN 0-941483-80-0   8.95

A ROOM FULL OF WOMEN by Elisabeth Nonas. 256 pp.
Contemporary Lesbian lives.   ISBN 0-941483-69-X   9.95

THEME FOR DIVERSE INSTRUMENTS by Jane Rule. 208 pp.
Powerful romantic lesbian stories.   ISBN 0-941483-63-0   8.95

CLUB 12 by Amanda Kyle Williams. 288 pp. Espionage thriller
featuring a lesbian agent!   ISBN 0-941483-64-9   9.95

DEATH DOWN UNDER by Claire McNab. 240 pp. 3rd Carol
Ashton Mystery.   ISBN 0-941483-39-8   10.95

MONTANA FEATHERS by Penny Hayes. 256 pp. Vivian and
Elizabeth find love in frontier Montana. ISBN 0-941483-61-4   9.95

THERE'S SOMETHING I'VE BEEN MEANING TO TELL YOU
Ed. by Loralee MacPike. 288 pp. Gay men and lesbians coming out
to their children.   ISBN 0-941483-44-4   9.95

LIFTING BELLY by Gertrude Stein. Ed. by Rebecca Mark. 104 pp.
Erotic poetry.   ISBN 0-941483-51-7   10.95

AFTER THE FIRE by Jane Rule. 256 pp. Warm, human novel by
this incomparable author.   ISBN 0-941483-45-2   8.95

PLEASURES by Robbi Sommers. 204 pp. Unprecedented
eroticism.   ISBN 0-941483-49-5   11.95

EDGEWISE by Camarin Grae. 372 pp. Spellbinding
adventure.   ISBN 0-941483-19-3   9.95

FATAL REUNION by Claire McNab. 224 pp. 2nd Carol Ashton
Mystery.   ISBN 0-941483-40-1   11.95

IN EVERY PORT by Karin Kallmaker. 228 pp. Jessica's sexy,
adventuresome travels.   ISBN 0-941483-37-7   11.95

OF LOVE AND GLORY by Evelyn Kennedy. 192 pp. Exciting
WWII romance.   ISBN 0-941483-32-0   10.95

CLICKING STONES by Nancy Tyler Glenn. 288 pp. Love
transcending time.   ISBN 0-941483-31-2   9.95

SOUTH OF THE LINE by Catherine Ennis. 216 pp. Civil War
adventure.   ISBN 0-941483-29-0   8.95

WOMAN PLUS WOMAN by Dolores Klaich. 300 pp. Supurb
Lesbian overview.   ISBN 0-941483-28-2   9.95

THE FINER GRAIN by Denise Ohio. 216 pp. Brilliant young
college lesbian novel.   ISBN 0-941483-11-8   8.95

LESSONS IN MURDER by Claire McNab. 216 pp. 1st Carol Ashton
Mystery.   ISBN 0-941483-14-2   11.95

YELLOWTHROAT by Penny Hayes. 240 pp. Margarita, bandit,
kidnaps Julia.   ISBN 0-941483-10-X   8.95

SAPPHISTRY: THE BOOK OF LESBIAN SEXUALITY by
Pat Califia. 3d edition, revised. 208 pp.   ISBN 0-941483-24-X   12.95

CHERISHED LOVE by Evelyn Kennedy. 192 pp. Erotic Lesbian
love story.   ISBN 0-941483-08-8   11.95

THE SECRET IN THE BIRD by Camarin Grae. 312 pp. Striking,
psychological suspense novel.   ISBN 0-941483-05-3   8.95

TO THE LIGHTNING by Catherine Ennis. 208 pp. Romantic
Lesbian `Robinson Crusoe adventure.   ISBN 0-941483-06-1   8.95

DREAMS AND SWORDS by Katherine V. Forrest. 192 pp.
Romantic, erotic, imaginative stories.   ISBN 0-941483-03-7   11.95

MEMORY BOARD by Jane Rule. 336 pp. Memorable novel
about an aging Lesbian couple.   ISBN 0-941483-02-9   12.95

THE ALWAYS ANONYMOUS BEAST by Lauren Wright Douglas.
224 pp. 1st Caitlin Reece Mystery.　　　ISBN 0-941483-04-5　　8.95

MURDER AT THE NIGHTWOOD BAR by Katherine V. Forrest.
240 pp. 2nd Kate Delafield Mystery.　　ISBN 0-930044-92-4　　11.95

WINGED DANCER by Camarin Grae. 228 pp. Erotic Lesbian
adventure story.　　　　　　　　　　　ISBN 0-930044-88-6　　8.95

PAZ by Camarin Grae. 336 pp. Romantic Lesbian adventurer
with the power to change the world.　　ISBN 0-930044-89-4　　8.95

SOUL SNATCHER by Camarin Grae. 224 pp. A puzzle, an
adventure, a mystery — Lesbian romance.　ISBN 0-930044-90-8　　8.95

THE LOVE OF GOOD WOMEN by Isabel Miller. 224 pp.
Long-awaited new novel by the author of the beloved *Patience
and Sarah*.　　　　　　　　　　　　　　ISBN 0-930044-81-9　　8.95

THE LONG TRAIL by Penny Hayes. 248 pp. Vivid adventures
of two women in love in the old west.　ISBN 0-930044-76-2　　8.95

AN EMERGENCE OF GREEN by Katherine V. Forrest. 288
pp. Powerful novel of sexual discovery.　ISBN 0-930044-69-X　　11.95

DESERT OF THE HEART by Jane Rule. 224 pp. A classic;
basis for the movie *Desert Hearts*.　　ISBN 0-930044-73-8　　10.95

SEX VARIANT WOMEN IN LITERATURE by Jeannette
Howard Foster. 448 pp. Literary history.　ISBN 0-930044-65-7　　8.95

A HOT-EYED MODERATE by Jane Rule. 252 pp. Hard-hitting
essays on gay life; writing; art.　　　　ISBN 0-930044-57-6　　7.95

AMATEUR CITY by Katherine V. Forrest. 224 pp. 1st Kate
Delafield Mystery.　　　　　　　　　　ISBN 0-930044-55-X　　10.95

THE SOPHIE HOROWITZ STORY by Sarah Schulman. 176 pp.
Engaging novel of madcap intrigue.　　ISBN 0-930044-54-1　　7.95

THE YOUNG IN ONE ANOTHER'S ARMS by Jane Rule.
224 pp. Classic Jane Rule.　　　　　　　ISBN 0-930044-53-3　　9.95

AGAINST THE SEASON by Jane Rule. 224 pp. Luminous,
complex novel of interrelationships.　　ISBN 0-930044-48-7　　8.95

LOVERS IN THE PRESENT AFTERNOON by Kathleen Fleming.
288 pp. A novel about recovery and growth.　ISBN 0-930044-46-0　　8.95

THIS IS NOT FOR YOU by Jane Rule. 284 pp. A letter to a
beloved is also an intricate novel.　　ISBN 0-930044-25-8　　8.95

These are just a few of the many Naiad Press titles — we are the oldest and
largest lesbian/feminist publishing company in the world. We also offer an
enormous selection of lesbian video products. Please request a complete
catalog. We offer personal service; we encourage and welcome direct mail
orders from individuals who have limited access to bookstores carrying our
publications.